The Sweet Spot

ALSO BY STEPHANIE EVANOVICH

Big Girl Panties

The Sweet Spot

Stephanie Evanovich

HARPER LUXE
An Imprint of HarperCollins*Publishers*

For my sister, Alexia Evanovich Rose, and her BFF, Mary-Jane Oltarzewski, for reading and encouraging the first story I ever wrote, many moons ago. And for letting me tag along way more than they had to.

HarperCollins books may be purchased for educational, business, or sales promotional use. For information, please e-mail the Special Markets Department at SPsales@harpercollins.com.

FIRST HARPERLUXE EDITION

HarperLuxe™ is a trademark of HarperCollins Publishers

Library of Congress Cataloging-in-Publication Data is available upon request.

ISBN: 978-0-06-232641-6

14 ID/RRD 10 9 8 7 6 5 4 3 2 1

Chapter 1

It was a top-down kind of day. The sky was blue, with a few passing clouds, and just a hint of breeze, indicating that winter was waving its final good-bye and that summer was just around the corner. The sun was bright and warm, encouraging buds to blossom into fragrant, glorious flowers. The very atmosphere spoke of all the things possible as the earth renewed itself after a cold East Coast hibernation. The day was just too tempting to leave the top up, even though Amanda never put the top down anymore—not since that first summer she'd had the Chrysler Sebring, anyway. She'd always wanted a convertible. At least fate had been kind enough to wait until August two years ago to sport around before a wasp tangled itself in her hair at forty miles an hour on her way to opening day at the Cold Creek. It ended up stinging her hand, her neck, and, inadvertently, her front bumper and an unsuspecting fire hydrant. She spent the night she had been meticulously planning for months moping in the ER with a slight concussion and a burn from the airbag. From then on, it had been air conditioning whenever she was in the car. But when she walked out the front door this late April afternoon, greeted with that first you-know-you-don't-need-a-jacket day, she was willing to take the risk. Today felt different. And wasps would still be drowsy. As she drove past Maxwell Place Park, Amanda watched ducks and geese and squirrels roaming in pairs, actually looking love-struck, ready to extend their respective species. People on the streets were smiling as they hustled about their day; others were acting flirty. It was nothing short of spring fever, and she couldn't help but catch it. At a stoplight, she tilted her face up toward the sun to let it shine on her for a moment as she offered up a quick prayer of thankfulness for this beautiful day, her wonderful life, and all the possibilities that came with it. Maybe she'd do some flirting herself. With that thought, she turned up the radio and began to bounce to the music. Yeah, it was a top-down kind of day.

And then the seagull flew overhead.

Amanda watched it all go down from the rearview mirror as she checked her makeup after pulling into the Cold Creek Grille's small parking lot. The white and green gloppy goo fell perfectly onto the right side of her head, a stark contrast to her long black waves. She stared at it for a few moments as the reality and the poop sank in.

"That didn't just happen."

But it did happen, and once again, Amanda Cole had been reminded: Never get too cocky. Avoid using words like *perfect* or *wonderful*. Never attach your own name. It was just an invitation to comeuppance. She wouldn't go so far as to say she considered herself particularly unlucky; she just knew her boundaries. She couldn't pinpoint when she'd learned it for sure, but it was probably somewhere in between not making cheerleading squad and being, as her mother put it, "twenty pounds away from prom queen."

Her mother wasn't cruel, but she was blunt. Sometimes it was hard to tell the difference, and every now and then, someone you loved said something thoughtless, and it stuck.

Catherine Cole didn't really want her daughter to be a prom queen, anyway. As Essex County DA, she wanted Amanda to be smart and shrewd and strong.

Amanda was beautiful and sensitive, in spite of herself, her retired family court judge father never failed to remind her.

Amanda stomped in through the Cold Creek's front door and slammed her purse on the bar with a loud thud. Two of her employees, Eric and Nicole, were going through the beer cooler's inventory, seeing what they would need to bring up from the basement for the evening ahead. Eric was a lanky, blond, blue-eyed surfer boy who had been accepted to Harvard, but opted for bartending school instead when he realized how late he liked to sleep. All his savings and vacation time were spent in search of the perfect curl. In between budgeting, he felt New Jersey waves were as good as anyplace else's, and here he could be close to his family. Nicki was a free-spirited Seton Hall dropout whom Amanda had known since high school who was trying to break into acting. She was a petite, vivacious brunette who had a great horror-movie-victim scream, but her booking-to-audition ratio was often disappointing. She did her best to stay optimistic, paying her dues, as they all called it. Eric was a few years younger but that didn't prevent him and Nicki from becoming fast friends as well as roommates. Although they weren't involved, it was common knowledge that the two were known to hook up now and again, usually the result of her not getting the call and his ability to make the best commiserating cocktail. Amanda didn't care if they shined the bar with their butts, as long as they could work together, did it after closing, and cleaned up afterward.

Eric looked up briefly from his clipboard and then did a double take as Amanda approached their end of the bar.

"Yikes," he said, his face scrunching up in distaste. "Hope that's not a fashion statement."

"Bird" was Amanda's one-word reply as she proceeded past them.

"Geez, what was that thing eating?" he said, casting a quick look at his counterpart.

"It's supposed to be good luck!" Nicki called out as Amanda disappeared into the ladies room.

"Not feeling it," Amanda snapped as the door closed behind her. She walked up to the mirror over the sink to best assess how to clean up the mess. The goo had begun to drip farther down and appeared to be soaking into the thick black hair she'd spent a half hour blowing dry. She took a deep breath. This was nothing more than a problem that needed solving—she had this. First she took some toilet paper and tried to scoop as much of the poop as she could with one grab. She managed to get the bulk of it, but what was left behind was now successfully smeared deeper into her hair and beginning to clump together. She wet some more tissue and tried to get the remainder out, but the tissue started to decompose in her hand and her hair, leaving bits behind and adding to the mix. She took one more handful of tissue and wet them again, but this time she got them too soaked. When she tried to gently squeeze it over the affected hair, the overflow dripped down her hand and onto the front of her blue silk Jones of New York blouse, leaving a wet spot directly over the center of her ample right breast.

"Really?" She shook her head in disgust at her reflection in the mirror. Not only did she have bird shit and toilet paper remnants in her hair, now she looked like she was lactating.

She had only managed to make things worse. Giving the shirt priority, she tried the hand dryer on it. After a minute, it dried up the moisture but left a rather large off-color stain where the water had been. It no longer looked like she was lactating, but merely that she had lactated. The right side of her head was now crunchy.

Strike two.

Amanda stormed out of the bathroom, back to the bar where Eric and Nicki were now waiting.

"You can barely notice it," Nicki said after staring for a minute.

"Are you kidding?" Eric took the more direct approach. "It looks like a pterodactyl flew over her after a chili cook-off."

Amanda closed her eyes, bit her lip, and began counting. When she reached eight the phone rang. She quickly fired off nine and ten out loud and went back near the front door.

"Cold Creek Grille. How may I help you?" She answered the phone as if her day were right as rain. She was a businesswoman, first and foremost.

"I need a reservation for tonight," a gravelly voice barked into the phone. The caller was either on a cell phone with a bad connection or had a mouthful of marbles.

"Of course, sir. What time are you looking for?"

"Seven," he said impatiently, and Amanda pictured him running to catch a subway.

"Let me make sure I have that available," she told him, trying to buy time while she booted up the computer at the podium a few feet away. She moved the phone to the other side of her head, forgetting it was a war zone, and her hair crackled near her ear.

"Trust me, sweetheart, you have a table available."

"Sir?" She didn't know what to be more offended by, his use of the word *sweetheart* or the underlying threat that she'd better be able to seat him. She came to the conclusion that he was just some arrogant blowhard who was sitting with his feet on his desk, overlooking the water with a fat stogie in his mouth.

"A superstar is having dinner at your restaurant; you don't want to make him wait."

"All of our guests at the Cold Creek are VIPs, Mr.—?"

"Maybe I should speak to the owner?" he said, cutting her off. She thought she heard more spit squish out of the end of his cigar.

"I *am* the owner. My name is Amanda Cole. To whom do I have the pleasure of speaking?"

"Don't seat us someplace high traffic like near the front. He's not there to be an advertisement. You'll get your photo op."

It sounded so scathing, as if she were some sort of a bistro whore looking to make a buck, as if she would be interested in taking a picture with him in the first place. Supreme Court justices and past presidents dined at the Cold Creek without incident. "Mr. Whatever-Your-Name-Is, I'm concerned not only for the comfort of our guests, but the safety of my staff. And we have had some high-profile guests in the past. Several are regulars."

"Yeah, yeah, I heard that. That's why I'm calling. But, lady, you never had anyone this big," he said with an air of superiority that was nothing short of skin-crawling. At least he had upgraded her to "lady."

If he wasn't being such a total jackass, she might have taken him more seriously. "Would you like to tell me who he is so that I might inform security?" she said with overt sarcasm. He could either take being spoken to in kind or start to ream her out and she would hang up on him and he could dine elsewhere, bad business or not.

There was a pause and she thought he may have hung up on her first. But then he said, "No. Better you don't know till he gets there. Someone tips off TMZ and the night's a bust. And he brings his own security."

"Will they be joining you for dinner?"

His laugh was particularly smarmy. "They're not paid to eat."

So he wasn't only rude, he was also a tyrant. "That's fine, sir, they can stand guard with mine." Only hers were imaginary. She no longer cared if the computer was ready. It was a Wednesday, when they were rarely fully booked, and this man and his famous guest seemed intent on dining there. He was probably going to be more aggravation than anything else, even if he was only half as self-important as his representative. "You're all set, dinner for two at seven. Would you like to leave me a name or is there a code word or what?"

There was another pause, and once again Amanda was given the false hope that he might have hung up, saving her from a night of inconvenient distractions at the very least. But then she heard him on the other end; the noise he made sounded like a snort.

"You're spunky, kid," he told her. "Name under Alan Shaw. I'll be there at six fifty. I don't like to wait, either. And make sure there are good steaks on hand, he's a meat eater."

There was no mistaking the disconnection this time. A security-conscious carnivore with popelike status was joining her for dinner tonight. One who had an obnoxious toady. She pulled the phone away from her ear, turned it off, and wiped the watered-down bird residue off it with the sleeve of her shirt before setting it down on the bar. She noted the time on the now fully booted-up computer, which opened to the day's reservation page. They were completely booked for seven. She had forgotten about the art house theater opening a few blocks away. Strike three. Her day officially went bust at 2:02 P.M.. That was fast, and on a day that had started off so well. When would she learn to keep thoughts of perfection out of her head?

Amanda took a look over at Eric and Nicki. When the telephone exchange had started taking a turn for the testy, they'd stopped what they were doing to watch, waiting to see if their usually competent boss was about to unravel. Amanda picked her purse up off the bar.

"Can you two hold down the fort for a couple hours?" she asked, more out of courtesy than concern, while fishing out her keys.

"Sure," they said in unison. Then Nicki added, "Where are you going?"

"I'm using a mulligan and starting the day over," Amanda said over her shoulder as she headed for the door. She wasn't sure it was going to help.

Chapter 2

Chase took a moment to appreciate the clear blue sky just before putting on his batting helmet. He loved the first home-day games of the season, before the humidity kicked in and the sun was so high at game time the ball was difficult to spot. Not to mention, crowds were much more forgiving and optimistic in April and May. When they were being baked in ninety-degree sun for two and half hours, unless the division title was already all sewn up, fans expected a win, and even then, they could be cranky.

But even in the dog days of summer, Chase Walker rarely needed to be forgiven. He had done his part since the day he put on the uniform as a rookie four years ago, a regular on the all-star roster. One of those years he'd won the home-run derby. He was what sportscasters referred to as "one of those naturally gifted corn-fed boys out of Iowa," all of which were true. He could always make it as a farmer, but he'd learned early on that as long as he kept hitting balls over outfield walls, he wouldn't have to. Luckily, the balls and the walls cooperated. The same could be said of his speed and agility. Given his size, neither was expected of him, but he worked on both anyway. He'd earned two gold gloves for the effort.

He walked out onto the field and, picking up a weighted donut, slid it down the end of the bat before stepping into the on-deck circle. He started haphazardly swinging to get the feel, and thought about Julie Harrison's five-year-old son, whom he'd signed a baseball for two hours earlier. Damn, that kid was cute.

Chase watched Baltimore's pitcher a moment. Brandon Howard didn't have a bad start; he had struck Chase out his first time up. But his curveball was coming in high and his slider had started breaking just short of the plate. His fastball had never been anything to write home about. If Troy Miller noticed it, too, he'd be working a walk and would load the bases. With the Miller's count going to 2–0, chances were he did.

Chase went back to reflecting on Julie, playing with his batting gloves, oblivious to the twenty-five thousand people around him. It was such a nice surprise when she showed up at the stadium during warm-ups. Eight years had changed her from a rebellious teenager to a graceful woman. When she'd called out to him from the row above the dugout, he recognized her right away. Some women just said his name differently. He had security bring Julie and her family onto the edge of the field, where Chase met her son, Milo, and Greg, her Marine Corps sergeant husband. Greg was tall, clean-cut, and sturdy with a firm handshake and good posture. Chase thanked Greg for his service, immediately offered them seats in his luxury box, and then signed the ball for Milo, all the while musing he wasn't the least bit surprised that Julie had ended up with a military man. Julie had a thing for discipline. But then again, so did he.

Troy Miller had swung on 2 and 0, and then took ball three. The catcher got up and ran out to the pitcher's mound to give a small pep talk to Howard. Troy looked over to the first-base coach, then back to Chase, and they exchanged small nodding grins. Unless the next pitch was perfect, Troy would be strolling to first. Chase pounded the handle of the bat on the ground, releasing the weight, and then leaned on it. The catcher and pitcher spent a few seconds conversing from behind their mitts before the home plate umpire started making his way to the pitcher's mound to break up the powwow.

Seeing Julie had made Chase nostalgic. After all, Julie had been his first girl. They had been seniors at Jefferson-Scranton High School in Iowa, long before he became a household name. They had been dating for several months when he dragged her kicking and screaming out of a party when the drugs appeared.

"I'm not about to blow my scholarship to Irvine over a buzz, Julie," he had calmly told her from the driver's seat of his father's pickup truck. Wise beyond his years, he was already good at impulse control. "You shouldn't want to get mixed up in that stuff, either."

She accused him of sounding like her father and told him to drop her off at home; she would find another way back to the party. He remarked that with the way she was behaving, if she were his daughter, they'd be taking a trip out to the woodshed. She threw down the gauntlet and replied she'd like to see him try.

He pulled the truck over into the driveway of a deserted farm and showed her in no uncertain terms what he thought about dares. After scorching the seat of her jeans until she screeched a promise to stay put after he dropped her off, he drove her home and they made out in front of her house for an hour. Julie would go on to dare him countless times before they graduated.

The night before he left for college she told him under a moonlit sky he was destined to be big and that she'd never forget him. He never promised he'd be back, and she had no means to follow.

Miller fouled off another two pitches before earning the walk. Chase heard his theme music start up and his name reverberating through the stadium's address system, followed by the accompanying cheer. He strolled up to the batter's box and went through his setup routine.

It was different in college. Girls were liberated and experimental; the dares became bolder, and antics to get his attention were brattier. He was more than happy to deliver, but it wasn't the same. It was purely for sex, and he couldn't get too invested in them. Baseball took up a lot of his time, and he took his education seriously, having never forgotten the words his father told him the day he left for California.

"Son, no matter where your talent takes you, you're going to be a man a lot longer than you're going to be a ballplayer. Knowledge is the only true power. Learn all you can."

Chase got a degree in business and stayed at university for the duration. He hit eighteen home runs his freshman year and only got better. It took him until his junior year to convince scouts he wouldn't be leaving

Irvine until he finished what he'd gone there to do. After graduating magna cum laude, he signed with the team he always wanted to play for and began to call New York home. His father died of a massive heart attack two years later, proud of the man his son had become. Chase convinced his mother to sell the farm and moved her into a gated community in Florida, where she ran one of his foundations, dated a doctor from the local hospital, and played a mean game of canasta.

"Strike one," Chase heard the umpire call. Shit, he had been so busy strolling down memory lane he had zoned out and completely missed the pitch, one that spent quality time over the plate. Not good. Not good at all. He'd better get his head back in the game and start getting down to business.

And that business was Brandon Howard. Chase Walker didn't take kindly to striking out. It'd be over his dead body that it would happen again. With the bases loaded and his current count, odds were he could expect some junk thrown at him in the hope he'd panic and swing. Or a pitch was coming down the pipe that he was going to send screaming out of the stadium. The latter sounded like the better scenario, if he could just get Howard to cooperate.

Once he hit the majors, all the rules had changed. It became all about excess. Women sought him out, his dominance like a beacon. Some wanted to be hurt. It was no longer about the give-and-take of mutual caring, respect, or even fun. Without the emotional attachment, the act often left him feeling hollow and sometimes guilty. After an array of one-night stands, he'd had a nearly yearlong romance with a well-known actress who indulged him occasionally. But her requests were few and far between, and when it was rumored she was having an affair with a costar, he promptly cut the relationship off. He didn't want to go back to arbitrary women who were vague memories the next day. He began to shy away from the scene altogether as his responsibilities and his stardom grew. But he missed the feel, the sound, the very company of women. He wanted it all, and he knew it was out there. He just had to be patient.

Patient. Like he had to be with Brandon Howard, who was busy shaking off his catcher, something Chase considered a very good indicator that Howard was losing his confidence, at least for the day. Chase set himself up, and Howard began to wind up.

"Strike two!" the umpire shouted, flamboyantly taking a step and pointing his finger to the side.

Chase backed up off the plate and out of the batter's box. Okay, this was serious. It was time to think of nothing but baseball. He adjusted his gloves while glowering at the catcher.

"Bet he doesn't have another one of those in him."

"What's the matter, Walker?" He heard the snicker from behind the catcher's mask. "The thought of going 0-fer giving you the willies?"

"Hardly," he scoffed, digging a small hole in the dirt with the toe of his left cleat before resetting himself. His sight zeroed in on the ball in Howard's hand. And as if imagining it was all it took to make it happen, Brandon Howard threw a lackluster fastball that landed smack-dab in the middle of the plate. And Chase Walker did what he did best. He swung. The resulting sound of the bat making contact told the rest of the story.

Chase took a few slower steps in the direction of first base until he was sure the ball was making its way into the parking lot and then he picked up his pace. He ran the bases at a decent clip into the awaiting high fives of his three teammates who had already touched home. They ran as a group into the dugout, and Chase tossed his batting helmet back into its slot, followed by his gloves amid all his teammates congratulatory slapping him on the back. He grabbed a paper cup full of water, and after pouring it over his head, took another and sat down next to Troy.

"What time is it?" Chase asked before swallowing the water in one gulp.

Troy squinted at the opposite end of the dugout and the digital clock near the phone to the bullpen. "Two past two. Why?"

Chase crushed the paper cup in his hand and tossed it in the direction of a nearby trash can. He reached for a towel, then held out a fist for Troy to bump.

"I just wanted to know exactly when I'd found the sweet spot for this season."

The Kings went on to beat the Orioles 8–3. And Chase had his first grand slam of the year.

He gave his interviews when the game was over and headed for the showers.

"Want to grab some dinner?" Troy asked him as Chase finished buttoning his shirt before tucking it into his trousers. Troy was new in town, having been traded in the off-season from Atlanta. His wife had stayed behind in Georgia until they decided what, if anything, to do with their house there. Troy's and Chase's lockers were side by side, which provided camaraderie, and Chase often asked Troy to join him after games for whatever he was up for. It was also a way for Chase to keep an eye on Troy, after it became apparent that Troy clearly had a drinking problem, which was only exacerbated by his wife's reluctance to join him in New York. Chase would never stand in the way of another guy's party, but he could make sure the man got home in one piece.

"Can't." Chase sighed and pinched the bridge of his nose in anticipation of his impending headache. "I'm having dinner with my agent."

"Sorry to hear that," Troy replied, understanding everything Chase implied. They shared the unique negotiating style of Alan Shaw, not that Troy got nearly as much attention. Chase would be working 365 days a year if he didn't keep Shaw reined in. "I hope at least you're going someplace where the food is good."

"So do I, but I doubt it, " Chase said, running his fingers through his full head of still-damp sandy-blond hair before he finished getting dressed. "It's someplace in Hoboken. One of those chic, trendy places that refuses to serve lunch. I'm totally expecting to need a pizza after they serve me four peas, half a potato, and a leg that belonged to the tiniest chicken on record."

Chapter 3

Amanda returned to the Cold Creek just in time for
opening. She had gone home, showered again, and
redressed. She'd redone her makeup, but hadn't taken
the time to blow-dry her hair again, and the result was
curly instead of straight, not the sophisticated look she
usually went for, but it would have to do. While at home,
she also rechecked the reservation list from her own
computer and saw that one of the parties was friends
of her parents. After a slightly awkward phone call on
her end and the promise of their next meal being on the
house, the couple politely gave up their reservation to
accommodate the guests Amanda had begun to refer
to as "the nuisances." She didn't bother telling anyone
about the phone call that resulted in the order to roll
out the red carpet; her being distracted by it was bad

enough. It was probably an actor; they usually came with the general sense the world revolved around them. Maybe it was a politician, though that was unlikely. Her parents were well-connected, and the reservation call would have reflected that. Odds were it wasn't a musician, which was something to be grateful for, since they tended to bring entourages.

Alan Shaw arrived promptly at six fifty. He was everything Amanda imagined he would be, right down to his overpriced suit, his prematurely receding hairline, and his creepy, flagrant once-over, although he looked younger than she imagined. She didn't see any sign of a cigar. She seated him at a booth in a quiet back corner, which seemed to meet with his approval. He dismissed her with the order of a Red Bull and vodka while pulling out his smart phone. She was more than happy to remove herself from his proximity, not bothering to tell him she'd send over his server. Amanda went back to the podium to seat another party after a quick stop at the bar to give Eric the drink order. Her smile started feeling forced and unnatural. Fussy customers she could handle; feeling manipulated by obnoxious superiority in her own establishment was nothing new, either. But today was a different story. The timing was awful and only added to the general feeling of malaise that always accompanied the cosmic forces of the world determined to keep her in check. She spent the next ten minutes awaiting the arrival of the man she had spent the better part of the afternoon thinking of as "the king."

She had no idea just how close to the truth she was.

It started precisely at seven o'clock, with a flurry of activity at the entrance. Patrons waiting for the rest of their parties to arrive and those lingering with their good-byes cleared a path when three exceedingly large figures seemed to fill all the remaining space at the front of the restaurant. Two of the men looked nearly identical. Both were burly and clean-shaven with short hair, matching blue suits, and serious expressions.

The third man was instantly recognizable.

His charisma had entered the room ten seconds before he did, branching out to everyone within its vicinity. And at its nexus was well over six feet of stacked muscle and magnetism presented casually in gray tailored slacks and a teal cashmere sweater. The collar of a button-down shirt peeked politely from beneath the sweater, the ensemble completed with thousand-dollar Louis Vuitton shoes. His movie-star good looks only added to it, from the perfectly mussed wheat blond hair right down to the cleft in his chiseled chin. It was a heady combination and the room began to buzz.

Great Caesar's Ghost! The Golden Boy is hot and then some. It was Amanda's automatic response to whenever he was mentioned in any capacity. It was the usual response of Nicki, too. Baseball was a mandatory tradition that started when Amanda was in grammar school. Summer in Jersey just isn't summer if you don't catch at least one baseball game. Nicki had had no problem jumping on that bandwagon, and the two of them went once a year, always to a Kings game. There may have even been a whistle or two in his direction from their seats once he hit the roster when they were in attendance. Other variations on the theme were: steamy hot, fig-leaf-wearing-in-the-garden hot, and fry-an-egg-on-his-left-pec hot. Amanda surmised sunglasses would have been a bit over the top, and as he moved away from the men who stood on either side of him, she waited for him to approach.

"Hi. I'm Chase Walker," he said when he reached her.

Amanda stared at him for a moment. He didn't say it in a way that was different from anyone else making an introduction would. But her rotten day dictated she heard him announcing his arrival as the final straw. It reeked of ego. Everyone on the planet knew who he was, even if they didn't know a thing about baseball. He was one of those extraordinary specimens that became a national treasure, probably against the greater good. You couldn't swing a dead cat without hitting something that had Chase Walker's face on it. He probably just liked to hear the sound of his own name, even if he was the one having to say it. And in that moment, for reasons she couldn't begin to explain, she chose to stand up for every person who was ever forced to cater to the perpetually pampered. Even on the best day of her life, people like him were difficult for her to take. She had the one luxury of not having to worry about getting fired; she was the boss. Her day already stank; she might as well make it memorable. When he and his goons left in a huff, she could have the added pleasure of tossing Alan Shaw out on his keister. She looked from one security guard to the other and then tilted her head at him, looking thoughtful.

"Mr. Walker, has anyone ever told you that your name is an oxymoron?" she asked, and then blinked at him with the subtle dare that he wouldn't make the connection and she'd have to explain.

He raised his eyebrows before breaking out into the most boyishly genuine smile she had ever seen.

"Not since the fifth grade." He chuckled, playing right into her observation. "Very funny, can't really chase anyone when you're a walker. Thanks for bringing it up. My therapist can probably start picking out his new car now."

His smile was disarming and his voice even more so. Both were warm and easy and terribly engaging. His reaction was completely unexpected. Suddenly she felt ashamed for acting so immature. He saw through her thinly veiled and well-mannered route into calling him a moron, and quick-wittedly called her out on it. He didn't seem insulted, nor did he seem ready to leave. She started to blush.

Chase studied her briefly before leaning back a bit and turning his head. One of the suits immediately rushed over, and he whispered something in the suit's ear. The man nodded and the two security guards left the building. Then he straightened and returned his attention to Amanda. He drew his head across the podium and closer to hers. Because of his height, he could've come clear across it and breathed in her ear, but he stopped just short of it. "I'm guessing my agent worked you over pretty good?" he said pleasantly. "Because back in fifth grade, I think I beat that kid up on the playground. I'd hate to think you really want to pick a fight."

"He does seem to bring out the worst in people," she murmured, trying to stand her ground and not apologize, but also feeling guiltier for having been so antagonistic and unprofessional. He was making her feel downright childish.

"He's a legend in his own mind," he whispered in her ear, all mirth and amusement. "He bullies me into bringing the security. He can be insufferable. But he acts that way so I don't have to. Can we start over?"

Amanda looked up into his sparkling green eyes and felt her breath catch. He was already towering over her and had moved in so close. His subtle hint of body wash surrounded by pure raw masculinity was intoxicating. It was hard to believe that Chase Walker could be bullied by anyone. And he was going out of his way to make her comfortable. He was a perfect gentleman. She blinked up at him, flabbergasted again, but this time for entirely different reasons.

"What's your name, darlin'?" His casual use of an arbitrary endearment had the opposite effect of his agent's use of one. It sounded warm and smooth, like honey.

"I'm Amanda Cole," she said, instantly playing along and extending her perfectly manicured hand with a more relaxed smile. "Welcome to the Cold Creek Grille, Mr. Walker. Your party is already waiting."

Then her hand completely disappeared within the grip of his. His hand was huge, in keeping with the rest of him. It was also surprisingly gentle.

"It's a pleasure to meet you, Amanda. Please call me Chase," he replied, refraining from telling her that her smile was radiant for fear it would sound condescending, since they had already started off on the wrong foot. In fact, she was beautiful in general. As soon as he'd walked in, he was drawn to her. Her big round eyes were so blue, her lashes long and inviting. Such contrast with the long ebony curls that framed her face. She had a pert little nose that looked adorable even when she'd wrinkled it up just prior to insulting him moments before. He could picture himself nibbling on her rosy bottom lip. He was surprised by the burst of kinetic energy, brought on just by placing her hand in his. She must've felt it too, because as soon as he lightened up on his grip, she quickly pulled her hand away and turned to lead him to his table.

Amanda Cole wasn't thin, but instead was robust and buxom. She had curves, lots of them, and in all the right places, he noted. Making sure she was several steps ahead of him, he pulled out his phone as he walked. The action served a dual purpose. If he looked focused on something, people were less likely to try to stop him. It was all about avoiding eye contact.

He could also discreetly look her up and down without looking like a letch as he followed behind her. And since it was his specialty, he could tell in one sweeping glance that beneath the lines of her royal-blue Halston dress, Amanda Cole was a brick house. Right down to her bodacious booty, which he guesstimated how much of his hand could cover in one shot. She had certainly given him reason to want to. She had a brat switch, and he had tripped it the minute she saw him. If she had spoken any louder, she would've cut him to the quick in front of half a dozen people, including his own employees. But she had been careful to make sure he was the only one to hear it. She wasn't flirting with him, though. She had reverted back to trying to act professional and move things along. Thanks to his agent, she'd probably spent the afternoon hating him. In too short a stroll, they arrived at the booth where Alan Shaw was waiting, and Chase took a seat. She wished them both a lovely dinner and promptly removed herself. He allowed himself one more thorough blink as she walked away.

"You had a good day," Alan said, taking another swallow of his drink as Chase settled into his side of the booth.

"All my days are good," Chase replied, gearing up for the onslaught that always came from dinner with Alan Shaw. He picked up his menu as Alan snapped his fingers, even though Nicki was already hurrying over.

"Mr. Walker," Nicki tried to stifle the giggling. "What can I get you to drink?"

"Please call me Chase," he said, thinking that that particular phrase was starting to sound like a broken record. "And I'll take a Heineken."

"Right away . . . Chase." Nicki giggled and scurried off.

"I should have ordered a waiter," Alan muttered before waving his own glass and calling after her, "I'll take another one, too."

"Nice play on words. Seems there's a bit of that going around," Chase commented dryly, casting another glance at Amanda. "I could have done without you pissing off the hostess. If she wasn't so cute and you weren't so pushy, I'd seriously consider complaining."

Alan turned his head briefly to follow Chase's gaze back to the front of the restaurant.

"That's not the hostess," Alan said indifferently. "She owns the place. She has no trouble turning on the bitch, but I hear the food is excellent."

Chase immediately bristled at the use of the word *bitch* to describe any woman, much less the one whom he currently had his eye on. But if that was as bad as Alan got in his description of women this evening, he'd consider it a win. "Know anything else about her?"

"Oh, great," Shaw griped. "I can tell already where this is going. If I answer your question, can we get down to business?"

Chase held up his hand. "Scout's honor."

"She's got a rich daddy."

"Daddy as in sugar?" Chase asked, feeling the disappointment of such a beauty going home to some shriveled-up geezer. But it would explain why she was so cantankerous.

"Daddy as in father," Alan clarified and Chase brightened.

"There's a rumor that he's going after next year's senate seat, and her mother is Essex County DA," Alan continued. "And she's single, which I'm sure is the only thing you really want to know anyway."

So she had breeding, Chase thought, not bothering to confirm or deny. It was best not to get too familiar with your agent. Alan Shaw was business. His glance swept one more time in her direction. Amanda Cole looked to be all pleasure. "How do you find out all this stuff?"

"I'm only as good as the knowledge I hold," Shaw scoffed.

"You always sound so shady," Chase said, "like you just came up with something from the seedy underbelly."

"I'll take that as a compliment," Alan remarked before switching topics. "Where's your security?"

"I told them to go get my car and bring it back. The crowd doesn't look too rowdy here and I want to take off as soon as we're done."

"Take off where?" Alan questioned suspiciously.

"Wherever I feel like," Chase replied easily, knowing it would aggravate him further. "It's my day off tomorrow."

"When are you going to learn you can't just venture off alone anymore?"

"Watch me," Chase said. "I don't have to always live in a bubble. And I like it when you don't know where I am, it keeps you on your toes. What's the agenda this evening?"

"I heard from Trojan again—" Alan began.

"I told you, I'm not doing a condom ad," Chase cut him off heatedly. "And if that's our only business tonight, I'm leaving right now."

"Relax, it's not." Alan was quick to defuse the mounting tension before adding, "but it's an incredible amount of money. And they don't just sell condoms."

Chase didn't bother responding and leaned back against the booth, crossing his arms and raising an eyebrow, signifying there would be no further discussion on the topic.

Nicki returned with their drinks, took their order, and left to go place it.

"Thank you, thank you, thank you," Nicki gushed to Amanda, who was standing with Eric at the bar. "I've never been so happy to wait on someone in my life. He called me *darlin'*. It sounded like something out of one of those Hallmark movies."

Amanda rolled her eyes and considered telling her he had called her the same thing. But then she might end up confessing that, at least for a moment, it had produced the same giddy effect. It also proved that it was a term he probably threw out to countless women. But Nicki was probably just his type: perky, freewheeling, and always ready for her close-up. If he played his cards right, he could be banging with her before daybreak.

"He looks like he's made of plastic. Why on earth would you want to get involved with someone who's more Ken doll than actual person?" Amanda asked.

"Do you know what someone like Chase Walker could do for my career?" Nicki couldn't contain her excitement.

"Make you forget all about it?" Amanda quipped, and Eric snickered. "Let me guess, they both want steak?"

"How did you know?" Nicki asked.

"A little bird told me," Amanda replied, fully appreciating the irony.

Chase covertly studied Amanda throughout his meal. His agent droned on, and he listened for key words signaling his full attention, a trick he had learned from being pulled in too many directions at once. He watched her go about her business. She was graceful, moving fluidly from table to table. She took a vested interest in every single one, sitting down momentarily at some of them with a wholesome familiarity. She seemed diligent and serious about her work, but with an appealing smile always at the ready. Not the fake, tight smile she'd first given him, but the one that showed she knew how to work a room. He looked around the restaurant, which seated about a hundred. It was tastefully decorated without being ostentatious. There was a cozy ambiance without it being too dark. It was also spotless. And the employees working seemed relaxed and happy enough to be there. It proved she knew how to run a smooth operation. It all added up to the fact that Amanda Cole had gotten his attention.

Chase also noticed that she left his table alone. The service was still impeccable, just not by her. She sent an attractive waitress to fawn over him. He liked that she wasn't impressed by him, even if his ego did take a hit.

She may have been fresh, but she was clearly also intelligent. She was class and sass, all perfectly packaged. Now he just needed to figure out if she was playing hard to get.

When they finished eating, Chase convinced Alan to leave with the promise that he was going to stay put for a while, have a few drinks, and let security drive him home. After a snide remark from Alan that if some tail was going to keep Chase from wandering off, he would take it and, with a leering smile in Amanda's direction, he left. Chase then took a seat at the bar, ordered another beer, and started chatting it up with Eric. He continued to flirt with Nicki when she picked up orders. Soon customers began to approach him, camera phones in hand. Amanda tried to distance herself from it and focus on doing her job, but she could feel him watching her in between the polite conversation he made with any and all participants. He didn't make any attempt to hide it. Whenever she glanced in his direction, he would give her a little wink, not the least bit concerned she caught him staring.

"You're going to sit here all night and remind me of my bad manners, aren't you?" Amanda said from behind him once the commotion had died down.

He turned around from his barstool to take her all in, appreciating what he saw. "I'm just waiting for security to come back with my car. I hope you don't mind if I hang out."

"They've been standing watch over a very nice Jaguar double-parked in front for the last half hour."

"In that case, I'm just an oxymoron fishing for a date," he said with a note of pure swagger.

"You know, one of those security guards is smaller than you," she continued, deliberately ignoring his attempt to extend an invitation. "It looks sort of counterproductive."

"He's the one I use when women poke fun of me in public."

"That hurt."

"Guilty enough to join me for dinner?"

"You just ate."

"Not tonight, tomorrow."

"Sorry, I can't. I have a business to run."

"Then let's do lunch? Or breakfast?"

"That's a bit presumptuous, don't you think?" she said, finding herself teasing back.

"That's what I'm talking about. What time are we getting off?" He was so annoyingly easygoing, not to mention gorgeous.

"Sorry, I don't date guys I can see half naked with a Google search."

"Geez, does that leave anyone else?"

"It leaves lots of people, Mr. Walker," she retorted snippily, as if she were engaging in a political debate. "It leaves teachers and doctors and policemen. Men who are a little choosier about whom they let into their private lives, who can go out for a hamburger without it making Page Six of the *New York Post*."

"I'm about as choosy as they come when it's about my privacy. It's not my fault I can't even spit dirt out of my mouth without someone taking a picture of it."

"You really don't spit all that much," she mused before catching herself. Dagnabbit, it sounded like she knew too much about him. But he did have a lovely mouth.

He smiled again. "I promised my mother I would try to curb it. So you watch baseball?"

"Occasionally," she fibbed, attempting to take another swipe at his swagger. "It's hard to turn off Derek Jeter, he's pretty dreamy."

But he only grinned at her. "You can meet him at our wedding."

"That's laying it on a bit thick."

"Maybe, but I'm just trying to illustrate how confident I am."

"More like stubborn. Don't worry, your interest in me will soon pass," Amanda told him, disappointed that she knew she was speaking the truth, even though she wished she wasn't. He was just killing time between models and debutantes. With the new day, this superstar would go back to his world of pomp and accolades. She wasn't interested in the dubious distinction of sleeping with him just for claiming the honor of having done so.

"I don't think so, angel," he replied. "I'm a little more one-track-minded than that. All you have to do is say yes, it'll make it easier for both of us."

"I beg to differ, Mr. Walker," she corrected him. "The way I see it, all I have to do is make it through to closing while dodging your cheesy advances."

But she had been wrong. The next day, Chase came back. Soon after opening, before the dinner rush, he arrived alone, wearing jeans and a button-down with his shirttail out. He'd dressed it up with an expensive-looking, soft gray leather vest that his biceps swelled out of. He took the same seat he had at the bar the night before. Then he proceeded to stay until closing.

"This is ridiculous," Amanda told him a little after eight, after he'd been there for more than three hours. She wanted to sound annoyed, but was secretly flattered. Not only was he pleasant and wonderful to look at, but he was also just so good with the banter. They had developed an easy rapport that she was beginning to find engaging.

"I know." Chase even managed to gripe with delight. "I can't believe you're making me do this. At least I'm getting the lowdown on you."

Eric took that precise moment to find his way to the other end of the bar after an apologetic shrug and a sheepish "It was all good." Amanda crossed her arms over her chest and narrowed her eyes at him as he walked away before turning back to Chase.

"Their opinions could be biased. They work for me."

"Then you better let me take you out so I can draw my own conclusions. If you'd just give me your digits, I'd be on my way."

"Then what?" she asked him.

"You're going to have to say yes to find out," he said, smiling.

"And if I don't?"

"Then I'm going to have to keep coming back here until I change your mind."

Amanda laughed. "I almost want to see that."

"Be careful what you wish for," he warned her.

And after politely rebuffing him again, Chase went about the business of doing just that. Every day he was in town, he found his way to the Cold Creek Grille. She started keeping his table open, and he began having all his dinners there. He sometimes dined with his security, and sometimes they discreetly sat at the bar or a nearby table while he hosted teammates or held other meetings. Kings games and their replays became a staple on the bar's television.

Chase got to meet Amanda's parents one night, when they came in after hearing the rumor that Amanda had an unconventional celebrity stalker. Chase had finished eating, but invited them for dessert, fully prepared to plead his case to the judge and the DA. They joined him, giving him a brief and prudent once-over. They were sophisticated and well put together, the DA in a no-nonsense business suit straight out of the court-room; the judge's attire straight off the golf course. They spoke about philanthropy and baseball, and Chase asked permission to date their daughter.

"Mr. Walker," Catherine Cole said in the same sassy tone Amanda used when addressing him by his formal name. What followed it was usually direct and pointed. And the same was true of her mother, even if she was impressed by his candor and manners. "My daughter is a grown woman, she makes her own decisions."

"Of course, ma'am," he said, laughing nervously. "But I was really hoping that I could get you to put in a good word."

Judge Rupert Cole chuckled with humor from across the table. Chase had integrity and humility, traits that were hard to fake if insincere. "Just remember, I can get a restraining order against you at a moment's notice."

"She's hasn't called the police on me yet, sir."

And when the verdict came in, they didn't think Amanda was going to. She was just being cautious, as they agreed she had reason to be. It didn't stop her parents from telling her they liked him.

Chapter 4

Chase became a permanent fixture at the Cold Creek. After the first week, word started to spread and there was a constant influx of people going there to dine in the hopes of seeing Chase Walker. And they weren't disappointed. He had dozens of pictures taken and signed countless napkins and random scraps of paper. He even autographed a few body parts. All with one single purpose: trying to score a date with Amanda Cole. The bar stayed crowded the whole time he was there. He learned the names of all the employees and went out of his way to engage them. If he was faking the Average Joe routine, he was an exceptional actor. Two weeks in, it became apparent he wasn't going to go away.

And it was impossible to deny: He was a wonderful flirt. He was also quick, intelligent, and confident, and every conversation ended with him asking her to join him somewhere, from Bora Bora to the coffee shop around the corner. He looked at her honestly when he did it, like he was soaking her in with his eyes.

Week three of Chase's staged sit-in began with a snafu that ended up working in his favor. It started on a Wednesday night with a dozen long-stemmed roses surrounded by baby's breath and arranged in a vase, delivered by the head of his security team. Blue roses, precisely dyed to match the color of Amanda's eyes, arriving a half hour before he did, and a hand-written note that read:

> *Blue roses symbolize something that is impossible to achieve. Not in my vocabulary. I apologize for the next two hours.*

It was vague and ambiguous, and he was already making apologies. The bodyguard, Jack, who often accompanied Chase, dropped them off with the same poker-faced expression he always wore and immediately left. Amanda didn't bother trying to interrogate him. Jack took his job seriously, and they both knew who signed his paycheck. The note and flowers set her on edge. Unless Chase had planted some vermin and called the health inspector, what could he possibly be sorry for? As the vibrant flowers were admired by everyone who passed them, Amanda's nerves stretched tighter, despite all her efforts to quell them. When Chase walked through the door, his message became as clear as the imported crystal the roses were presented in. She didn't know whether to feel insulted or relieved. He gave her a quick, crooked smile while the three other members of his dining party entered after him.

"Well, what do we have here?" Eric snickered quietly from behind the roses at the end of the bar nearest to Amanda's podium workstation, the only spot roomy enough to keep them from getting in the way. Amanda was suddenly bemused.

Chase Walker had brought a date to the Cold Creek, a date of the waiflike supermodel variety. She was long and lean and stood naturally on six-inch stilettos, making her nearly as tall as he was. Her skirt was a respectable length, but the sequined, belly-button-ringed-revealing tank top was the complete epitome of skimpy. Her skin was porcelain. She looked disinterested, if not snobbish, and in Amanda's opinion, hungry, as did the other woman who was with them. The only difference was Chase's date had a mane of flaxen, stylish hair, while the other woman's was more platinum highlighted. Their superfluous, wispy giggles were exactly the same.

Amanda kept her poise, smiling brightly as the four approached. He was free to bring whomever he wanted to dinner, but flaunting his desirability wasn't how to earn brownie points with her.

"Good evening, Mr. Walker. I have your table ready."

"Hi, Amanda," he greeted her, only the slightest evidence of his discomfort betrayed by his hand-caught-in-the-cookie-jar expression. "I'd like to introduce you to my good friend Logan Montgomery."

The remaining person in their group stepped forward, hidden behind that first gust of charisma that accompanied Chase. Logan Montgomery was probably the most handsome man on the planet. He was dark and swarthy, with jet-black hair and expressive brown eyes. His skin was so tan it suggested he'd just returned from some exotic island. His face was classically chiseled and his physique nothing short of astounding. She couldn't help but stare. His smile was easy as he joined them, but if she'd known him better, she would have noticed he was also suffering from his own faux pas.

Amanda also would have been able to tell by the quickly concealed, edgy glare Chase shot at him, but Logan had the sort of looks that when you saw them for the first time, you needed a moment to take them in. "Logan, this is Amanda Cole, the woman I obviously didn't tell you enough about."

"My pleasure, Amanda," Logan drawled before returning Chase's look with an amused one of his own. "Sometimes, when texting, one doesn't get a full picture. For some reason, my host still insisted on dining here."

Amanda didn't see the need in letting the introductions continue. Clearly a miscommunication had taken place, and Chase had made his choice with regard to the situation. He apologized ahead of time, which was rather egotistical for someone she wouldn't give her phone number to, yet incredibly romantic in a peculiar sort of way. And she didn't want to know anything about either man's date. Still, he had to have some reason for bringing a date here. Maybe it was a last-ditch effort to illustrate she was missing her opportunity, and Amanda was interested in seeing how the evening played out. She nodded a hello and, grabbing four menus, asked them to please follow her. As she led them to Chase's regular booth, no mention was made of the glorious bouquet taking up one end of the bar, by either of them. The gentlemen motioned for the ladies to be seated on the inside, and as they slid in, Chase and Amanda's gazes met and locked. A brief moment passed as Chase took her in, having not seen her for the last two days, Mondays and Tuesdays being the Cold Creek's "weekend" and was closed. It was the look that he gave her when she was across the room, too far away for them to have a real conversation. The look that suggested he was deep in thought, hinting that some of those thoughts were indecent. Then he did what any gallant gentleman would do.

He slid into his seat and proceeded to completely ignore her. His attention centered solely on entertaining his date. He sat so that if Amanda glanced over, his back was presented to her. There would be no cat-and-mouse game of him trying to catch her eye, no drama played out from behind the scenes. He didn't use a trip to the men's room as an excuse to exchange a few words with her. He never looked over, not even once. Chase appeared to be enthralled with whatever was going on at his table, which from what Amanda could tell, was a great deal of laughter and waify giggling.

Amanda found out through Nicki that both women requested specially prepared salmon, grilled and basted in olive oil and lemon, with steamed vegetables, no carrots.

Figures, Amanda thought, as she saw to it that the order was expertly prepared. Within fifteen minutes, interest had passed into pique. It was unexpected and startling. She had no justification; she had told Chase all along he didn't stand a chance. And it wasn't necessarily the presence of the woman that irked her. Amanda wasn't even sure she saw her as a threat. It was the pure, unadulterated snub from the man who'd spent every spare minute he could until tonight catching her eye from wherever he was seated. Who wrapped her up in his unabashed affection and delighted in it. She hated having to admit she was hurt because Chase Walker wasn't showering her with his attention. And even though she really was flustered, there no way in hell she was going to show it. She wanted him to get back to living the high life, she told herself. She was just having second thoughts about seeing him do it in her restaurant.

As Chase and his companions dined, and the more she tried to ignore them being there, the more Amanda couldn't refrain from looking over. He wasn't touching his date, hadn't moved in too close, but he was fully engaged in his tête-à-tête with the woman. It was all very proper and genial, and by the time they ordered coffee and one dessert, Chase's favorite, Amanda was fighting off a full-blown snit.

Amanda didn't check on his table as she would've normally done with most guests, mostly because she didn't think she could trust herself. What she did, in her opinion, was the next best thing: Anybody who showed the slightest interest in the celebrity dining in the back of the room, she sent them right over to his table. Normally, when Chase was eating, she would smoothly point fanatics over to the bar, telling them that Chase hung out there after he ate and loved a good conversation. But tonight, Amanda told a dozen people in the most encouraging voice she had that, yes indeed, that was Chase Walker, and he loved meeting his fans, even when having dinner. Half of the people she told shied away and left him alone. The other half paraded right up to him and, if nothing else, momentarily broke up his love-fest. And she quietly enjoyed the small vindication from afar, until she got what she wanted: He looked at her. After getting out of the booth to stand at the table and accommodate a picture, he faced her direction. He smiled for the picture and then scanned the room, instantly finding her. It was brief, and it was perceptive. Or maybe she just felt guilty for the immature way she'd resorted to rattling his cage while still keeping her distance. He gave her a tiny smile before returning to his seat.

They finished their coffee, Chase paid the bill, and then they got up to leave, passing by Amanda on the way out.

"Thanks for a wonderful meal," Chase said brusquely, taking his date by the elbow to escort her out the door.

"Thank you for dining with us, Mr. Walker," Amanda replied with the same sass she employed every time she used his formal name. "Please consider coming back again."

Logan and his date followed in Chase's wake. Logan was shaking his head, with a small knowing smile of his own. "It was nice to meet you, Amanda. Sorry about the mix-up."

And then he was gone. All that remained were her unjustifiable wounded feelings and an exorbitant bouquet. She sullenly got back to work while business slowed down and, nearing the end of the night, she went back to the roses, dejectedly touching the petals and rearranging the stems.

"For Pete's sake," Eric eventually said from the other end of the bar before approaching her. "How much longer are you going to let this go on? He's starting to tell people he's eaten everything on the menu twice. The guy is really starting to get the sympathy vote. If you don't say yes soon, you're going to look like you're shooting him down to build your clientele."

Eric wasn't far off. It was starting to feel like saying no to him was akin to burning the American flag.

"He's got you batting for him now?" Amanda asked, still concentrating on the flowers. She had started to find all the good-natured teasing a bit intimidating. She never expected him to make good on his threat of becoming a pest, but she had gotten used to it. She couldn't throw him out now. From the sound of it, her entire staff would start a mutiny if she did. And when all was said and done, after the evening's events, she didn't want to. She had started looking forward to his arrival, more than she would've wanted to admit. She felt a spike in her heart rate every time he came through the door, a sudden hitch in her breathing that she attributed to his charisma sucking all the air out of the room.

"Yeah, what are you waiting for?" Nicki chimed in, having been his waitress and witnessing the whole bizarre evening from both sides. "He's not perfect enough for you?"

Amanda didn't take what Nicki said personally. Nicki had tried her best to hide her disappointment when it became apparent Chase was indeed interested with someone at the Cold Creek, and it wasn't her. It was a tough pill to swallow. Rejection was rejection, no matter how you look at it. Amanda knew that pill, and the current pill didn't taste much different. She continued to study the flowers. She had just been rejected, by a guy slick enough to believe he could honestly play both ends against the middle, with a swankier consolation prize.

"No one is perfect," Amanda stated, hoping she was effectively downplaying his actions and that using the word wouldn't set off a chain of events ending up with her in the hospital. "There's always that fatal flaw and I'll bet his is a doozy."

"Fatal flaw?" Nicki repeated with interest.

"Yeah," Amanda explained. "It's a theory we figured out back in college. When you first start dating a guy, he's busy saying all the right words and acting like Prince Charming, trying to get you naked. Then if he likes the outcome, it's all about trying to get you to stay naked, but the flaw is there, lying dormant, until you're hooked. By then it's usually too late; you're all wrapped up in the memory of when you first met and everyone was on their best behavior. Then you ride the breakup-makeup carousel until you both can't stand yourselves. Our final analysis was, until you find the fatal flaw in your potential partner, the relationship can't ever be real."

"That's stupid," Eric remarked, free to speak his mind. There were times when Amanda was a boss and there were times when Amanda was a friend. Most of the time, she was both. "People are always changing.

What's a flaw in someone who's twenty-five could be a nonissue five years later."

"So what happens when you find it?" Nicki asked curiously, ignoring Eric. Boys knew nothing of the sisterhood.

"Then you decide if it's something you can live with, and if the good makes the flaw worth it," Amanda continued. "For instance, you can take a guy who enjoys his free time with the boys, but one who spends every weekend drunk is a no-go. Maybe he's a real cheapskate when it comes to showering you with gifts and expensive dates, but he's all about you when you hit the sheets. Or you don't mind that he doesn't have a really great job, as long as while you're working he's not at home cheating on you."

"You realize that every situation you just described has nothing to do with the guy who's trying to get your attention," Eric pointed out. "For crying out loud, talk about an overreaction. He just wants to take you for dinner."

"Guys like that don't just want dinner," Amanda said, thinking Chase was not just any guy. He was more of a stalker who just happened to win everybody over, a drop-dead sexy stalker with electric eyes, a teen-idol smile, and a butt worthy of an underwear model—and those were just the parts of him she could see. "I'm telling you, he's only pushing because I had the nerve not to melt in his presence. And how do you know he isn't a cheater? For all we know, he's the biggest philanderer on the planet."

"Oh sure," Eric snorted, rolling his eyes and shaking his head, " 'Cause all the best womanizers sit alone at a bar being shot down for nights on end."

"Need I remind you, he just left with a contestant from *America's Next Top Model?*"

"Hard to forget; we're all still looking at the flowers he didn't need to send you," Eric retorted.

"He's like your own personal Norm from *Cheers,*" Nicki said, giggling, "except he's gorgeous."

"And he has a job," Eric added.

"And a million women want to have his baby," Amanda concluded, not needing Eric and Nicki's sudden bustling to tell her that Chase had reentered the bar. She could feel him.

Chase came in and sat down in the seat next to her after the failed attempt at sneaking up on her. Eric and Nicki said their hellos, and Eric handed him his usual Heineken before returning to continue closing up.

They spent a few moments in silence while Amanda tried to decide if she was still peeved or elated that he was back.

"Thanks for the flowers. Aren't you supposed to be somewhere unhooking a bra and rounding second base?"

"Do I detect a hint of snark?" Chase smiled with relief. " 'Cause if I do, it just made my night. I was starting to wonder if you really didn't care."

"You mean these aren't your way of inviting me into a threesome?"

"I don't share," he told her seriously. "Thanks for being such a good sport. I know it was awkward."

"But that didn't stop you from doing it," she said snippily. "The least you can do is give me your motive."

"I told you, I'm going to keep coming back here until you let me take you out," Chase said with single-minded determination. "Logan is my best friend, and I wanted him to meet you. He'd just gotten back from vacation, and when I sent the text that I wanted to have dinner, I couldn't bring myself to type the part about the girl who was still giving me the brush."

Amanda's giggle bubbled up and overflowed. The most famous man she could think of went trolling for chicks with the handsomest. "Logan is your choice for a wingman? That's got to be risky."

Chase laughed along. "Not in this case. It was the other way around. Logan really wanted to impress his date. When he brought her to my game, she called her friend, and they saw to the details while I was warming up on the field." He didn't tell Amanda about the mad rush he sent Jack and the boys on to make the roses happen or that Logan was hopelessly stuck on blondes.

"So your solution to the problem was to bring everyone here to taunt me?"

Chase reacted unfavorably to her accusation and adopted a more weighty tone. "I didn't do it to tease you. I'm on a mission. There was no way I wasn't seeing you tonight, even if you are starting to make me look like a chump with your phony-baloney reluctance. But it's the height of bad manners to make a lady feel uncomfortable. Like it or not, I was on a date and she deserved my full attention."

Amanda pursed her lips together. She was the one who was supposed to be offended, yet it felt more like she'd just been given a lecture on etiquette.

"And none of this would've happened if you didn't insist on stringing me along with this game you're playing," he continued, chiding her.

He wasn't angry with her, but there was a definite switch in his approach. His easygoing, valiantly persistent persona was now overshadowed with a strength that hadn't been there previously. It created a new, different sort of rush and she didn't mind he was about to force her hand.

"Come on, angel," he said, his eyes as deep as his voice. "Give me my shot."

Amanda hesitated and debated the pros and cons one more time of the word that, once out there, she wouldn't be able to take back and would probably end up regretting.

"Yes," she said quietly.

Chase shook his head dramatically, as if he couldn't believe what he'd heard, then broke out into a full-blown grin.

"See?" he asked happily. "Was that so hard?"

Chapter 5

Amanda sat on her couch, wringing her hands and lecturing herself. It was just a date. There was no need to be so nervous. Then why did she feel like a long-tailed cat in a room full of rocking chairs? Because while her date was known for playing first base, he could've been a pitcher, given the way he knew how to throw curveballs, starting with his departure from the Cold Creek as soon as she'd accepted his invitation.

She had thought she was so cunning, feigning ignorance to the prior knowledge of his schedule. After saying yes, she figured she had bought herself some more time and gave him one more chance to get permanently distracted. Chase already knew the Cold Creek was closed on Mondays and Tuesdays, the only days she would consider accepting a date. She had had the foresight to agree to an invitation that fell when he had to leave for a road trip to Cleveland. She never expected him to phone both his coach and the Kings' general manager immediately from the bar. He informed them that something important had come up and he would not be flying out with the team on the designated travel day, but flying out independently, and assured them he would arrive in plenty of time before Tuesday's game. He apologized for deviating from the normal practice, but gave no excuses or explanations and none were asked for. Then he called his own pilot and told him to be ready Tuesday morning to take him to Cleveland. The moment he pushed the Off button on his phone after making his final call, Chase asked for her address and told her he would pick her up Monday at seven. Then, with what Eric described as a "shit-eating grin," Chase abruptly left the Cold Creek and didn't return in the interim. Four days of her watching the door, only for him to suddenly become a noticeable no-show.

She should've figured he had his own plane. She would've never guessed he was a master at how to create buildup and tension.

So now Amanda waited, glancing at the clock again. The five-minute countdown to seven was in motion. Maybe he would be late, and she could be righteously ticked off at his discourtesy. At five minutes after seven she would grab her keys and take a powder.

But she knew he wouldn't be late; he ran like clock-work. For the past three weeks, whenever he had a home game, he arrived to occupy his barstool or table exactly an hour and twenty minutes after the last pitch was thrown, even if it was near midnight when he arrived, as had occurred when a night game went into extra innings. Of course, her entire staff was more than willing to stay past their usual closing time of one A.M. to accommodate him, and not just because he was such a generous tipper. He had won them all over after his third night there.

He probably owned a helicopter, too, although she hadn't heard any reports of one landing on the street. He could be the speedboat type. Or maybe he just made use of a phone booth, Superman-style.

She considered quickly changing her clothes again, for the third time. He told her to wear whatever made her comfortable. She finally settled on a burgundy Anne Klein dot flared sweater dress with three-quarter sleeves. Something about the spin-worthy flared skirt called out to her and against Nicki's choice of the stan-dard little black dress.

There was a knock at her door. He was three min-utes early, curse him. Amanda took a deep breath and squared her shoulders.

The charisma blew in like a wind gust as soon as she opened the door. The good looks, polish, and impeccable

fashion sense were hard enough to handle, but the charisma got her every time. She could blame his clean,
expensive cologne, but she knew she'd only be fooling
herself. And this was no time to take a departure from
reality. It didn't help that his absence had made her heart
grow fonder, which in turn was cause for more worry.

"Hi," she squeaked, then gulped for air.

Chase smiled at her as if he hadn't seen her in months
and she was a sight for sore eyes.

"Hi, beautiful," he said. "You ready to go?"

"I already agreed to this," Amanda said, regrouping
and irritated by her own greeting. She reached for her
purse. "You don't need to keep flattering me."

"I'm not flattering," he responded easily. "It's more
like an observation. And you better get used to it, because
I'm very observant and fully appreciate the finer things."

Boy, is this guy smooth, Amanda thought as they left
her apartment and she locked her dead bolt. Finding
his flaw was going to be a challenge. *Stop it,* she told
herself, *there is no flaw to find. This one just isn't for
you.* Together they made their way down the hall to
exit her building.

"No security guards tonight?" she asked dryly.

"I didn't think I was in any danger this evening," he
replied. "I need security?"

"One never knows."

"I'll take my chances." He chuckled as he ran a few steps ahead to hold the door open for her.

The same British metallic green Jaguar XKR-S she remembered from the night she met him was parked in front of the building. It was sleek and beautiful and looked powerful. The same could be said of its owner.

"This car looks familiar," she commented as he rushed to open the car door for her.

"You sound disappointed," he replied as she slid into the car and onto the soft camel-colored leather seat. He closed the door and ran to the driver's side.

"Aren't people like you supposed to own a car for every day of the week?" Amanda said after he took his place behind the wheel.

"I can only drive one car at a time." Chase laughed, buckling in and starting the car. Then he looked at her, a look of warmth and attraction and way too much hidden meaning. "I get attached."

He let the gaze linger and comment hang in the air before revving the supercharged 550-horsepower engine and adding, "Would you feel better if I told you I got a new one every year and also have an Escalade for when I need more room?"

Amanda slightly shook her head in an effort to break the spell. "I'm sorry. I didn't mean to make you sound so spoiled."

"It's okay, I'm nervous, too," he replied quietly before looking away. He shifted the car into gear and pulled out of the parking lot.

Amanda would've told him she highly doubted that. She made Chase Walker nervous? The thought alone was laughable. But he sounded undeniably sincere.

"Where are we going?' she asked, avoiding the topic altogether.

He smiled and his eyes never left the road. "It's a surprise."

"I'm not sure I like the sound of that," she said. "Your arsenal of surprises is probably pretty big. I'm starting to wish security was with you after all."

"You think I'm going to take you someplace and attack you?" he said, laughing.

"No!" she quickly backtracked, laughing as well, mostly from how infectious his laugh was. He was making it difficult for her to keep her guard up, and they had been alone together for only five minutes. It was going to be a long night. "I meant that maybe there should be someone around if we're going to do something extreme. You know, to pick up the pieces, yours and mine."

"Amanda, whether you know it or not, I'm all the security you'll ever need. I would never let anyone harm a single hair on your head."

She wanted to scoff. She wanted to call him Casanova or something equally fitting for sounding so schmaltzy. But she was afraid all the butterflies in her stomach would try to escape if she opened her mouth. The line between charm and earnestness, which had already started to blur, was being swept away. He always seemed to be one step ahead of her, disarming her logic and ability to stay realistic. He met her sarcasm with sincerity. He knew how to hit all the right notes, push all the right buttons. She looked out the window at the scenery as he expertly maneuvered the car through traffic down streets she knew by heart, saying nothing. Where was he taking her? She glanced at the dashboard; he didn't have GPS on, no clue to be gained there. She should've known. One step ahead of her, she repeated to herself.

"What's it like to be living a dream?" she asked impulsively, thinking it might have some curveball of its own.

If she caught him off guard, he didn't show it. He responded without hesitation. "It feels pretty good. Except you always have to find another dream after the other one comes true. Do you think it's too late for me to be a cowboy?"

"If you mean play for the football team in Dallas, I wouldn't be surprised if the answer was no."

He took the compliment in stride. "No, I mean the real deal. Ride the range. Live in the saddle."

"I'm not the right to person to get that opinion from. I used to dream of being in the rodeo after hearing stories about my dad growing up on a Texas ranch. As soon as I was old enough, he bought two horses so he could teach me to ride."

"Then I'm not too late," Chase said, trying to tempt her. "To share the dream, you know? We could still go riding off into the sunset together."

"I don't think so." She was torn between the discomfort of the memory and his latest endearing come-on. "On my second visit with the horses, my nose started to run, I broke out in hives from my neck up, and my eyes swelled shut."

Chase chuckled, trying to remain empathetic. "That's terrible."

"You're not kidding." She tried to sound light, but there was a sad truth in her jest. "I spent a night in the emergency room and two days in bed. I was never allowed near them again; so much for the rodeo."

Amanda didn't tell Chase that she believed Rupert Cole never fully recovered, and she failed him in his turn at influencing his only child. The Thoroughbreds, Carlos and Santana, were sold and the incident was never mentioned. The father and daughter went on to pursue things they could still enjoy together, like sports and how to grill the best baby back ribs, but he also turned off "Black Magic Woman" whenever it came on the radio.

She also left out the part where her mother, during one of those days sitting bedside with the temporarily blinded ten-year-old Amanda, took the opportunity to tell her there was absolutely nothing wrong with second place, as long as you were consistent at it, because it meant that you never gave up. It was an odd logic that would twist around Amanda's psyche for years, and she experienced multiple examples that seemed to reinforce the rule. Funny she would recall that conversation when she was up to her eyeballs in Mr. First Place.

"That's okay," he said cheerfully, already mentally crossing it off his list. "I also dream about being a pirate."

"Just for the record, you do mean shiver me timbers and not playing for Pittsburgh?"

His eyes flew wide in reproach. "As far as baseball goes, I only dream about being a King."

"The rest of the king stuff come with the territory?"

"Amanda, I wish you wouldn't use my being famous as a strike against me. I swear to God, I'm a regular guy."

There ain't nothing regular about you, guy, she thought.

They drove the rest of the way to his secret destination while listening to his iPod rotation. He had a good balance of ballads and beats. Some of it was surprising. He liked a lot of old-school music. Scenery that looked familiar ended with Chase turning his car into the Cold Creek's nearly deserted parking lot. She instantly recognized Eric's old Chevy Blazer.

Eric had a set of keys to the restaurant and was supposed to be in a wet suit somewhere off the coast of Belmar. Chase pulled his car haphazardly into a parking space and cut the engine. She turned back to him, but he was already out of his door and dashing over to her side to open hers. He reached in for her hand to help her out.

"You want me to cook for you?" she asked, thoroughly puzzled and taking his hand.

Chase smiled and shook his head, his dazzling green eyes bright. "Absolutely not, but I did want to make sure you had the best dinner in town."

He didn't let go of her hand and instead began leading her toward the front of the building. He had gotten physical so quickly, but she didn't try to pull away. Resistance seemed futile and her hand in his felt uncomfortably reassuring—he really was an oxymoron in motion. When they got to the front of the building it was no surprise when he finally let go of her hand and reached for the door, pulling it open for her to enter.

Confirming her suspicions, Eric was at his usual spot behind the bar. Sitting at the bar was Freddy, another one of the Cold Creek's waiters. Both were fully dressed in uniform and broke into sly, knowing smiles. Fantastic and familiar smells wafted from the kitchen, and Amanda didn't have to go in there to find Phillip, her chef, and Pam, his assistant. Both were peeking out through the round windows of the kitchen's in and out doors. They watched Amanda and Chase enter, enjoyed the moment, and then went back to put the finishing touches on the meal that was being prepared.

"You surprised?" Chase asked.

"An understatement," Amanda replied.

The lighting was dim and romantic. Music played softly in the background, Earth, Wind & Fire. Chase's corner booth was set, complete with additional candles, and he led her to it. A bottle of Dom Pérignon White Gold Jeroboam chilled in a bucket next to the table. As they sat down, Eric joined them to open it. With a resounding *pop*, the seventeen-thousand-dollar bottle of bubbly became worthless and he poured it neatly into two crystal flutes, refusing to spoil the ambiance by looking his boss in the eye and giving her the opportunity to reprimand him. He quickly left while Chase picked up his champagne glass and extended it in her direction.

"Here's to our first date," he toasted.

She lifted her glass and touched it against his with a gentle *clink*. She took a sip.

"How did you manage to pull this off?" she finally asked.

He released a single chuckle and shook his head slowly. "Amanda, I've been planning this for weeks. You really don't understand, do you?"

What was to understand? A handsome man with too much money was pulling out all the stops to get what he wanted, even if it meant taking over her restaurant and getting her own employees to conspire against her. If she had given in to his advances that first night, they wouldn't even be sitting here. She didn't feel flattered and she didn't feel special. What she felt was manipulated and duped, which were pretty much the same feelings she had from the moment she first picked up the phone and Alan Shaw was on the other end. More Earth, Wind & Fire started playing—this time "Love Music." Tears started to burn her eyelids and she reached for her glass in an effort to hide them. She took another sip.

Chase watched the emotions play across her face. Damn it. He had pushed too hard, come on too strong. All he wanted to do was impress her, and he'd ended up completely overwhelming her. He kept getting his signals mixed. A minute ago she seemed flirty and at least open to him. He rose from the table.

"I'm going to go and check on how dinner is coming along. Do you mind if I go into your kitchen?" he asked, trying to give her some sense of control back.

Amanda shook her head, not trusting herself to speak.

"Do I need a hairnet or something?" he asked, trying to lighten the moment.

A giggle bubbled out of her and she shook her head again, grateful that he was willing to give her a breather. As soon as he disappeared behind the kitchen door, motioning Freddy to follow him, she turned her attention to Eric, who was watching the whole scene take place from behind the bar. She crooked her finger at him, beckoning him over.

"Just who do you work for, anyway?" She got right to the point, aware she didn't have much time before Chase returned.

Eric took a deep breath and released it before giving her what sounded like a well-rehearsed speech. "Amanda, you are hands-down the best boss I've ever had. You're an amazing lady that I'm proud to work for. But sometimes you don't know how to get out of your own way, especially when it comes to matters of the heart."

"Well, I did ask." She sighed. Eric hadn't answered her as an employee, but as a friend. And as both, his words held merit. She didn't see the point in trying to argue with him. Besides, he wouldn't understand. She wasn't really cynical about love; she just knew she wasn't the hitting-the-jackpot type.

"This isn't some creep who just wants to get into your knickers. Why don't you do yourself a favor and just enjoy all your favorite foods and a nice evening with a man who went the extra mile to show he's interested? You can worry about his being Chase Walker tomorrow."

"By then, it could be too late," she said sadly. But she knew it was already too late. To keep from falling victim to vibrant green eyes, a million-dollar smile, and his all-consuming magnetism.

"You know, the best waves to ride come from the roughest seas. Risk it."

Eric didn't wait for her to respond. He turned and went to resume his post behind the bar and began to wipe it down, even though they both knew it was already clean.

"You're too young to be so smart," she called out to him.

Eric looked up briefly from his chore, giving her a grin and a nod. Chase came out of the kitchen and tentatively resumed his seat.

"Can we start over?" Amanda smiled at him from across the table and he visibly relaxed.

"Hey, that's my line." He laughed, then said earnestly, "You don't even need to ask. I'm sorry if I came on like gangbusters. I really thought this was a good idea, with you being so leery and all. I wanted to take you someplace familiar where you'd be comfortable."

"It was a very sweet gesture," she told him honestly, even if it was a little too sweet.

"Dinner is coming right out. I asked if maybe we should be starting with salads and your chef told me that you're not a fan."

"That's not entirely true," she said, laughing, trying to heed Eric's advice to look at him through different eyes. "I just think if you're going to go for the gold, calorie-wise, why fill up on greenery?"

Chase smiled again and reached for the champagne, refilling their glasses. "A woman after my own heart. Nothing bugs me more than a healthy girl pretending it's attractive to starve herself. When we were going over the menu, I gave myself a high five." He took a hearty swallow.

"It's probably wrong to ask, but I'm dying to know just what it took to get these guys to come in tonight."

Chase leaned across the table to divulge only part of the secret. His breath was sweet with champagne, and his eyes were warm with admiration. "They have been very well compensated for their time. But the truth is that at first, they all refused my offer and were willing to do this for free. It seems they're very fond of you, as am I. It's easy to see why."

With perfect or not-so-perfect timing, Freddy arrived at the table with his serving tray. And just as Eric had alluded to, it was laden with painstakingly garnished plates consisting of her favorites from the menu. Pecan-encrusted chicken resting on a bed of risotto, and string beans sautéed with mushrooms and almonds.

He even sacrificed his love of beef, she mused when the same meal was placed in front of him, even though Phillip could have easily prepared any number of the dishes Chase usually ordered. After draping his napkin across his lap, he dug in, encouraging her to do the same. He always ate with gusto, but never like a heathen, even if his portion was double the size of hers.

He cut his meal into manageable bites, never spoke with his mouth full, and knew how to use a napkin. He asked all the right questions.

"What made you want to open a restaurant?" he politely inquired.

"Neither of my parents wanted me to follow in their footsteps and get involved with law," Amanda answered.

After years within its trenches, both the Coles viewed the judicial system as little more than an assembly line of tortured souls who had seen the worst of mankind, in themselves and others. Her father retired as early as he could, while her mother trudged on, determined to make a difference while occasionally facing injustice. They'd both wanted to spare her that sort of jading. Her father loved cooking and grilling, often throwing parties in the summers and welcoming her involvement. When he suggested Johnson & Wales in Providence, Rhode Island, to learn all about cooking, she thought it was as good a place to start as any. She could even venture into pastry baking. But her natural propensity for organization and leadership soon had her gravitating toward restaurant management. She had the fair-minded compassion of her father perfectly blended with the attention to detail and tenacity of her mother. In homage to her mother's influence, she completed a double major in Food Service Entrepreneurship and Culinary Arts. There was no question in either of the Coles' minds any investment in their daughter's future was a wisely judicious one. When she expressed the desire in owning and operating a small restaurant, they didn't hesitate to back her. They used their influence to cut through miles of red tape and were the holders of her liquor license. They saw to all the small details to set her up for success, including getting the best location and making sure it included a parking lot. From time to time, her father could be found in the early mornings dabbling in her kitchen, secretly overjoyed that his passion for good food had been passed on to his daughter. The Coles dined and entertained there, sometimes with high-ranking government officials, and word began to spread. She had an innovative chef and adequate portions. Amanda had turned out to be everything the Coles' images dictated she should be. She was proper, intelligent, and graceful in every sense of the words, even if she was a little too cautious.

In turn, she asked him about baseball, and he lit up with the same boyish enthusiasm conveyed in every interview she ever saw him give. It was a fascinating transition, and Amanda caught herself smiling when he did it. It was clear he was passionate about his sport.

But other than that, he appeared to be way more interested in learning about her.

"You really are big enough to play football," she said, trying to even out the exchange of information.

"I did play in high school," he confirmed, "mostly because my dad said if I wasn't doing something productive with my time off, he would put me to work on the farm. He was a big believer that kids with too much free time often found trouble."

"He sounds like he was a smart man," Amanda said, suddenly remembering footage she had seen. A snippet, the image of a stoic, glassy-eyed Chase walking his unsteady and red-eyed mother briskly to a car outside a church, flashed across her mind, reminding her that even in grief, he was denied privacy. "I'm sorry you lost him so young."

"Thank you," Chase replied soberly. "He was a smart man. When I was offered scholarships for both, he was the person to suggest I stick with baseball, because it would be easier on my body, not to mention my mother. I don't think he ever gave me a piece of bad advice. And I'm comforted by the fact he died exactly the way he wanted to. Quick."

Amanda nodded; there really was nothing to say. But she was sad for him, too, even if he was little more than a stranger whom she had to fight off to keep that way.

"He'd be real disappointed in me if he knew I spent the rest of my life mourning him. He wanted me to do great things," Chase said by way of closing the subject. He didn't want to see pity in her eyes; he much preferred her feisty. He wiped his mouth with his napkin and took a hearty swig of champagne before standing up and holding out his hand.

"Dance with me." It sounded more like a command than a request.

She stared at him blankly before looking out into the restaurant. Several tables had been pushed to the sides, creating a space in the middle of the room. Had they been moved before she got there and she just didn't notice? Earth, Wind & Fire was still playing, rich and soulful. Eric was still behind the bar. minding his own business and working on what Amanda was sure was a crossword puzzle. She took Chase's hand and he led her to the impromptu dance floor and pulled her in close. Although it required a reach on her part, one of her hands rested on his shoulder. Her other hand, secure in his, was placed directly over his heart. Together they began to sway to the music.

Finally he had her in his arms, which was right where she belonged.

"We fit together well," he whispered in her ear, and the pressure of his fingertips on the small of her back increased. "Don't you think?"

It was likely her neck would need a chiropractor if she spent too much time looking up at his face. But staring at his chest had its benefits. Despite his size, he was light on his feet. She resisted the urge to melt into him and he dipped them a little.

"You are just full of surprises, Mr. Walker, right down to your choice of music. Isn't your theme music the chorus from 'Head Like a Hole' by Nine Inch Nails?"

He chuckled. "I have my aggressive head-banging moments, but they don't make for good romance."

"And once again, I need to remind you, romance with you is not part of my equation," she reiterated, hoping she sounded convincing. It felt good, huddled up against him, so good.

"Aren't you even the least bit curious to see what a guy like me has to offer?"

"I already know what you have to offer, being on the road for half the year with the added bonus of women throwing themselves at you." The argument was as weak as the accusation.

"I never took you for a gal who reads the *National Enquirer*," he mused, foiling her again.

"I don't need a tabloid to get a good read on you," she said, wondering if every woman who danced with him wound up feeling like putty.

"You're not going to be one of those people to whom I'm going to have to say 'Having my picture taken at a party with Kate Upton doesn't mean I slept with her,' are you?" He didn't ask it as if he thought he needed to try to change her mind. He had an air about him as if he already knew she was going to become what he probably referred to as "a done deal."

"I can't get wrapped up in a guy like you," she said, mostly to herself to fight it off, although he clearly heard her.

"Why not?" he queried.

"Because you're so very nice and way too complicated," she was able to say automatically, since it had become one of her mantras.

"And you're way too pragmatic. I'm the simplest guy there is. I remember everything my parents taught me. Do the right thing and everything turns out right. Stay loyal to those you want loyalty from. I have almost everything a man could want; I'm a complete tool if I don't appreciate it."

"See? Now that's the kind of stuff I'm talking about. You sound too good to be true. And why are you even interested in someone like me? You're supposed to be hooked up with some Southern belle who's got a waistline the size of my pinky. *Sports Illustrated* will take pictures of you both in your bathing suits, you holding her over your head."

"What's so difficult to believe? You're a natural beauty who's smart and witty, even when trying to keep your defenses up. You would never be so impolite to me if you weren't attracted. I watch you with other people. You have perfect decorum even with total asshats."

And then Chase smiled, still sweet but with the tiniest touch of sinister.

"But you try to tell me, usually in the freshest way, my own mind. I think I know why you're doing it, too, but we can talk about that later," he said, his hand curling tighter around her waist. "And don't be so foolish to think I'm not strong enough to hold you over my head. The only question would be for how long. You're no Kelly Ripa."

Amanda laughed. He wasn't insulting her. It wasn't a backhanded compliment, either. The way he said it was more in appreciation. It wasn't like he compared her to his ex-girlfriend, who had a celebrated figure and her size 8 earned her the Hollywood assessment of obese. Besides, Amanda was comfortable in her double-digit size. The extra weight made her feel strong and powerful, a force to be reckoned with and not a pushover. Of course, next to him, it was hard not to feel like a dwarf; he was just too intimidating.

He finished up with, "As for me, I've been totally blessed. The least I can do is not be a jerk about it."

How was she supposed to come up with an answer to that? He took every argument she had and charmingly shut it down. There was no denying that from the second she met him, Chase was polite and chivalrous and way too accommodating. And it wasn't an act, but who he naturally was. He was warm and approachable, and it was clear people mattered to him. But she also knew that he was rich and powerful and accustomed to getting what he wanted. It was also clear that apparently what he wanted at the moment was her, for whatever reason. The only thing she could do was continue to keep him at arm's length physically and hope that he would lose interest because it was too much effort, and then they could both go back to the very different lives they knew.

Neither of them said anything more and continued to move to the music. Earth, Wind & Fire switched to "Reasons." It was one of the most random and romantic songs in her own repertoire, handed down from when all her musical influence was reflective of her parents. From when as a tween in her bedroom she used to dance with her pillow and dreamed of being a princess, not a contender. It was only after she felt his fingertips curl in on her back that she realized she had rested her head on his shoulder, well mostly his chest, and closed her eyes. She could've easily stepped on his feet and let him do all the dancing, but they weren't doing too much moving anyway.

They continued to slightly sway, even after the music stopped until Amanda realized it. She had gotten caught up in the closeness. His touch, the scent of his Burberry cologne, even his heartbeat through his shirt was mesmerizing. They hesitantly separated and she looked around. The place was empty. The table where they'd dined had been cleared of dinner dishes and replaced with tiramisu and coffee. The kitchen was dark. Everyone else seemed to have left. She had been so wrapped up their dance; she didn't even notice any of it taking place. She could add *magical* to the list of adjectives she had started compiling to describe him.

They had their dessert and returned to small talk. He quizzed her about baseball, and she wowed him with her knowledge. She didn't just know the basics, but the intricate points of the game, why the infield fly rule was important, why bats came in different weights and sizes, and why a player would choose one over another. She was able to talk about strategy. His face briefly clouded over defensively while confirming that he never took steroids, and they both agreed it was cheating, but that players who took them before they became illegal shouldn't necessarily be denied entry into the Hall of Fame. By the time they left and caught Eric napping in his car, waiting to lock up, Chase knew Amanda Cole was the woman he'd been waiting for. There was only one question left to answer: Could she—would she—be willing to play all his games, even the kinky ones? Something in his gut told him no, and then his head told him he could worry about it later. His heart told him none of it mattered.

He held her hand as he drove her home, and she let him, though she wasn't sure why. It felt wrong to encourage him only to leave him hanging when they said good night. There was no way she was going to invite him in. If he and his magic magnetism got past her threshold, she'd be a goner.

But he didn't ask to come in. He didn't even suggest it. When they reached her door, she had already fully prepared her excuses, but none was required.

"I had a great time tonight," he said politely. "Thanks for a wonderful evening."

Once again, he had thrown her a curve. "I did, too," she murmured.

His hand reached out to brush his knuckles across her cheek. When she didn't protest, he cupped her face in his hand and bent his head down, bringing his lips to hers.

The kiss was warm and gentle. He took his time, savoring it. His mouth opened slightly, but his tongue didn't probe. Instead, Chase softly drew the breath right out of her. She couldn't recall anything quite like it. The man knew how to kiss. And then it was over.

He pulled away to stand up straight and she swallowed a mouthful of disappointment that it ended.

"I'll see you when I get back on Friday. Keep my barstool warm?" he said.

She nodded, still trying to catch her breath and wishing that he would kiss her again. And it was a wish that he fulfilled, but this time quickly, mostly because he couldn't stop himself from stealing one more taste of her delicious lips. And then, as if by magic, he was gone and she was standing alone in her living room. She didn't remember saying that final good-bye or opening the door. Chase Walker's kiss had nearly caused her to black out. All her excuses were silenced by the memory of it; her logical reasoning was nothing more than white noise. But of two things she was certain: The time had come for her to begin her quest in earnest to find his fatal flaw. And she couldn't wait for Friday.

Chapter 6

While in Cleveland, Chase called Amanda every day. When she was too busy to talk, he also began to text. He sent a random stream of amusing anecdotes about his travels or questions about how her day was going. His texts were playful but benign, no requests for sexting or even a hint of impropriety. But before her day was over, without fail, the same text arrived, often right before she got into bed: "Sleep well, angel, miss you."

She spent all her free time researching him. As soon as she entered his name in her browser's search engine, she had a plethora of ways to peek into his world. Countless glimpses into his history and his lifestyle were made available with a single keystroke. Like her, Chase was an only child, which seemed unusual for a farmer's son, unlike her upbringing, which Amanda had surmised was a case of two career-driven people who thought procreation was expected of them, at least once. Upon further investigation, she uncovered that while he was growing up, his parents ran free summer camps out of their farm for urban youth designed to introduce them to animals and teach them about agriculture. They took in foster children and sponsored local athletic programs. His mother won national awards for her volunteer work. On his own, he was charitable almost to a fault, his focus mostly on family issues; literacy, terminally ill children, and wounded veterans in particular. There were no stories of mayhem or debauchery, no reports of him partying too hard or getting into bar fights. He was never busted for drunk driving or trashing a hotel room. He had no axes to grind with other baseball players or team management or celebrities. As far as Amanda could tell, Chase Walker appeared to be the offspring of Gandhi and Mother Teresa.

It was maddening. The flaw had to be somewhere. It seemed silly to take comfort in thinking that maybe he was a Satan worshipper or spent his off-season participating in human sacrifices.

He did seem to like his women, though, and there were plenty of pictures to prove it. She scrolled through hundreds of photos posted to the web. There were dozens of him with the actress she already knew about, but there were also ones with pop stars, models, and baseball fans, his arm always curled around their waists and his smile a clear indicator that he didn't mind the closeness. And at the end of that arm was the same hand that had held hers when they danced and brushed against her cheek.

It was terribly disconcerting that she did mind. As the days wore on and she continued to peruse the women he'd dated, Amanda realized that she minded very much. Maybe that was it? He really was a womanizer who collected orgasms like he did awards. But while he had all the makings of a playboy, it was completely contradictory. He was just too attentive and accessible. That could be his modus operandi; shower with attention until the mission is accomplished, then on to the next conquest. And then she thought that maybe it would be best if she got her fling over with so she could be free of him. Amanda did have several casual hookups on her sexual resume, the result of her being single-minded on the success of the Cold Creek and unwilling to commit to potential long-term boyfriends who were too eager to give her unsolicited business advice. When she was first starting out, it was easy to shake her. She was too strong in her business decisions now to ever consider a man's opinion a challenge, and had several failed relationships to prove it. But she had made an error. She should've had her one-night stand that first night, before he started turning on the charm. When he stopped doing all the little things that had romance written all over them she knew the outcome wouldn't be the same. And overruling all logical thought was, she wanted to try out his kiss again. She got the distinct impression that letting Chase have her body would result in her wanting him to have her heart and soul, and that was a losing proposition.

As she continued to browse and discover, she began to conjure mental images of Chase seducing and deflowering virgins and swinging from the rafters with prostitutes, all with Earth, Wind & Fire playing in the background. Jealousy mounted and then turned irrational. By the time he surprised her and showed up on his way to the stadium before his Friday-night home game, unwilling to wait until after it to see her, she didn't know whether to throw herself into his arms or slug him.

Because the restaurant was already open and there were witnesses around, she refrained from doing either.

"If you're in this to add me to a list of conquests, turn around and leave right now," she hissed quietly at him from across the podium where she was standing as soon as he walked in.

He looked momentarily shocked, and then the smile appeared.

"Either you've been doing some homework while I was gone or your workstation is the portal to hell." He chuckled, delighted by her outburst. "You get pretty brazen behind that thing."

He got as close as he could to her, much closer than the last time he did it with the podium still between them. "Over the years, I've gotten very good at reading signs. You sound jealous, and I think it's adorable," he whispered, then pulled back enough for her to see him raising both his eyebrows, daring her to dispute it.

She didn't answer him because she didn't know how, and he had just prevented her from making a scene. She did sound jealous, because she was. It was unsettling, having to acknowledge that whenever she was in his presence, she was so willing to forsake her good manners and instead become bitchy and shrewlike. Since meeting him, she had slowly become a walking contradiction. One she had moved to blaming on that first kiss, which still made her tingle. Why was she so dead-set denying the attraction to him? Maybe it was time to just sit back and enjoy the attention, but be mindful that it was most likely temporary. If promiscuity was his flaw, it was sure to show itself. And if she didn't just hop into bed with him, it was likely to show itself sooner rather than later. He had already wedged himself into her life.

"I can't keep fighting you, Chase, but I'm scared to death you're going to use me," she said, finally blurting out the confession.

He straightened back up and looked down at her from across the podium, shaking his head. "What's it going to take for me to prove to you I'm not that guy? I think I'm in this one for the long haul."

He had already proven it, in every conversation they'd had and every overture he'd made. She glanced past him and saw a party of four waiting patiently to be seated. She could tell they knew exactly who he was, with only having the back of him to go by. She saw the two camera phones ready for when he turned around.

"I need to go slow," she murmured.

"However long it takes," he promised.

"Will you be back after your game?"

He merely smiled before turning and getting ready to have his picture taken. "Silly question."

They began dating and the game changed. She dropped the attitude and focused on enjoying his company. That following Monday and Tuesday, she tagged along with Chase on some of his routine. She went with him to the gym, and won what she secretly named "the eye-candy sweepstakes." Chase's friend Logan Montgomery was also his personal trainer. She used a treadmill while the pair worked out in Logan's private Englewood facility, and she tried to keep from ogling the men as they pumped iron. Not that the beautiful Logan could hold a candle to Chase's rugged athleticism. But it couldn't be denied, the view was spectacular. It also confirmed that he really was strong enough to hold her over his head. Chase knew how to beast up a weight bench. The only way it could've gotten any better was if the whole workout was done with both of them naked; however, seeing them in shorts and T-shirts gave her imagination a good sweat.

She went with him to his games Monday and Tuesday night. She had her picture taken from yards away by questionable-looking characters while he was on the field. He answered a question at his postgame about whether they were an item with a boyish "Yep." He picked her up early before his Tuesday-night game and took her on a road trip to nowhere, just drove a few hours in a random direction to check out weird stuff, then turn around and headed back, the GPS at the ready if needed. She enjoyed that for all sorts of reasons. At sixty miles an hour, she had him all to herself since he shut off his phone. And he wasn't able to concentrate on giving her all the looks that made her question her ability to keep her hands off him. She wasn't going to be able to hold him off much longer. She was losing all her motivation to try. She wanted to make out. A moving car gave her an advantage, but only a slight one. Because as he drove, he touched her always, mostly stroking her forearm with his free hand, sometimes taking her hand and lightly playing with her thumb. If he was able to incorporate the look into that, she'd be hard-pressed not to start ripping his clothes off. By the time they got to the stadium for Tuesday night's game, Amanda had determined that the next overture he made, she was taking him up on it.

She loved to watch him play; he was larger than life. As soon as he stepped onto the field, the fashionable, polished luminary celebrated his truest essence. Not an act, but the ultimate extension of everything he was, minus the baggage of being a role model. He played hard but he wasn't intense. He didn't punch or throw things, never mouthed an obscenity or took on an umpire past a polite inquiry. He was carefree and playful, enjoying every moment of being a grown man lost within a boy's game. It was incredible to witness. Amanda roamed the stadium, finding her way to the bleachers and the upper decks to watch him on the big screen, secure in the knowledge he had no idea where she was. It gave her the opportunity to let her guard down and observe him in his element without any regard to his focus being on her. He always watched her. Whenever they were together, she was always in his sight line, often with the same look he wore the first night at the Cold Creek. But from the cheap seats, she was able to spy on him with thirty thousand other people; only the rest of them had no clue as to what they were seeing.

She was there waiting for him when he came out of the locker room, because she liked the thought of his seducing her most of all and couldn't wait to clue him in. First, she had to dutifully fade into the background while he met his responsibilities to be accessible to his fan base. She offered to take some of the pictures in the spirit of being a good sport. She ignored the rush of peevishness that accompanied watching him do the familiar arm curl around another woman's waist. Having to endure the few women who insisted on kissing him presented more of a challenge.

Chase didn't kiss back, but graciously presented his cheek. Then his eyes met hers and he gave her a little wink, the affectionate reminder that he appreciated her tolerance. It teasingly conveyed that he knew about her jealous streak. It also reminded her that he was thrown

temptation on a regular basis, and by the time they finished dinner, she had waffled on the topic again. But
after he walked her to her door and gently drew her
into his powerful arms it was impossible to think of
anything at all. Each kiss was more electrifying than
the first had been, since he had started brushing his
tongue across her lips and sometimes into her mouth,
all smooth and warm and soft. His fingertips traced
down her spine and came to rest on the small of her
back. Both nights she was dizzy afterward and was left
wondering if the entire day had been a dream and her
gentle giant nothing more than a mirage. But the text
would soon arrive afterward, confirming her reality:
"That was fun. Can't wait to see you again."

He left that Thursday for a short stint in Boston,
and in his absence, Amanda gave herself the "fish or
cut bait" lecture. He was who he was, and nothing was
going to change that. She couldn't keep viewing women
coming on to him as a roadblock. If they were to have
any hope at a relationship, she would have to get used
it. He had kept his promise and was willing to abide
by her timetable. He couldn't keep that promise and
hit on her at the same time. She was going to have to
make it obvious she was ready. Whatever his flaw was,
it was becoming less important. On a balmy Sunday
evening in June, while he was finishing up game three

with the Sox and she was still feeling the afterglow of a particularly romantic phone conversation from the night before, Amanda impulsively referred to Chase as her boyfriend.

The repercussions soon followed.

Luckily the following stormy Monday changed the game again.

She hadn't answered his call all day or the night before, either. Vexing but not surprising. Amanda often neglected her phone. Still, he wasn't used to people ignoring his calls and definitely not women. As soon as word came down that the game had been officially rained out, Chase quickly showered. Then he went straight to Amanda's apartment, knowing the Cold Creek was closed. He would surprise her, offer to take her to dinner. Have her for dessert. Four days with nothing but her occasional voice over the phone only heightened his resolve. And he decided the weeks he spent at the restaurant winning her over counted as time served. He had just about reached the end of his rope when it came to waiting her out. She'd put him through his paces longer than any woman before her. He'd been patient, respectful. She was a good girl, not a tramp, he got it. But even he could tell there was more passion building up when they were together. She had to be convinced by now that he was more than just a muscle-bound overindulged jock. Tonight Chase had every intention of breaking through the cool exterior to what he just knew was a sex goddess underneath. She might even find herself on the receiving end of a hand tattoo. He jumped out of his car and, whistling his way through the building, stopped in front of her door and knocked.

The door opened as far as the chain lock would allow. Round blue eyes widened in surprise as they peeked through the gap in the door.

"Chase!" she gasped, and then failed at the recovery with a stammered, "H-hi."

"Hi yourself." His smile was strained. She was still behind a fully chained door and hardly appeared happy to see him. "My game got rained out. I thought maybe you'd like to go have dinner."

"I-I wasn't really expecting you." Amanda continued to stutter, making no move to unchain the door. "I wish you had called."

He did call. About fifteen times. His face clouded over with the realization. She had no intention of letting him in. Then his eyes flashed with anger. Maybe she was entertaining. He still couldn't see anything past the crack in the door and her dismayed cobalt blues. For all he knew, she was buck naked behind that door, ready to get busy with someone less "complicated" than a playboy baseball player. That would certainly be a reason to avoid calls and be so distressed by his arrival. He could feel his blood starting to boil.

"You're right, of course," he said, stiff and restrained. "I didn't mean to surprise you. This was a bad move on my part. Good night, Amanda." Chase turned on his heel to make a hasty exit out of the building before he did something he knew he'd regret.

Amanda quickly unchained the door and pulled it open, stepping out into the hall.

"Chase, wait!"

Chase stopped. He clenched, then unclenched his fists before turning around, determined not to let her see just how furious he was. Damn, he cursed himself, why didn't he just keep walking? Because he knew even now, there was just no way to deny her.

His jaw went slack as soon as he pivoted and got a decent look at her.

"Holy hell," he breathed, rushing back toward her. "What happened to you?"

Amanda peered up at him sheepishly, still keeping her head down in the effort to continue hiding the damage. "I committed the cardinal sin of the restaurant business last night. I tried to go in the out door."

He cradled both sides of her face in his hands and tilted her head upward for a thorough inspection. Her upper lip was swollen and split. It looked raw and painful. He could forget about kissing her any time soon. He whistled through his teeth.

"Wow. Good one. I had no idea your job was so dangerous."

"It didn't help that thanks to Freddy's height, his tray was perfectly level with my face. An inch or two in either direction, I probably would have been okay. Or lost an eye. Amazingly, he didn't drop the dishes. It was in the middle of the dinner rush, it was just so hectic." She laughed weakly and flat-out lied about the dinner rush, which had already petered out. She had no intention of telling Chase that she had been watching him turn a double play from the TV over the bar when her lapse in good judgment occurred and she collided with the waiter at full speed. It was bad enough she had to endure the endless teasing of the staff, many of whom were instantly suspicious of any reason she would give for faltering. She blinked up at his concerned face again, whispering, "I didn't want you to see me like this."

He studied her a minute more before planting a solid kiss on her forehead and proclaiming, "Nope. Still beautiful. Is this the reason for the locked door and the dead phone?"

"Yes," Amanda admitted bashfully.

"Don't ever hide from me again," he said sternly before releasing her. "Do you still want me to go?"

Amanda was all at sixes and sevens. She had been having trouble thinking of anything besides him. Now he was here, in the flesh. Barking orders and being generally domineering. It was a departure from his seemingly limitless tolerance and definitely hot. But she didn't want their first time to be like this. It was going to be extraordinary. She was supposed to look like a temptress, not a platypus. Whisper words of love, not sound like Mushmouth from the *Fat Albert* cartoon. But he was still as charming and sexy as sin. She must have been crazy to think she could avoid him until she was more presentable once he showed up at her door. His affection had become addictive and impossible to fight. She shook her head. "Of course not."

There was no mistaking the look of relief that passed over his face. She turned and he followed her back into her apartment.

"Amanda Cole," he said from behind her after closing the door, his voice full of barely contained delight, "what exactly are you wearing?"

Amanda froze, squeezing her eyes shut tight. She had completely forgotten. He wasn't talking about her jeans or her bedroom slippers. She waited for the first wave of the flush to pass through to her hairline.

"Angel girl," she heard him breathe softly from behind her. He had gotten closer. "You're wearing my number."

She couldn't deny it. Figures it would have to be the one with his name stitched in bold letters across her shoulders as well. She certainly wasn't expecting him to show up unannounced when she bought the jersey from the local Modell's the day after their first real date. She wasn't about to admit she had been wearing it exclusively for the better part of a week when home alone, either. She struck an overly casual pose and then turned back around to him.

"This old thing?" she asked breezily in spite of her flaming face.

He was staring at her, eyebrow and head both cocked, grinning from ear to ear.

"Caught," he mouthed to her.

"Don't go overboard, Walker. It's just a shirt," she scoffed, then added a *tsk*. "Of all the arrogance."

In the fractional moment of silence that hung in the air before he could respond, his name was said loudly and clearly. They turned their heads in unison to her high-definition fifty-two-inch flat screen mounted on the wall. For several seconds, they both watched the image of Chase filling the screen, adjusting his gloves, the bat neatly tucked under his arm. He tapped the bat one time against each of his spikes and took several practice swings while masculine voices talked about him in the background using words like *impressive* and *stellar*. His batting stats appeared in a box on the bottom of the screen. Chase turned back to Amanda, his eyes wide and bright with wonder.

"This game is from four days ago." An ecstatic, boyish smile took over his face. "I had a really good night. I think I dove into the stands."

Amanda hastened around the couch to reach for the remote, her face already feeling the rush of heat making its way up and into her cheeks. *Hell's bells, the television got me again.* She internally whined. There was no point in continuing the façade anymore. Any chance of pretending she wasn't preoccupied with him was dashed. She looked at him a second more on the screen, in the batter's box, where ten minutes ago she'd been safe to admire him without his knowing it. She pointed the remote at the television and turned it off. She looked back to him timidly, hoping he would go easy on her.

"So caught," he whispered, his eyes aglow. Then they began to devour her, one blink at a time.

"I DVR them so I can see you up close," she offered up feebly, her mouth suddenly dry. His gaze was hypnotic. Playing hard to get was no longer an option.

Neither was lying to him. Not when he was looking at her like that. And he hadn't run away when he saw her all banged up, like that jerk did to Marcia when she broke her nose on *The Brady Bunch*. Chase Walker looked like the only taking off on his mind involved their clothes. "When they show you before you're getting ready to swing, you get a look I like. I certainly can't see it from any seat in the stadium."

Chase casually stroked his chin as he slowly took several long strides to join her near the couch, his eyes never leaving hers. "A look you like? And just what sort of look might that be?"

Amanda felt like melting under the heat of his stare burning into her. It should be illegal for a man to be that handsome. He was going to laugh at her after hearing her silly reasoning. He was going to know he had her hook, line, and sinker. The rain was pounding against the windows. Her heart was pounding in her chest. As if in a trance, she answered him, her voice soft. "The same kind of look you get right before you kiss me."

But he didn't laugh at her. Instead, Chase took another step closer, his gaze finally coming off her eyes and drifting down to her puffy upper lip again. He sighed and shook his head. "You're so clever, Amanda. They both require the same level of focus.

You've barely begun to see that look. But it almost pains me to say, if you're intent on getting that look out of me tonight, you're going to have to get more creative. That shirt is a pretty good start. I'm up to it if you are."

She swallowed, but it was difficult with the lump that was now fully formed in her throat. She knew if she tried any sort of comeback, it would result in saying the only words that kept repeating in her head: *I want you.* She had pretty much given him the go-ahead to sweep her up and have his way with her, but he was just standing there, staring at her mouth, his arms casually flung across his chest. He appeared to be thinking. Dear God, if he didn't touch her soon, she thought she might spontaneously combust.

He looked back up and dropped his arms. He began smiling, the same sort of smile that a cartoon cat gets when it eats the canary with one bite. She fully expected to see him hiccup and a yellow feather fly out of his mouth.

"Amanda, do you touch yourself while you watch me? Do I make you come?"

She dropped her head and began to blush furiously again, refusing to respond. She'd be taking that answer to her grave. The question itself was so personal and he asked it as though he had every right to do so. Chivalry was indeed dead, at least for the moment, and its replacement was oozing pure sexuality. Her skin began to prickle with excitement. He reached out and took her chin, lifting her head to meet his eyes.

"I think I feel cheated." He grinned wickedly down at her. "I'm doing all the work and some vibrator is getting all the glory."

With his strong fingers still on her chin, Chase carefully brought his mouth down to brush against her neck, just below her ear.

"No toys needed." Amanda swooned, her eyelids heavy. His fingertips left her face and began to trace a path down the front of her jersey. Her hands ran up the solid wall of his chest before coming to rest on his granite shoulders.

He grunted in approval, his lips traveling farther down her neck and his hand to her jeans. He unbuttoned them without her even noticing. She barely heard her zipper going down. She was lost in the sensations of his mouth on her skin. It was all she could do to remain standing. Despite the size of his hand, he was able to nimbly and easily dip it inside her panties. Her breath quickened and her grip on him tightened. As soon as he heard her tiny moan of appreciation at his intrusion, he drove his thick middle finger inside her and exhaled a groan of his own.

"Shit, I wish I could kiss you," he murmured into her neck as he began to move his finger in and out of her slowly, his hand snug within her silk and lace.

"Me, too." Amanda nearly cried in frustration, squirming into him. Her lip was no longer the only thing throbbing. In fact, it paled by comparison. She tried to bring his head down to her mouth. "I don't care."

He pulled his head from her grasp to look down at her.

"But I do, angel," he told her, carefully kissing the corner of her mouth while his finger continued its torment. It tickled at her soul while his other fingers toyed with the velvet lining that surrounded her. It soon left her witless. With the whispery pant of his name from her, Chase realized his wait was over. No ifs, ands, or busted lips, he was going to claim her as his own, once and for all.

His free hand moved to the small of her back, just in time to steady her as her knees started wobbling. They buckled completely when he abruptly withdrew from her. He caught her, lifted her, and raced the short distance to her bedroom, depositing her on the bed. He quickly removed his own shirt and unzipped his pants while kicking off his shoes. With the slacks open and slung low on his hips, he reached into his back pocket and pulled out his wallet. From inside it, he took out a condom and held it up.

"Amanda," he said in a rush, "I use one of these every time. I don't want to use one now. I promise I'm disease-free. Are you protected and safe, and do you trust me?" Chase didn't actually care if she was protected or not. He couldn't think of anything he'd like better than holding the shotgun at the wedding. He didn't really care if she was safe, either; the seed had already been planted in his mind that he'd be willing to die for her. But her trusting him meant everything.

From the middle of her bed, Amanda tried to concentrate on what he was saying because his tone was certainly compelling. But seeing him for the first time without his shirt was fueling her already overloaded senses. She had seen multiple pictures of him shirtless when she did her research; the spread from *Fitness* magazine instantly crossed her mind, followed by the same lust-producing chill. She saw his abs and pecs in at least one commercial for a well-known sports company. He didn't need Photoshop to do any of it justice. He was beyond splendid. Hulking and muscular, he was tan and defined and smooth, except for the appealing pattern of light hair that started on his chest. It narrowed down his solid belly in an inviting path to the elastic waistband of his designer boxer briefs. She couldn't tear her eyes away from them, until she noticed them swell further, fine baby blue cotton straining against the still-half-closed fly of his black, tailor-made Armani trousers, a tidbit of information she obtained courtesy of an extensive article in *GQ*. When it dawned on her that she was gawking at his arousal, she brought her eyes swiftly back up to his. They were smoldering and serious and waiting with hard-won patience for her answer. What was the question again? Her gaze shifted briefly to his raised hand, then back to his face, and she wordlessly nodded. He tossed the condom and his wallet in the direction of his discarded shirt. He pulled at her jeans, and in one fluid motion, they and her panties were off, like a magician pulling a tablecloth out from under a completely set table. But he wasn't ready to see her out of his shirt, not yet anyway. She wore his brand so well. He joined her on the bed, unbuttoning her jersey without taking it off. He kissed her just above her navel while his hand took full advantage of no longer having to work around her panties. Chase lingered there, the sound of her breathless pleasure music to his ears. Her hands ran along his back, and her nails tickled him. She was sweet and soft; everything he had convinced himself was worth waiting for. But he was finished with waiting. His lips finally moved upward only to meet up with her bra. In a quick, efficient motion, the bra was unhooked and he pushed it aside to allow himself access to her generous breasts. He kissed each one and his fingertips toyed with hard, responding nipples. She moaned and his erection raged within his clothing. He stood up, encouraged by her involuntary sigh at his withdrawal and he quickly finished stripping down. The time to get her fully exposed had arrived.

Amanda sighed again, but this time in full appreciation. Any further comparisons to him resembling a Ken doll were permanently put to rest; Chase Walker was completely in proportion. She reached out, hungry for him to return and resume all the amazing ways he made her feel when he touched her most intimate places. He rejoined her and began peeling off her jersey.

"Ouch," she whimpered when she couldn't resist and her lips made contact with his jawline.

He instantly stopped and pulled back briefly, admonishing her with look.

"Boy, are you stubborn," he said, his voice raspy with passion. "Not on my watch." He finished removing her shirt and lingerie, gently turned her over onto her stomach, and took a moment to feel the rush.

He thought he had seen the best backsides the world had to offer. But he wasn't prepared for the sight. Her cheeks were smooth and plump, feeding into curvaceous legs. He stared, captivated, his neurons firing full throttle as he envisioned all the sounds they and she would make as he ministered to them.

Amanda had turned into one raw nerve ending. She wanted him —no, needed him. It was as intense as the desire to kiss him was. The ache to feel his hands on her again, the ache to experience everything he had and everything he was. She needed all of him. It began to wane as seconds dragged on while he denied her and was then followed by a moment of gut-wrenching clarity. She peered over her shoulder at him from the pillows, suddenly wishing she could cover up. He was no longer turned on.

"You think I'm fat, don't you?"

Chase wasted no time lying alongside her, covering half her body with half of his own, pinning her beneath him. She didn't fight it; instead lowering her head back onto the pillow and facing the wall, his warm, hard muscles against her back and shoulder acting like a blanket. He ran his large strong hand from her leg and over her bottom, slowly dipping into the indentation at her waist, along her rib cage and under her breast, then down her arm before settling possessively on top of hers, separating her fingers with his own. With his mouth less than an inch from her ear, he meaningfully whispered.

"Please listen carefully, Amanda, because I intend to explain this only once. You take my breath away, as much right now as the first time I saw you. And now I'm seeing all of you, so you can imagine how hard it is for me breathe. I am almost six and a half feet tall. On a good day, I'm pushing two hundred and sixty pounds. My ego does not require I have a girlfriend half my size to make me a bigger man. I am already a monster. I do not want or need a woman I can bench-press. I prefer a woman of substance, with softness and curves. One I know is able to handle my passion, one that can nurture my babies. I have no desire to bang into your bones when I take you, which I am most certainly going to do, and soon." He shifted, deliberately maneuvering his long, hard length down the crack of her behind to settle at the triangular juncture of where her treasures met. She spread her legs slightly to ensure him a better fit, and he was satisfied with the chill he felt blow through her. After her confirming shiver, he continued to breathe into her ear. "Do you feel that, Amanda? Do you think I want to worry about whether or not you can handle me? I was caught up in thinking how you were made for me. You're so perfect I was taking a moment to give thanks for it. You should be spanked for even thinking anything else."

It would have been right there that she would've given him the go-ahead. An insolent comeback, a coy giggle, an issuance of a dare; but there was nothing. Not even the feigned indignation that cleverly disguised encouragement for him to take the leap. It didn't make any difference anyway—overruling everything else was the burning need to be inside her.

But she had stopped hearing his words long before then. Combined with the feel of him pressed against her, they had blended into one long buzz of yearning.

"If you promise not to try to kiss me again, I'll turn you back over. I would much rather look into your beautiful face than the back of your head, but I'm serious, you have to let that lip heal."

His voice was husky and authoritative, replacing all his prior crooning. She would've agreed to anything to be wrapped within his steel arms. She murmured in pledge while turning back over, and unable to wait a moment longer, he entered, then filled her, and they stilled. The tidal wave of sensation it caused left them both momentarily stunned. They stared at each other for a moment in awe, and then both blinked in mutual recognition. No words would do the feeling justice and neither of them bothered trying to say any. He began to worship at her altar slowly, but they both knew it couldn't last. They had held back too long, teased each other beyond what either of them could tolerate. His movement within her rapidly increased and she clung to him, praying for him to release her and at the same time for it never to end. Her climax exploded into a kaleidoscope of uncontrollable tremors and her back arched in an effort to keep him securely inside her as they overtook her. As she repeatedly cried out his name, it was more than he could bear, and he began to stiffen above her. While continuing to hold her tight within his grasp, he joined her.

Chapter 7

C hase had started listening to love songs. Sappy, saccharine bona fide love songs. His iPod became one long playlist of Barry White, Drake, Bruno Mars, and the like. And of course he could never get enough of Earth, Wind & Fire. There was always a team grumble when it was his turn to choose the locker room music and he tried to slip in a few too many. But Amanda crying out his name in ecstasy was by far his favorite song. He had that one on repeat.

A picture he took of her with his own phone became his screensaver. It had been taken nearly a week after the first time they'd been together, taken at one of those tucked-away twenty-four-hour diners he sometimes found his way to in the middle of the night. Her lip had healed to his satisfaction and she immediately took advantage, leading to fiery results. She was still slightly flushed and her hair was an array of still-damp curls from hours of sweat-producing passion. Her smile was shy yet beguiling, her blue eyes containing a different kind of sparkle, and he took the credit for creating both. He looked at it a hundred times a day when he wasn't with her, the memory of her mouth being added to their sexual equation as vivid as the day he hit his first home run. A single moment in time, captured in the same way she had captured his heart. And as soon as he saw her in person, the only thing he could think of was getting her to look that way again. The urgency of their first time was gone, replaced with a bottomless pit of exploratory lust. They wouldn't rest until they were completely exhausted from touching and tasting and sexing.

But something was missing, and as much as he tried to ignore the thought, there was no denying it. Amanda Cole was a good girl, in every sense of the word. Her lovemaking was as wholesome as she was. Even as her mere touch set him ablaze, she was temperate. She never talked dirty. She didn't bite or scratch him. She was warm and giving, taking as much care with him as he did with her. And when they were actually together, it really didn't matter. But when Chase was alone and he had nothing but her picture, his mind would venture to a different place. A place where she cried out because of him, but more from pain than pleasure, although he knew they could be synonymous. He couldn't be sure, but all indicators pointed to the fact that he had fallen for a vanilla.

She continued to send out mixed signals, and he was having trouble reading them. Shades of bratty were recalled in a hurry, as soon as he took on a dominant tone, often with an apology on her part. He had tried to introduce it once playfully, a sharp swat with an accompanying threat after she made them run late one evening, but his timing was off. He had been too concerned with the outcome and hadn't realized how seriously she took punctuality. Her wide-eyed look of shock had stopped him cold.

It was clear that nobody had ever laid an assertive hand on Amanda Cole. She spoke little that night at the function they attended and on the way home apologized for not being on time like it was really important to him, and he ended up feeling like a heel. If she had been receptive, he would've blown off the event altogether and sated his lust for it. He didn't know how to tell her without jeopardizing the illusion he had worked so hard maintaining to impress her.

The funny thing was, the longer he was with her, in her actual presence, he hardly thought about it at all. While he was going to meet her, it consumed all his thoughts. But once he was with her, Amanda wove a web of sensuality around him that made it impossible to concentrate on anything besides her, and his desire faded into the background. Making love was truly about turning her on and reaping the rewards of the end result. He was completely enchanted with everything about her. He juggled all his responsibilities effortlessly until Amanda wanted his attention and then he was willing to abandon them all. And it was something she didn't take advantage of. She never pouted while he met his obligations, always the first to make things as easy for him as possible.

The solution in Chase's mind was a simple one: just never be without her. He already knew he wanted to marry her. He had all the means. She would never have to work a day in her life. They could play all day, every day, and he could introduce it to her slowly. And it seemed like the natural progression, at least to his way of thinking.

The suggestion came up the first time he brought her to his penthouse apartment, figuring it gave him the home-field advantage. Her place was nice, but didn't possess the same luxurious opulence his did. He would woo her with amenities and then present her with an offer she couldn't refuse.

As he showed her around, all Amanda noticed was how big everything was. She fleetingly wondered if the elevator they took to get there was secretly located inside a beanstalk. From his bulky square furniture to his eighty-inch-screen television to his choice of artwork, everything appeared oversized. Even the clocks were huge. She noted she would likely need a tugboat to get her in and out of his bed.

"I want you come on the road with me," he told her once they settled back in the living room.

"I don't think I've ever been to Arizona," she replied after sinking into his enormous couch, then struggling to sit back up and perch herself on the edge. She tried to make it look smooth by toying with what appeared to be a ten-pound remote that was sitting on the football-field-sized coffee table in front of her.

"I'm not talking about this trip," he said. "I mean all of them."

She stopped what she was doing as she looked up at him. She didn't know if he was still standing to be daunting, but in response to it, she stood back up as well.

"You're serious?"

"Some things you don't kid about," he told her.

Amanda walked past him to the windows looking out onto Central Park. Here it comes, she thought. The slow disintegration of everything that was important in her life to accommodate every notion of his. He didn't even ask if this was something she'd be interested in; it was issued, more like a mandate. She crossed her arms over her chest and turned to face him.

"I already have a career," she told him, unable to keep the disdain out of her voice. "Looking after yours isn't what I had in mind. I didn't spend four years in college to carry your bags."

"I can look after my own career, thank you very much," he replied defensively. "And I haven't touched my own bags in years."

"Thanks for the clarification. You have the nerve to sound surprised. I realize that most women would jump at the chance to be your kept little plaything, but I think I'm going to have to pass."

She was annoyed with him, and he struggled between the disappointment of her refusal and wanting to tell her he was trying to find a solution to his real issue, which he now felt the urge to reveal in a very real and disciplinary way. He loved that she had a mind of her own and that she didn't look at him as some sort of gravy train. But he wanted her to bend to his will on this, which he hardly considered a sacrifice. He knew he couldn't have it both ways. Chase held up his hands. "Whoa. Back up. Let's start this over. Yes, I do want you with me, Amanda, but not because of the reasons you're thinking. It's not about keeping you. I want you there because I never want to be without you. I want to be able to see you in the stands when I'm playing ball, because it's the closest we can get to you being able to play with me. I want you to be the last thing I see every night and the first thing I see every morning. Yeah, I guess it is selfish, but it's not because I want you to cater to me."

He had returned to being disarming and noble, but for the first time Amanda felt like it was contrived.

"Those sound like wonderfully romantic intentions," she said.

"Most women would think they are."

"Then why do I suddenly feel like we're in the middle of a showdown?"

"Because stubborn is your middle name," he grumbled, looking away and asking himself when exactly coward had become his.

Amanda felt his tension. It had to be hard for him, being shot down in such a fashion, especially when he was offering her something that would appear to be the ultimate in spoiling to anyone else. She approached him and wrapped her arms around his waist and rested her forehead on his chest until he returned the embrace and relaxed.

"It's moving too fast," she told him honestly.

Chase wanted to yell that her excuse was lame, they had been moving at a snail's pace since they met. He wanted to bellow until the walls came down how dare she refuse him and the real reason he made the offer was because she was too genteel to give him what he wanted, and it seemed like the only viable solution. He wanted to follow that up by forcefully taking it, with her kicking and screaming until she submitted to him. He wished he had the strength to go and seek what she withheld from another avenue. But he was caught within her web of beauty and desire. He took her head in his hands and tilted it up toward his, praying that none of his thoughts was conveyed through his eyes.

"I understand," he told her before lowering his lips to hers and taking her right there on his couch, without bothering to remove her clothes.

He left for Arizona the next day without her and embarked on the worst play of his baseball career. He made several errors, lost all focus and timing at the plate. The ball seemed to be in the catcher's mitt before he even started to swing. His all-star average started dropping rapidly and there was a real danger of losing his spot in the batting order.

It didn't take long before the conundrum began overshadowing his every waking thought. Overcautious soon turned into temperamental. There was nowhere for him to find release. He didn't want to blame her, so instead became moody whenever they were alone. He was aggressive and demanding when they made love. Amada felt guilty although she wasn't sure why. There was something wrong between them that she could reach out and touch, but he wouldn't let her in or share it.

After two weeks of his increasing alienation and an agonizing Tuesday night of watching him struggle at the plate, Amanda had had enough. They went back to his apartment and his sulking continued.

"Chase, I'm tired of playing this game. Trying to figure out what's wrong with you. You've been checked out for, like, a week now. Your strained politeness is starting to get on my nerves. If I've done something wrong, just tell me."

The only thing she had done wrong was become his obsession. And she had just caught him obsessing how because of her, his life was now out of control.

"I'm not always in front of a camera, Amanda. I don't always have to be on, do I? I'm in a slump; it puts me in a bad mood." Slump. Shit. He said it. It had just slipped out. He wasn't ready to give voice to it yet. Once he acknowledged it, it was free to run roughshod over him until he confronted what it was that caused it. But if he had that confrontation and it played out wrong, he could end up losing it all. He didn't want to confront it, even though it was standing right in front of him. But stripping it naked and making love to it wasn't going to solve the problem, either. He wanted to share his deepest, darkest secrets with her, but he had waited too long to take the risk. He was so far beyond that now. He needed her, ached for her above all else. And he didn't want to tell her like this, with hostility the motivating undercurrent.

"Funny how you used the word *slump* there," she said, tuning right into his superstition.

His voice took on more of an edge. "It's a baseball term, for times when a player isn't hitting the ball."

"Yes, I know. Ever have one before?"

"Not that I can remember," he grumbled irritably.

"Didn't you once tell me that slumps often occur with major changes?"

"What are you saying?"

"I'm saying that you have a girlfriend. That's pretty major. I think I heard someone call me Jessica Simpson the other day. That just won't do, I'd have to stop wearing her line. Maybe we should cut back on some of the time we spend together?"

She didn't really want to be without him. The thought alone was a depressing one. But maybe he was ready for a change and didn't know how to tell her. She could test him with the opportunity and see if he made any move toward it; then all she'd have to make was a heartbreaking decision. She had no intention of being his hometown stadium girl as he coasted from city to city. And if all he needed was some alone time to get him back on his game, she was willing to make the sacrifice. Anything would be better than the cloud of surly that now followed them around.

"Out of the question," he instantly rebuffed, more like a bark, as if she were daft for making the suggestion.

"Thanks for giving it consideration," she replied with a touch of sarcasm.

"I don't need to consider it," Chase continued heatedly. "It's not going to make things better. If you were really concerned about helping me out, you'd start packing your bags."

He wasn't talking about breaking up with her. And she really was flattered that he wanted her so close. "I worked really hard to build up the Cold Creek," she said, trying to let him down easy and keep him from getting further agitated. It was the first time he'd mentioned it since he brought it up the first time.

"I know you did," he admitted, trying not to convey the built-up resentment. "I'm not insisting on it, am I? You asked me what's wrong, I'm telling you."

"Insisting?" Amanda blinked indignantly. "When did I give you that sort of license?"

"You didn't," he quickly clarified angrily. "I just couldn't think of a better word. Don't read into it."

"So the alternative is I get to deal with your bad mood till you spank one out of the park?"

Spank. One out of the park. When one of the guys on *SportsCenter* said it, it didn't have the same effect. But she had introduced it into conversation and so casually. The one word he'd been thinking all night. The word he imagined he heard coming from her lips on a daily basis. But she was being rational and capable. She wasn't saying it to turn him on. She wasn't trying to antagonize him, either. He knew he was acting off. Why didn't he just come out and tell her? Because he needed to believe he was bigger than his secret. He couldn't bear the thought of her reaction if she wasn't into it. The look of distaste or, worse yet, revulsion as her opinion of him diminished right before his eyes. Or the capper being she indulged him and then cut him loose after labeling him a pervert. For the first time in his adult life, he questioned his ability to make the right decision.

"It's probably best if I take you home," he said abruptly, rising from the couch where they'd been sitting to retrieve his keys. "I don't think either of us is having a good time."

"Chase, I don't work for you. You're not allowed to dismiss me when you don't like what I have to say."

"I'm not dismissing you I'm trying to spare us the aggravation of a useless argument, and give us both a chance to cool off."

"But I'm not mad," Amanda said slowly and deliberately, feeling as though she had pieced together a puzzle. "This *is* about me not willing to follow you around, isn't it? You're mad because you're not getting what you want. What would you have me do, Chase? Show up at the Cold Creek tomorrow and tell thirty people they're out of work because their boss decided to close the place and follow around her favorite baseball player? I realize that they're not as important as you, but their families think they're pretty special and are depending on them. And while I'm not an important cog in the world dynamic either, if I don't show up, the place can't stay open."

She was completely right and he knew it, and it only irritated him further. His alternate excuse for being distracted wasn't sounding much better than his real one.

"I'm trying to be a gentleman here," he growled. "But I'm warning you, if you push this, you're going to find yourself someplace you don't want to be."

"I'm already someplace I don't want to be. You know that place where you always want me around only to shut me out, all with your cool courteousness? This certainly makes me want to give up my career and be at your beck and call, although I don't know what Jack will do with all the free time now that he won't be spying on me anymore."

Chase had positioned his most trusted security at the restaurant in response to some threatening jeers from the stands referencing why his head wasn't in the game. He knew Jack wasn't exactly inconspicuous or personable, but the last thing he needed was her questioning him on it, given she inadvertently was the cause.

"He's not spying on you." Chase could feel his teeth starting to grind. "He's there to protect you when I can't be there."

"I never knew I needed protecting until I met you."

"Don't be childish, Amanda. There are people out there who are truly crazy, take it all too seriously, and know exactly where to find you. Why do you think I have them?"

Childish? Amanda thought, enraged. If anyone was acting like a spoiled child it was him, only he was hiding behind all his gallantry and nebulous attempts to scare her. "I have an idea," Amanda said with over-zealous sarcasm as she rose in agreement to call it a night. "Why don't you blame your slump on me? Looks like you're doing it anyway. Tell your coach you're not getting enough rest because I'm not there to suck your dick when you're on the road, and it's throwing your timing off."

Amanda knew she struck a nerve when his face immediately fell in response to the shock of her crudeness. "What did you just say to me?"

Sparked by her own gumption and charged by his reaction, Amanda switched course. Spitting out the obscenity felt good; so did watching the drastic and sudden change in his disposition. It was one moment where he looked dark and primal and about to lose control, then successfully reeled it back in. Clearly he wasn't used to being spoken to like that, probably by anybody. There was an exhilaration that came with seeing him go from considerate and polite to as frustrated as she was. If they were going to have their first fight, they might as well have it. Finally, she was getting a glimpse of what in all probability was his flaw and could begin to view their relationship from a level playing field. And that flaw was he expected her to agree and go along with whatever he thought was important. Apparently, he also expected her to saddle the blame when his rose-colored glasses got fogged up. How he acted when he didn't get his way and she called him on it spoke volumes. If he thought he was going to manipulate her with great sex and an abundance of cash, she was going to set him straight here and now. Closing the distance between them, Amanda stood confrontationally in front of him. With her hands planted on her hips, she recklessly continued. "You heard me. You can tell everyone at your next press conference that you're not making your numbers because your latest fling is fucking all the power out of you with her voodoo pussy."

And just like that, she triggered him. Her vulgarity was not only deplorable but completely unexpected and he instinctively reacted to it. With well-honed reflexes, Chase grabbed her upper arm and spun her halfway around. Seconds later, she felt the stinging slap of his free hand connecting smartly with the right side of her behind.

"OH!" Amanda squealed with surprise and indignation, trying to pull herself out of his grip.

His hand swung again and her left side received the same stinging treatment. Then, with her arm still solidly in his grasp, Chase began to march her in the direction of his bedroom. She planted her heels into the hardwood floor in protest, her bare feet sticking on the thick shine and acting as a momentary stopper against his momentum. Further determined, he effortlessly hoisted her over his shoulder, applying another well-placed swat. He bore her the rest of the way down the hall, with Amanda pounding his broad back and swearing at him with every step. He slammed the bedroom door shut with a backward kick. When in his room, he set her down briefly.

"You kiss your mother with that mouth?"

Before she could decide how best to answer him, Chase took a seat on the corner of the bed, hauling her with him. He unceremoniously tossed her facedown across his knees.

He flipped up her flowered sundress in one hand and pulled her panties down to her thighs with the other as she demanded an explanation. His arm clamped firmly around her waist and his other hand rested ominously on her now bare bottom. With her only view that of the floor, he said in a voice she'd never heard before, "Amanda, in ten seconds, I'm going to full-on spank you. If you really don't already know why, we'll discuss it later. You can fight me, accept it, or call the cops when it's over, but make no mistake, little girl, it's about to happen."

Without another word, Chase Walker raised his hand and changed the game again.

Chapter 8

Amanda woke up the next morning in Chase's ginor-mous bed alone. All snuggled within his zillion-thread-count cotton sheets and his downy comforters.

She knew she wasn't free of him. He was located somewhere inside the penthouse apartment. She sat up, pulling the bedding with her, unconsciously reclaiming her modesty and remembered the night before.

Last night was hot and steamy and wild, she thought. And kinky.

Amanda Cole was not kinky. She was gracious and refined. She wasn't a prude, but she shied away from the fethishy stuff. Last night was all evidence to the contrary, however. And this wasn't about toe-sucking or him wanting to drink something out of her shoe. What he did to her actually hurt, enough to make her cry. And that almost seemed like the least of her worries.

The whole episode only lasted about two minutes. A tiny span of time that opened up a floodgate of more feelings than she thought a person could have. She fought him as hard as she could for that first minute, so incensed by what he was doing, but there was no way to match his strength. Chase said nothing as she struggled, simply kept to his word and saw to his task. With uncanny expert precision, he maneuvered around her squirming and kicking to connect with his target every time, using just enough force to remind her of exactly where she was. But as soon as she stopped trying to escape, worn out from all the thrashing, his as well as her own, he began to scold her, something about soap and her mouth. The words were all jumbled in her mind. But she couldn't forget the same crisp, authoritative tone that continued since he informed her of his intention. It was curt, resolved, and disappointed, definitely disappointed. It demanded her attention, and she found herself getting caught up in it. The more he scolded, the worse she felt. The absence of his generous loving affection cut into her like a knife.

Then they seemed to combine, the pain of his voice with the sting of his hand, and she gave over to it all. It was like she had risen out of her body and was watching it all take place from the ceiling. And whether it was from the ceiling or nothing more than a picture in her mind, she was able to see his handsome face, a mask of determination and control. It was strangely comforting. It matched the look he got when he kissed her, and when he made love to her. Which meant it was a look that was erotic as hell.

It was too many feelings all at once, vying for space in her brain. Pain, shock, frustration, disappointment, love, trust, eroticism, control. Control. She crashed back down to the floor, and once again it was the only thing she could see.

It was then that Amanda really started to cry.

As soon as he recognized her tears for what they were, Chase stopped. He waited a moment, caught his own breath. Then he helped her to stand and stood up next to her. All traces of fury in him had vanished. He almost appeared serene. He certainly didn't look like he wanted to hurt her any further or force himself on her in any way. He took a few steps back to give her some space, crossed his arms over his chest, and watched, waiting to see what she would do next.

Although her dress fell back down, her panties pooled at her feet. She could feel them around her ankles. She wanted to reach back and try to rub at the burn, but refused to give him the satisfaction of letting him know just how well he'd done the job, as if there were any question. Embarrassment tried to cram its way into her skull. There was just no room for anger. And she didn't want to be angry with him anyway, she wanted his laughing, loving voice back. If she didn't hear it, and soon, the absence of it would be more than she could bear. The longer it continued, his silence created an expanding void that grew bigger and she didn't have the strength to climb out of. She didn't know how she would be able to stand one more second of it. She swiped at her nose with the back of her hand and choked on a sob the only word she could think of, part question, part exclamation, and all distress signal. "Chase."

And then he was there, scooping her up and holding her close against his chest. He went back to the corner of his bed, only this time to sit her on his lap. She bit back the wince while he held back a smirk and he settled her more comfortably against him. He held her quietly as she cried incoherent, random words, trying to make sense of it all.

When her last tear was shed and the last word babbled, he kissed her. It was tender, conciliatory, but by no means remorseful. With each kiss, she wanted to coax the words out of him, words to explain, words to forgive. Only he wouldn't say them. He adoringly hummed and hushed but his mouth was far too busy doing other things. Instead, he tumbled her backward onto the bed and helped her work through each of the feelings that were bottled up inside her, one by one. As each feeling exploded out of her body with the force of a line drive coming off a fastball, he caught it, made it his own, and joined her in it. He matched her emotion for emotion, and it was manic and chaotic and euphoric. . . .

Amanda vigorously shook her head. She could never be accused of being a delicate flower, but last night went beyond aggressive sex. And her feminist school of thought was, if you let a guy hit you once, it's like giving him permission to make you his punching bag. This felt different and only added to the confusion.

Where had this man come from? This was not the completely gallant gentleman who politely pulled out her chairs, opened all her doors, and held her hand. Who took chivalry to a whole new level. The Chase from last night was forceful, intent on overpowering her and refusing to stop.

Had she even said stop?

No, she hadn't. She fought and she swore and called him every name she could think of. She even made up a few. It had become an accelerating battle of words and wills until it was clear who was going to come out the victor. But at no time did she tell him to stop. At one point early on, she actually sank her teeth into his side, a decision she could probably thank any lingering soreness for. The resulting volley of sharper swats was a stark reminder of just how much restraint and control he wielded over her. How helpless and completely at his mercy she was. The mind-blowing sex afterward was born of the adrenaline created from the whole experience. It was wrong for him to take that sort of advantage of her. It was even more wrong that she let him. And there was no way to rationalize how, through it all, there was this out-of-body element that she had never felt before. It was feral, hedonistic, and uninhibited.

One of his bathrobes was lying across a corner of the bed. *Was he being thoughtful, presumptuous, or just plain lazy?* Amanda pondered, standing up. She slipped on the heavy terry cloth. It was completely dry; he hadn't used it. She settled on thoughtful while tying it at the waist and pulling up the extra material to ensure she wouldn't step on it when she walked. She tiptoed down the hallway, the same hallway that only hours ago he'd tried to drag her down, peeking into open doors for any sign of him. She encountered his cleaning lady in his memorabilia room, an entire room full of trophies and other dedications to his greatness. Lena was a stout Latino grandmother with a ready smile whom security picked up every morning at five A.M. and drove home at the end of each day since she was hired three years ago. She politely directed Amanda to the kitchen at the opposite end of the hall. Chase's magnetism started creeping up on her as she got closer and hit her full force before she made it to the entranceway. She drew in her breath and held it. She thought she was ready to face him. She was wrong.

Chase was sitting on a stool at the kitchen's long center island, which also served as a breakfast bar. He was freshly showered and fully dressed in Kings work-out garb, sans his hat and spikes. His blond hair shone under the bright lights overhead in the windowless kitchen, making him look more angelic than mortal. He held on to a coffee cup. The heavy ceramic mug looked normal in his large hand, and probably held a quart of coffee. The remnants of his Paul Bunyan–sized bowl of Cheerios sat beside a stack of newspapers, one opened directly in front of him. Chase always had his morning papers delivered by six and tried to be done reading them all by seven. When he caught sight of her in the entranceway he smiled brightly.

"Morning, angel," he greeted her, pointing to the opposite end of the long counter near where she was standing. "Coffee's ready, over there in the corner." He went back to reading.

Amanda suddenly felt shy. Silly even. Something about the way he'd said "corner." How could someone telling you where the coffee is sound so dominant and sexy? He was completely relaxed. That was fine. She could follow that lead. She was still feeling the aftereffects from what he'd done to her last night; he was engrossed in the box scores, no big deal. She ambled across the kitchen floor to where her Gulliver-made-it-home-sized mug waited and made herself a trough of coffee. As she methodically poured coffee, then added milk and Splenda, she tried to work up the nerve to broach the subject. To inform him in no uncertain terms she wasn't that kind of girl, no matter how much she may have acted like one. Nothing came to her mind that sounded even remotely plausible. She didn't need to rush; she told herself. She could do small talk.

"I thought all you big shots only wore your play clothes when at the field?" She stirred her coffee with a teaspoon that looked more like it was made for soup.

"I have clothes everywhere," he replied cheerfully. "Sometimes I need to make a sudden appearance. Today I just overslept a bit and wanted to get a jump on the day." He looked her up and down while her back was turned, before adding, "Lots of great energy."

Energy, Amanda repeated to herself while she stirred her cup. That would help explain all the electricity that left her feeling so jittery. Maybe it was the way he said it, so at ease with the dimension he was trying to add to their relationship.

He went back to reading as she turned around. She stared at the contents of her mug and took a moment to appreciate that there was no way she could convincingly pretend nothing had changed with so much being left unsaid. If he wasn't going to bring it up, she was going to have to. He wasn't focused on her and she considered it a benefit.

"Chase," she began steadily, but her voice cracked as soon as she said his name, "about last night?"

"Yes?" he asked casually, not looking up from his paper.

"You seemed like you really knew what you were doing there." She tried to sound snarky, but it came out more flummoxed.

"I do," he stated, very matter of fact, still seemingly engrossed in the paper, but with the corners of his mouth starting to turn up.

"Like you've done that sort of thing before."

"I have." He grinned, turning the page and scanning it.

"And that if we keep seeing each other, it's something you'll want to do again?"

"I will." He nodded, still grinning. He took a sip of his coffee, his eyes focused on the comics.

His two-word, nonchalant answers and perceived lack of interest was starting to completely unnerve her. She hadn't even come out directly to say what she was talking about and he was behaving like they had entered into a pact that only he was privy to.

"What if I don't want you to?"

Chase finally looked up from his paper, his eyes spearing her from across the granite island. "Then you better not be naughty."

Any bravery she had mustered up evaporated when he focused on her. The temperature in the room turned up a hundred degrees and his robe became more like a straitjacket on her body. Amanda felt as though she were slowly being smothered in his hotness. Even when he wasn't looking at her, her heart was racing. Now he was grinning at her as if she were standing there naked. His eyes shot green laser beams from where he was sitting that effectively drilled into her core, impaling her into the counter she was leaning against, rendering her immobile.

Naughty. The word, spoken by him, was like a caress, an ardent invitation daring her to be just that. It had a hundred different meanings and every single one of them led straight back to last night.

"You might want to start by watching your language," Chase added, still smiling but shaking his head reprovingly.

From across the room, his confidence was like a force field that radiated out, pushing her up against the counter and ravaging her. He wasn't even apologetic. He had just alluded to the fact he would spank her whenever he felt she needed spanking.

She tried to scoff in bravado, but it was ineffective. "That sounds like I have no say in this whatsoever."

"Doesn't it?" He went back to reading the paper, chuckling.

"What if you decide you want to do something crazy, like snap my neck?" she sputtered, detesting that it had started to sound like they were entering into negotiations.

"That's not how it works," Chase told her, laughing and looking at her again, this time with his heart-melting boyish sincerity. "And why would I want to see anything on you snapped? In case you haven't noticed, I'm completely in love with you."

"You have a funny way of showing it," she mumbled, looking down at the floor. She hoped he couldn't see how he was affecting her. She knew it wasn't working. His gentle teasing served only as a reminder of how comfortable he was with all of it. Or that her having stayed somehow signified an acceptance of terms.

Chase patiently waited for her to look at him, and then cleared his throat to get her attention when he felt she'd stalled enough. When she finally brought her face back up to meet his, he smiled again, his eyes crinkled at the corners in amusement.

"Amanda, there's nothing wrong with you liking it."

"I never said I liked it," she replied too quickly, blushing furiously in her epic-fail attempt to stare him down.

"Women don't make the kind of love you did last night after being deeply offended. You were amazing." He winked at her.

Amanda blinked, and her eyes filled with tears. It was like he was poking fun at a weakness in her. She wasn't supposed to be acting like she'd be willing to let him do it again, let alone at his discretion. She was supposed to be breaking up with him, telling him to find some crazy party girl who lives her life with all bets off, a girl who likes it rough.

"Oh, baby. It's okay." As soon as Chase saw her well up, he put down his coffee and rose, going to her. He cradled one side of her face in his hand, gently kissing her other cheek. He wove his hand in her hair and swiped at her tears with his thumb before kissing her again. He was sensitive, but also familiar, and inadvertent chuckles continued to roll out of him. She was tousled and muddled and fretful, all swallowed up in his bathrobe. She was completely irresistible. Heaven help him, how was it possible to be more infatuated with her? He pulled her to him and wrapped his arms around her.

"The first time is always overwhelming, so many emotions and sensations going on. It's a lot to come to grips with. Not to mention I probably wore you out and you're exhausted. I don't blame you for being confused. It's gonna be all good, I promise." His voice was a mellow coo even with the underlying chuckle.

"You sound so sure of yourself." She wept angrily into his chest, further distressed that she couldn't ignore how secure she felt in his arms. "You're always so sure of yourself, it's just not fair."

"I just trusted you with the only secret I have; does that make you feel on more solid ground?"

She stopped weeping, lifting up her head. "This is your secret?"

A loud laugh erupted with his exhale. "How'd you hear about it?"

It was true. There was a definite ring of scandal to it. It was the kind of quirk that if found out would stick him into that category of smarmy bad-boy pro athletes who never quite shake the status. Chase was the spitting image of virtuous morality. He had easily kept this side of himself from her until she demanded he show it. Or maybe not so easily. He had become increasingly irritable, which had prompted her to push for an explanation. One she acted completely out of character to get, which coincidently summed up how she conducted herself since their relationship started.

"People with reputations for my sort of thing usually end up wearing it as a moniker, whether they want to or not. I'd like to keep this one to myself. I'd appreciate it if you did, too. No matter which way you end up going."

"Going?" she repeated. It was one thing for her to consider leaving him, but his mentioning it didn't sound remotely the same.

Chase took her hand and, grabbing her coffee cup with the other, led her over to where he had been sitting. He placed her mug on the island in front of the chair next to his and sat back in his own, watching her climb up onto it. Once she was seated, her feet dangled almost a foot off the ground.

Good God, she thought as she settled and folded her hands in her lap, is everything in this house tailor-made for a giant? Or did she just feel suddenly small and childlike? He wasn't reading the paper anymore. As she got into her chair, he had gathered them and put them to the side. His eyes were still bright, but no longer teasing. She had his full attention.

"You probably have a lot of questions. What do you want to know?" Chase said seriously. "Ask away."

"This is a sex thing for you?" Amanda dove right in.

"Mostly, but not always," he answered before narrowing his eyes at her. "I certainly wasn't turned on while you were hurling obscenities at me."

She flushed anew at the change in his tone before remembering that he was the one with the explaining to do. She threw the inquisition right back on him. "If it's a sex thing, why didn't you tell me about it before? We've had lots of sex. You really could have inducted me into your inner circle in a way slightly less jarring."

Chase shrugged and for just a moment looked boyishly contrite. "You really didn't seem the type or pick up the vibe. Girls with a taste for it usually tip their hands pretty quick. I don't even have to make like it's my idea. They practically throw themselves over my lap when I even hint at it. Girls who aren't into it are pretty clear it won't be happening and that's fine, too, but I have to admit, I lose interest. I never expected finding you would hit me so hard. I'm just so smitten with you. I didn't want to take the chance of scaring you off. And you never misbehaved. Although"—his eyes began to gleam—"you zeroed right in on my biggest pet peeve. Ladies should talk like ladies. You timed it perfectly; my palm had really begun to itch. You've always made me work for it, why should this be any different? After last night, I'm confident you felt the vibe just fine."

Amanda tried to sound offended, and couldn't quite pull it off. "You think I provoked you on purpose?"

Chase smiled again, but he was regarding her closely. "I don't think any of that really matters now, does it? It happened and you stayed. And I'm so glad you did. Like I said . . . amazing."

"Are there any other surprises? Like is this an ass thing for you? You know, a fixation? Are you going to want to . . . ?" The question trailed off and her eyes grew wide.

Chase chuckled at the transparent look on her face. "Relax, angel. I crossed that one off my bucket list a long time ago. It was overrated. Of course, if it's something you insist on trying, I'll be happy to oblige, but it's really not on my radar. I'm not interested in your gorgeous booty for that."

"How'd you manage to keep it a secret?"

This time he laughed, deep and rich, in reaction to just how fast she wanted off the anal topic. Then took a moment to consider just how truthful he should be. There was no need to tell her about pain sluts or women so turned on by it, they often wanted more than even he felt comfortable giving. "It's not the kind of thing people generally shout from the rooftops. But to give you the short version, a lot of one-night stands with horny groupies, women who drink too much and think too little. They come on stronger than a freight train when I'm on the road. I threaten, they request, everyone's happy."

Amanda's mouth formed a thin, tight line and then twitched it from one side to the other. Yeah, that wasn't going to work at all.

Chase grinned at her, delighted. "Security sweeps everywhere I go since I met you. As soon as you stop being stubborn and come with me on the road, you can tell me if they're not doing a good job and I'll fire them. And I've never brought a woman here."

"Never?"

"Not for that," he clarified with a wry grin. "Even if you believed only half of what you've heard, that still makes me fifty percent playboy. But I've always been careful about the women I have my picture taken with more than once. Women greedy for fame often don't have a moral compass, and it's hard to tell the difference. And this is my thing, the only thing I have that I can call my own. A lot of responsibility comes with being on a box of Wheaties. I may have played around a little at my places in Tampa and California, with women who had as much to risk as I did, but not here. This is where I call home. I made up my mind a long time ago that there was only one girl who would go over my knee here. I've spent a long time looking for you. I can't believe you fell right into my lap."

He indulged himself in a chortle at his own pun before grinning at her, his eyes shining like a kid who had gotten everything he wanted for Christmas. "Baby, I got it so bad for you, I can't even stand it. You're my total package."

It couldn't be happening. He was the walking, talking, living definition of the total package, with the possible exception of being able to go from zero to Neanderthal in under a minute. And he had just confessed he was mad about her, had been searching for her even.

"This is like the most jacked-up version of *Cinderella* ever," she finally said.

Chase laughed again, and then settled his gaze back on her affectionately. "I never thought of it like that."

"Maybe you'd prefer to hear my Superman theory?" Amanda giggled at the mental picture of him in full costume, swooping down and adjusting bad attitudes, one naughty girl at a time.

He actually looked like he was considering it, but he was really just enjoying the relief of those blue eyes looking at him playful and flirty, and all the things that look really meant. "Cinderella works for me. I have no problem getting in touch with my feminine side. And after all, I would like to believe I've found my princess. So now you know. I'm sorry I didn't tell you before. I should never have tried to keep it from you. But it's who I am. I think it's who you are, too, if you're willing to trust me and explore it. I promise you, it can be downright fun. A steady partner in this particular crime is all new to me, too. We'll figure it out. I have no desire to make you a submissive who does everything I say. Lord knows I have enough to do running my own life. You turned into an exceptional woman without my help—if it ain't broke, don't fix it. There's no dungeon here where I want to tie you up and make you suffer. No deep, sinister plot. The worst thing that'll ever happen is that every now and then, like last night, you may end up taking one for the team."

"Take one for the team?" Amanda repeated. In baseball, it meant getting in the way of the ball and letting it hit you. She didn't like the sound of that at all.

Chase gave a half laugh, then went serious, his eyes darkening like turbulent deep sea waters. "It means there may come a time you get spanked when you don't think you deserve it."

She gasped at the change in his expression. "I don't ever deserve it!"

He just looked at her, a small smile playing at his lips; so much for her to learn. He'd bet dollars to donuts she'd be trying to find ways to "deserve" it before nightfall.

"Of course not, precious, you're my perfect angel. But I'm a typical alpha male and a straight-up old-fashioned guy. This one is going by my rules. If you remain, your job is to stay beautiful and think up ways to entertain yourself. Hopefully, most of them include me. My job is to cherish and protect you. Fulfill all your heart's desires." His eyes began to narrow again. "And make sure you mind your manners."

"What's wrong with my manners?" she asked with a pout. It was her first pout and he adored it.

"Absolutely nothing, that's why you caught me by surprise last night. Vulgarity is not your bag. Frankly, it might have been a deal breaker when I met you if it was. I'm out in the public a lot. I have to be able to trust that I won't end up embarrassed. I look at last night as just another instance of you making me earn it. You have all the grace of a princess. My princess."

It's hard not to feel just a little bit special when a gorgeous, hunky gazillionaire keeps calling you his princess, no matter how overconfident he sounds when doing it. He certainly had all the makings of a prince, albeit one who was part teddy bear, part brute, and all sorts of dangerous. If nothing else, he was a royal pain in the ass, on several levels. And he was handing her the keys to his kingdom. She smiled at her own train of thought until his voice brought her back to the reality of the conversation.

"There's just one thing you must always remember. You're not a prisoner here. If you stay, with all the perks and perils of this relationship, it's because it's your choice. You can leave at any time and for any reason. But you can only leave once."

She heard the door to the kingdom slam shut, and she was tossed back into the moat. She wasn't completely sure what he was talking about, but he sounded very serious for someone stating the obvious. It had all the earmarkings of an ultimatum.

"Okay?" She stared at him blankly, waiting for him to elaborate.

"It may not be as easy as it sounds, especially if you don't like when I lay down the law."

She wanted to be afraid, but it was impossible with the way he said it. It sounded foreboding, but at the same time tempting.

"There's a lot of power-playing involved, for both of us. I may have the upper hand on you physically, but you'll have total control over me mentally. You withdrawing from me when I make you uncomfortable can't be a weapon you use against me. We would get toxic fast. And committing to something like this based on one experience is never a good idea." Chase leaned over and kissed her forehead while slipping off his barstool. "You have a lot to think about, angel. In the meantime, I'm going head out to the stadium and catch some batting practice, work out with the team. Feel free to stay as long as you'd like. Take a bath, go back to bed. Your clothes are already clean and hung up in my closet. When you're ready to leave, just tell Lena and she'll call downstairs for a car to take you home."

Chase reached into a drawer near the kitchen entrance and pulled out a baseball cap. He put it on and the boy appeared, carefree and playful, his recent trouble on the field already in his rearview mirror. He stopped just short of exiting the kitchen and turned back to her, his grin slightly penitent.

"You know, the minute you tell me you're sure, we'll be picking out the ring. And I support whatever you want to do with the restaurant. The following-me thing was the lame excuse I was using because I couldn't tell you why I was all pent up. That problem's solved." He smiled at her from across the room, all confidence and compromise. "But spring training is going to be awful if you're not in Tampa with me. I don't sleep well on the plane. I'll see you tonight."

And then he was gone. She heard him holler good-bye to Lena, the woman's "Adios" from a safe distance, then the echo of the front door closing and she was alone. She flushed anew with the thought of his housekeeper hearing any part of their discussion. Amanda looked around the kitchen, toying absently with her coffee cup. He was right. She had a lot to think about. Was she ready? Could she handle the sort of relationship he had proposed to her? And if she couldn't, would she be able to say good-bye and not feel a heartbreaking void? She already felt his absence, and he hadn't been gone more than a minute. She wanted to be angry with him. He had no right to wait until after he sucked her in with all his appeal to reveal this side of himself. He was offering her everything he had in exchange for her pain threshold and willingness to submit to him on his whim. That she was even considering it disturbed her. Equally disturbing, he acted like already knew what her answer would be.

Chapter 9

Amanda did take a bath in Chase's Olympic-sized tub. Lena insisted on drawing it and added a ginger-coconut milk bath and salt mixture she said Chase used for aching muscles and moisture.

Lucky guess on the muscle aches. Amanda smirked, gingerly stepping into, then settling in the sunken tub. She soaked mindlessly to the hum of the luxurious jets for almost an hour before getting dressed and leaving. How was Chase able to feel so energetic when she was so languid? A car dropped her off at home and she changed for work, even though her clothes were clean. Wearing the same outfit two days in a row screamed "hussy," at least in this case. Driving to the Creek, she decided she didn't want to think any more about Chase's proposition for the time being. She still had more questions, wanted other things more clearly defined. Like would it now turn into a caveman open season? Was he one step from dragging her around by her hair?

She got into work early and went about her usual business, blessedly mundane things that she could focus on. Tasks that were mindless because she'd been doing them for years. Eric and Nicki arrived forty-five minutes later, but not with the tomfoolery they usually exhibited with each other. Eric came in first. Amanda looked up from her linen order expecting to see Nicki following right behind him, or at the very least expecting to get a hello, but Eric went directly behind the bar and put on his apron, yanking on the strings a bit as he tied it.

"Nicki come in with you?" Amanda asked.

"Yeah," Eric said in disgust, grabbing the bin to start his routine of getting ice from the machine in the kitchen for the coolers at the bar. "She's having a cigarette, 'cause that's how those Hollywood actresses stay thin."

That was random. "Nicki went back to smoking?"

Nicki came in the door and Eric immediately went into the back. Nicki plopped down on the barstool next to Amanda's and began digging around in her purse.

"You're smoking again?" Amanda asked.

Nicki gave a shrug while popping the Tic Tacs she'd been looking for. "I never completely quit. I sometimes grab a few when I'm stressed."

"You're stressed?"

"I wasn't until yesterday," Nicki jeered, then said loudly, "And I shouldn't be now!"

Eric came from the kitchen with the bin full of ice, and Nicki promptly went into the ladies' room. Eric muttered something under his breath. This didn't resemble the being-able-to-work-together policy at all.

"I hate to be a jerk about this," Amanda said, getting right to the point. "But you guys assured me you'd be able to keep it professional. If there's an issue we have to work out, I'd rather it gets done before we have customers."

"There won't be any issue. We won't be working together anymore," he said curtly, throwing the ice all around the cooler.

"Don't even kid," Amanda said flippantly.

Eric stopped what he was doing to stare at his boss, demonstrating how serious he was. Amanda began to frown as Nicki came out of the bathroom. Eric went back to dealing with the ice after giving a wave in Nicki's direction. "She can tell you all about it." He took the bin and went back into the kitchen, while

Nicki rubbed the side of her nose purposefully with her middle finger.

Amanda looked at Nicki and said, "Somebody better start telling me something."

Nicki took a deep breath and extended her middle finger right at the kitchen door before saying, "I guess there's never an easy way to do this."

Amanda, like all good employers, knew what usually followed an opening like that. "You got another job?" she asked, trying to be supportive. She knew it was never supposed to be permanent, but she would miss Nicki. Working with a friend had been fun.

"I'm moving to California," Nicki blurted out excitedly.

Amanda was equally excited after her initial surprise. "Did you get a gig?"

Nicki crossed into rehashing the argument as she must have presented it to herself. "I have an audition for a pilot with USA Network. But more than that, I made a connection. Well, a connection's connection. The pilot's a long shot but some extra work rolls through this woman's agency. At the very least, she knows a restaurant that will hire me when I get there. I have to try. I really feel like I have to take the chance."

"Of course you do!' Amanda enthusiastically agreed. It was thrilling to watch people take risks, even if she was leery to take any herself. Nicki was always willing to work hard; she deserved to try to make her dream happen. "You can work as many hours as you want before you leave. Do you know how fast you're going to make the move?"

Eric came out of the kitchen glowering, and Nicki snorted in anger. "That's the hard part. Seems my roommate is a real buzzkill and doesn't want to let me out of my lease."

Amanda sat between Eric and Nicki as they stared each other down. Was Amanda the only one to see that this was about more than a roommate moving? Or was she starting to see everything with romantic overtones? Eric dumped another bin of ice and said, "I told you, get a suitable roommate to replace you and you can do whatever you want."

Nicki made a face at him and then spat dramatically, "Remember that flaw you told me about before, Amanda? I think I found Eric's. He's a monkey-wrench-throwing motherfucker!"

Amanda was grateful they were busy shooting daggers at each other. Now was not the time to inform Nicki or anyone else that she had discovered Chase's fatal flaw. But damn if Nicki dropping the f-bomb wasn't an instant and blush-inducing reminder.

Eric and Nicki did maintain a cordial picture as they worked that evening. Amanda would've given more thought about what they would do once they had to go back to the same apartment after work, but as Chase's estimated arrival time drew closer, all her thoughts centered on him. As soon as he came through the door, her excitement gave way to shyness after the first initial rush that seeing him provided. The way he looked at her now held a different type of warmth, the supersecret kind. She didn't want to ask him any more questions; she just wanted to get back to feeling his hands all over her. She left Eric and Nicki to duke it out and retired for the night after the last customer left. They could make up or lock up. She hoped they would consider doing both.

In the end, Amanda stayed. At first it was under the guise of Chase's challenge that submitting to him could actually be enjoyable. And it was. She liked it a lot. When she surrendered all her control, the result was the most intense freedom. She could put all her fears, worries, and decisions into his strong, powerful hands, and he took them willingly. From across his knees, she was released from all her anxiety. It was amazingly cathartic, but still left her conflicted. His reward had to be greater, because he was still a man, and a spoiled one at that. But she couldn't quite find the words to question him about it without becoming tongue-tied. And he was so comfortable with it. There were no secrets from his past he was tortured by, no deep-seated desire to abuse women hidden behind his long list of good deeds and magnetic smile. He genuinely saw his role as her protector and was a natural at it. She knew there would never be anybody she could ever trust enough to confide in about her newfound fetish, as much for her sake as for his. He'd asked her to keep it to herself, and that wouldn't be a problem. She didn't even know exactly how to share it with him, much less anyone else.

Now that Chase no longer had to concern himself with the outcome, he came in contact with her bottom whenever he could. His rascal-like quality was sent into overdrive and it made him all the more lovable. He was a real ass man, and she wondered how he'd been able to conceal it as long as he had. It became a veritable world series of pats, swats, and grabs whenever he was presented with a really clear opportunity. But those opportunities were rare, since there always seemed to be someone in their space. In public they were always proper. Discretion really cut into their fun time.

She waited for him to become an unofficial dictator, ordering her around and forcing her to see his way on any and all things. But that never happened. It was quite the opposite. Chase doted on her in every way possible. He gave no indication he wanted to run her life any more or less than he had before. He valued her opinion and didn't always have to be right. If he had strong feelings on a topic, however, she better be able to sway him. That was the hitch: If he said no and he meant it, he expected her to abide by it. Not doing so resulted in ramifications that were quick, effective, and came with the voice. She wanted to avoid that.

But he rarely said no. He was usually so indulgent, she felt childish for not going along with him. The pedestal that he put her on was high, and he still was able to shine down on her from it. In turn, she wanted to make him happy. But what do you give the man who has everything, including the ability to make a woman willingly submit to corporal punishment?

"I just hired a manager," Amanda told him one evening when he came to pick her up.

"A very wise decision." He couldn't help beaming.

"I'm glad you think so," she replied. "Since you're the one trying so hard to get me to leave the place, it's only fair you pay half his salary."

"Angel, I'll pay all of it. Best money I ever spent."

She originally was going to hire Liam to take over for Nicki, but he was just so skilled. And the former NYU graduate had such panache. It was a good fit that seemed to come at the right time. He walked in off the street within an hour of Amanda placing the ad online. Nicki was still making her arrangements but took immediate time off to make her West Coast audition and check out the lay of the land. Amanda put Liam on the books the day they interviewed. He worked well with Eric, who looked a little too pleased as the weeks wore on and Nicki struggled to find Eric a roommate, working almost all her regular hours when she returned.

Amanda continued to work when Chase was in town, but she went on the road with him more. They began to play their own kinky versions of beer-swilling games, started innocently enough when he came into the Creek and she bought him a beer, ordering his postgame favorite, Heineken.

"Give him a Heiney, Eric," she said, smiling at Chase, delighting in the coincidence.

From that moment on, whenever the word in any format or context was mentioned, they would share a quick look and have a brief stare-down. She started dropping words with intentional double meanings— words like *discipline*, *punish*, and *disobedient*, words Chase immediately picked up on, no matter how innocuously she introduced them. "That's a punishing rain, don't you think?" she would ask . They were always said in public but never directly connected to avoid drawing attention. Amanda presented a gracious and reserved picture. It was the way she was raised. She was generally more of an observer and still getting used to the attention. So she got to work on her timing, which was excellent. But she never under any circumstances could bring herself to say the word *spank*.

Sometimes Chase forced her to say it by refusing to do it until she did; a sensual power struggle he was certain he'd win, and for which they would both be rewarded.

She went back to doing research, this time not about him, but them. And the amount of information to be found was mind-boggling. There were videos, chat rooms, and stories written about role-playing, age-playing, and domestic discipline. People had parties to meet and greet. There were entire communities dedicated to it. Some of it was frightening at first. People told stories with corresponding photos of being tied up and essentially whipped with all sorts of implements, leaving welts, cuts, and bruises. Some took it a step further and introduced additional body parts to the mix. Others got trussed up and shackled to contraptions. There were videos with sessions lasting extended periods of time. Chase was nothing like any of that, but came closest to the domestic stuff. And he didn't like it when she cried, even when that was his intention. When she started crying, the spanking was over. What she found was, when they were doing it for fun, she could take a lot before actually crying. She tried throwing in some role-play scenarios, and while he admired her braided pigtails, the little plaid skirt, the white button-down blouse with the matching cotton panties and knee socks, he much preferred being Chase Walker to a strict high school principal.

Who wouldn't?

"Chase? What exactly is topping from the bottom?" Amanda asked him one afternoon, a few weeks later while he was driving to drop her off at work before heading to the stadium.

He took his eyes off the road for just a moment and cast an amused sideways glance in her direction. "Doing a little more homework, were we?"

"Trying to," she said, "but a lot of it doesn't make any sense."

"Probably because it doesn't pertain to you," he told her. "We're making our own rules, angel, you should know that by now."

"Does that mean you aren't going to tell me?" She huffed, leaning her arm along his on the center console and her head on his shoulder.

He chuckled a little before kissing the top of her head and humoring her. "Topping from the bottom is an S and M phrase, as you probably know from whatever mischief you've been up to. It's used by insecure doms who don't know how to handle a sub who's always looking for some attention. It's when they accuse their subs of trying to control the action or the dynamic of the relationship."

"Sounds like you're not big on the concept."

"You're not my sub, you're my girlfriend. And I'm no insecure dom, having to battle you for control. You have a mind of your own, I think you should use it every chance you get. You're all I think about when I'm not on the field, so it's safe to say you have my full attention. Not only can I give you everything, I want to. There's only one rule, act like a lady, which you already do. If you want me to spank you, all you have to do is ask me. And if I think you've earned one, there's nothing you can do to stop me. I thought we went over this?"

Amanda waited a few moments, staring at the dashboard before quietly asking, "But what if I don't want to ask?"

Chase chuckled again. "How about just give me a hint?"

She didn't answer him and tried unsuccessfully to hold back the sigh. Either he was being dense on purpose, to partake in one of his particular forms of enjoyment, watching her fumble while trying to talk about it, or he really didn't understand her conundrum. There were times when she made it all about him—she wasn't putting on nurse and school-girl uniforms for her own enjoyment, although she certainly didn't mind. But there was an indescribable excitement that came from watching him get all worked up and react, knowing she was the only one with the ability to make him. It took the intimacy of their relationship to a whole new level, pushing him just far enough for him to go from doting to domineering, minus the voice, of course. If he was really upset with her and he used the voice, it would take all the fun out of it and she'd end up miserable. Occasionally, it was so much more rewarding to tease him into it, just short of making him mad. That certainly seemed to qualify as topping from the bottom. If she was going to embrace the lifestyle, shouldn't she be getting it right? Would she blow her chance at happiness by being a bad fit for an alpha male? Even in the air-conditioned car, thinking about it suddenly made her backside feel warm and tingly.

"I can practically hear your brain working," Chase mused into her ear, and the warmth increased just a bit, radiating slightly onto her thighs. "It's my job to know what you need, and you're a pretty easy read. It's all about control for you. You can't stand the thought of relinquishing it, but because you trust me, you don't mind my stripping you of it. I fully realize the sacrifice you make by giving it up to me."

"I can't tell if you're being sarcastic or sincere. You don't think this has anything to do with you challenging your own control?"

"As soon as I lay my eyes on you it challenges my control. But I have to be in control at all times or I could hurt you. It's taxing enough that you're practically insatiable."

If he thought he was being cute, it didn't translate. In fact, it irked her. "You make that sound like you're doing me a favor. I don't appreciate it. My sex life was fine before you got involved."

His Jag came up to a stoplight, and he nearly slammed on the brakes. His right hand white-knuckled the steering wheel and his left hand swept across his chest, his face tight with anger, all playfulness gone. He pointed a deliberate finger at her. "Hey. We had a deal. We don't talk about the people we've touched in the past. I admit I'm a possessive savage. Don't ever talk about another man touching you again. It makes me see red."

Amanda quickly sat back up straight, startled by the distinct edge of the voice now reflected in his tone.

She detested that her stomach immediately dropped in response to it. Curses, she made that deal when it was going to curtail the revolving door of women in his past, not the three buffoons from hers. Damn it, would any of these conversations ever go in the direction she wanted? Every time she tried to illustrate a valid point on this particular topic, he would turn all toppy and arrogant, never failing to reinforce their roles. There were times when she really resented the power he had over her. This was rapidly turning into one of them. She crossed her arms, sitting fully back in her own space.

"Okay. I get it. No dirty words, no ex-boyfriends," she said, trying unsuccessfully to ignore the heat on her backside intensifying yet again. She wriggled the tiniest bit in her seat to try to relieve it.

"I'm not trying to get into an argument with you here," he said, his ire dismissed as quickly as it appeared and replaced with congeniality, completely unaware that anything was amiss. As if he didn't know he was mentally paddling her to tears, the bastard. "I'm just saying that I've been at this a lot longer than you. I've honed the skills. If I don't know how to handle the likes of you, I need to hang it up."

"The likes of me?" Amanda asked, equal parts intrigued and annoyed. She tried to make the shifting in her seat to face him look like she was becoming fully engaged, but she was really trying to alleviate the inferno raging on her behind, which was slowly driving her mad. Surely he was some evil wizard disguised in adorable man/boy packaging. "That almost sounds like a challenge," she snapped.

"Baby, if issuing me a challenge makes you happy, I'll do my best to rise to it. You don't need to get so worked up. You're getting all flushed."

He was confident to the point of sounding condescending; self-assured to the point of being smug. She resumed the crossed-arm battle stance in her seat, fighting back tears of frustration at the whole exchange and his ability to roast her derriere without laying a hand on her. And then she caught sight of it, in the far right corner on the digital display in the center of the dashboard. A tiny icon of a car seat appearing, then disappearing, intermittently flashing, and underneath it read, 86 . . . then 87 . . . and then 88. As soon as it fully registered, Amanda dug her feet into the floor mat, heels and all, and arched her body off the seat as best she could.

"What's the big idea!" she shrieked.

"Just a little reminder, angel." He chuckled, depressing the button on his steering wheel with his thumb to shut off her seat warmer. Watching her subdued squirming reach its crescendo was easily the best thing he'd see all day, at least until he picked her up after his game when all her seat warming would be courtesy of his right hand. "You really hung in there. I was beginning to worry the leather would start smoking."

"You're not funny, Chase," she said, unable to keep from laughing at her own stupidity for thinking he had that sort of mental hold over her. At the same time, she was also relieved.

"Sorry, baby," he said, smiling out his window, completely unrepentant.

She gingerly settled back down, satisfied the seat had cooled. And then she thought about how he could use a little reminding of his own. They drove the rest of the way to the Cold Creek in silence. He was thinking about how endearing all her wiggling was. She was thinking about how to up the ante. When he pulled up to the curb, he grabbed her hand to pull her in for a sound kiss. "I'll see you tonight," he said after grudgingly unlocking their lips. "Stay off the Internet. It gives you bad ideas."

"Have a great game," she told him lovingly, pulling away and reaching for her door handle. Once safely outside the car but before closing the door, she leaned back in and added, "This means war, you know."

"I would expect nothing less from you," he replied happily. "You have my debit card if it can be of assistance. Give it your best shot."

She closed the door and he watched her walk away, his view from the passenger-side window a perfectly framed picture of her behind provocatively swishing within the confines of a respectable Ralph Lauren dress. He smiled; the game was already afoot. He watched her until she disappeared into the restaurant, thinking she should be glad he didn't believe in topping from the bottom since it was becoming apparent she had a real knack for it.

"Bring it on, baby," he said out loud to himself, pulling away from the curb and back into traffic, admitting he wouldn't have it any other way.

Amanda walked into work and found Eric on his side of the bar. Sitting across from him was a tearful Nicki. They were holding hands. It was drama of a different kind, and she approached the pair cautiously.

"You found a roommate?" Amanda asked.

They both turned to her with bittersweet smiles.

"Sort of," Eric said, squeezing Nicki's hand again. "I'm moving to California."

Amanda smiled, spreading the bittersweet around. "Now I also have to find a bartender?" She thought on the matter logically. It could be Liam's first real test. It was all so serendipitous. Liam had shown up with all his zeal at precisely the same time she began to feel left behind when Chase had to travel. Even more cosmic timing, Eric and Nicki had been with her since she opened. They had helped her with their own blood, sweat, and tears for a lot of sixty-hour weeks.

"Afraid so," Eric said, biting his lip and looking Nicki up and down. "They have some great waves in California. And curves, lots of great curves."

Nicki returned his look with a little lip-biting of her own, and it was easy to see that she and Eric had left the friends-with-benefits zone.

"Was I the only one who didn't see this coming?" Amanda exclaimed.

"You're busy being swept off your feet," Nicki told her. "Whether you want to admit it or not, your luck's about to change."

It wasn't said with malice. It was a complete revelation. One that Amanda's friends had come to before she did.

"Yeah, don't blow this," Eric agreed. "You just won the love-story lottery."

"And it's funny," Nicki continued. "Watching the whole thing go down is what really gave me the push to make the move. It's like watching your dream come true made me really want to go for mine."

Amanda nodded, saying nothing. She wasn't sure when she gave anyone the impression that being the trophy of a well-known sports figure was her dream, but apparently she had. Or was she just having other's dreams projected onto her? Either way, whatever it took to give someone a rush of perseverance was a good thing, and she was glad she could help.

Eric cast another affectionate look at Nicki before adding, "And watching you make excuses to try to fight off the man who adores you made me realize that the person I loved was right in front of me. I just had to get over thinking it was too much to compromise. As soon as I opened up to the possibilities, it dawned on me, I can tend bar anywhere."

"What about your lease?" Amanda queried.

Nicki smiled smugly and shot Eric a look before informing Amanda, "Well, see, that's the thing. I called the landlord asking if he could be of any help, to see if maybe knew of someone looking for a place. He thought I was being awfully nice about it, that trying to find Eric a roommate was really going the extra mile. Turns out we've been month to month on our lease since our renewal back in March."

"Can't blame a guy for trying," Eric remarked, stone-cold busted. "I only did it because she sounded like she didn't want me to tag along."

"Maybe you should let a girl know you're interested." Nicki reiterated something that sounded suspiciously like it had been previously discussed. "I didn't invite you because I think your exact words were you would never move *there*. You didn't need to board the crazy train at the first stop."

"I'm really going to miss you guys," Amanda said.

"We're only going to be a private jet ride away," Eric replied.

Eric and Nicki set their definite date of departure for two months. And Amanda felt a very real shift in what she thought was important. Like the intelligent, handsome wise guy who thought he couldn't be outsmarted.

Chapter 10

Her chance to get even with Chase came less than two weeks later, when, on his day off, Amanda told him she had a surprise for him. The word *surprise* tipped off the other to be alert. They drove away from the city and closer to her hometown to a local spa named Vita, located on a golf course and in a country club that her father was a member of. After leaving the car with the valet and entering the spa, Amanda took Chase to the front desk, where a flustered receptionist, blushing profusely, asked him his shoe size and if he would mind taking a picture with her. After Amanda snapped the shot with the girl's iPhone, they were handed pairs of spa sandals and directed to their respective changing rooms, where plush robes awaited them.

"I'm not getting a facial or a pedicure, am I?" Chase joked as they moved away from the reception area. "It's a little too girly for me."

"Of course not, silly," she replied.

"Are we going to roll around in mud? 'Cause that I could get into."

"We're getting massages."

"Baby, I'm really touched. But you know I get rubbed down several times a week. I can think of better ways to spend an hour naked than with you in another room."

"I agree," she said over her shoulder, right before disappearing through her changing room door. "This is different. We're getting a couple's massage."

When she ventured out into the relaxation area a short time later, Chase was already in his robe and on a chaise longue in front of a wall-length tropical fish tank, waiting for her.

"I think I've figured out what you're up to," he said suspiciously, quirking an eyebrow.

"I'm up to something?" she asked, stretching out on the chaise next to him. "I just thought this would be something different and relaxing that we could do together."

Before he could open his mouth to take it a step further, a shapely brunette floated in and joined them. She greeted Amanda and introduced herself to Chase as Bobbi. They chatted a few seconds about the weather, then Bobbi requested they follow her. She led them down to the last room at the end of the hall leading away from the fish tank area. The room had been made up with two massage tables side by side, with about a three-foot gap between them. Sconce lighting fixtures shaped like clamshells on the walls were dimmed and made to look like candles gently flickering. Soft music consisting mainly of pan flutes, harps, and pianos played in the background. The whole mood of the room was designed to mollify. Amanda hoped it would be enough to keep him from going ballistic when the time came.

"I'll give you two a minute to get all comfy under the sheets," Bobbi said soothingly before leaving and closing the door behind her. "Kelly and I will be right back."

"Bobbi certainly is attractive, isn't she?" Amanda remarked off-handedly, reaching to untie the bow of her robe's sash. Chase brushed her hands away and, grabbing the knot, pulled her to him.

"Oh yeah, I've got you all figured out, baby. I can't believe how enchanting you are," he said after kissing her and pulling at the bow until the sash untied and her robe opened.

"I needed figuring out?' she queried innocently as he shrugged the robe down her shoulders and completely off, kissing the hollow of where her neck met her shoulders. He took a moment to admire her naked before reaching for the knot on his own robe. As he took both robes over to hang them on hooks on the wall designed specifically for them, she waited, taking a few moments to do some admiring of her own before lifting up the sheets and blanket and lying facedown on her table.

"You think I'm not going to be able to keep from getting turned on by another woman touching me," he said confidently after hanging up the robes. "I promise you, it isn't going to happen, but I dig it when you turn on the jealous."

"You haven't seen Kelly yet," she hedged, testing her head's alignment into the cushy face cradle.

"Bobbi, Kelly, Megan Fox, it doesn't matter who you throw at me. I only have eyes for you. All my other parts, too," Chase remarked, also lying his bulk down beneath his own sheets on his stomach, adjusting them to the middle of his back.

There was a soft rapping on the door and Bobbi's soothing "We all good?" from the other side of it.

"Nothing ventured, nothing gained," Amanda replied wistfully. "Enjoy your massage."

Amanda blew him a kiss before calling out, "Yes, we're ready," and placing her head into the hollowed-out oval pillow. The door opened and the two masseuses entered the room.

She could feel the energy shift in the room with the very masculine "How we doing today, Amanda?"

"Very well, thank you, Kelly. My shoulders are a little tight," she replied with familiarity, her face still fully into her face cradle. Was it her fault Kelly happened to be a unisex name and that Chase would lean toward the feminine? If nothing else, she just managed to catch him unaware. She listened carefully to the movement about the room and for any signs of protest from a certain Chase Walker. He didn't want to hear her even mention other men; certainly one touching her was bound to get some reaction out of him. What would he do, cause a scene by demanding that Bobbi and Kelly switch clients? She felt the warm lotion followed by the firm hands that couldn't possibly belong to a woman begin to rub her right shoulder. Too late on the switch, she noted; their treatments had begun.

"Mr. Walker, is there any area you want me to specifically work on?" Bobbi asked, sounding as if she knew she had her work cut out for her.

"Please, call me Chase," he responded politely. "Anything you can't break up, my trainers will take care of."

He didn't sound upset at all, she thought, a tad disappointed. He sounded more like he was talking to a reporter than a naked man with a pretty woman's hands all over him. His self-confidence foiled her again. She had spent nearly a week avoiding his hard-core attention in an effort to keep her skin free from the occasional bruise and it was all for naught. But if the end result was they would share a nice massage, enjoy a tasty lunch, and go back to his place to spend the rest of the day in bed, the day was still hardly a failure, even if she did end up having to put on a costume.

"Chase, your shoulders are pretty tight, too. Would you like me to try some deep tissue?" Amanda heard Bobbi ask several long minutes later, and suppressed a giggle. Her shoulders weren't really tight when she said it, but his obviously were.

"Do the best you can, Bobbi," was the response, stiff and monotone. It had taken a turn from accommodating and friendly. Maybe he wasn't relaxed at all. Maybe he'd come to his own conclusion about her intentions, and there *was* a real and imminent danger. Maybe there was a chance that he would enjoy another woman's hands on him, a little too much even? He'd be getting a taste of what he'd been missing. And now he had to focus on not reacting to the woman's touch in a very manly way. What a colossal misstep on her part. She had just handed him the keys to the candy store. And if that were the case and there was the slightest evidence of arousal, she was going to kill him. Completely intrigued and unable to resist any longer, with Kelly moving farther down her back, Amanda picked up her head to sneak a peek in Chase's direction.

Chase wasn't looking at Bobbi. His head wasn't resting snugly in his oval pillowed face cradle while he enjoyed his massage, either. His eyes were glued to the pair of hands now reluctantly swirling over the skin on the small of her bare back.

And then he blinked and his eyes were on hers. Dark green peeked out from around fully dilated pupils as they bore into her from four feet away. Chase Walker was furious. He was practically vibrating in anger. She blinked at him, wide-eyed and apologetic, but he just continued staring. She couldn't bring herself to look away. A shiver started at her toes and worked its way up and out through the top of her head. As soon as he broke the stare, returning to watch Kelly move on to pulling at the blankets to reveal her full leg, unable to keep from torturing himself with the sight, she quickly placed her head back into her pillow.

"My glutes are tight, too, Kel." Amanda didn't know what possessed her to go into overkill, but she didn't see the point in being half-assed about it. He couldn't get much angrier.

"Too many squats at the gym?" Kelly laughed uncomfortably, the kind of stilted laugh that came from the discomfort of being watched. Chase wasn't making much of an attempt to hide it. Amanda thought how grateful he must feel that there were other people in the room, because she felt the same way. She wanted to warn him: If the behemoth on the table next to you makes any motion to rise, make a run for the door. She'd be right behind him.

"Stairmaster," Amanda murmured and she felt the cool rush of air down the left side of her body when Kelly folded the bedding so that nearly the entire left side of her body was uncovered. She could almost feel the stinging slap on her now-bare flesh that she was certain Chase itched to deliver. What she got instead was Kelly's normal, almost dainty hands by comparison, followed by his elbow and forearm trying to act as clinical as possible as the barely contained nuclear energy took over the room, threatening to suffocate them all.

Amanda kept her head in the face cradle, completely daunted by the glare Chase had given her. It was impossible to enjoy the massage, but she relaxed a little, resolved that even if the consequences were more than she'd bargained for, she had set things in motion and was prepared to accept them. The masseuses finished their legs in unison and Bobbi requested they both turn over before presenting her back and lifting the sheet and blanket to keep her client from getting tangled in the transition. Kelly had already turned around and lifted Amanda's, trying to hide the deep, centering breath he was taking. It gave them a moment of relative privacy, and she could feel Chase staring at her again the second he was given the opportunity. She afforded him the look, trying once again for apologetic, but probably overshot. Chase was leaning on his elbow, an eyebrow fully raised, his face otherwise impassive. He continued staring until she blinked; then he shook his head slowly and lay back down on his table. Amanda took a quick glance down at Chase's torso and gave a little smirk of satisfaction. His sheet and blanket were flat against his rock-hard belly; Bobbi's touch meant nothing to him.

Chase continued to watch Kelly massage his girl-friend, vexed but now also fascinated. He had calmed down considerably the farther Kelly got away from her behind, and now that they were on their backs, he could easily monitor the other man's hands on her shoulders. He looked detached, the sure sign he was comfort-able with his own firm resolution and willing to wait for its moment. He watched the hands rub her supple flesh in a way that suggested he had mentally replaced them with his own. He was engrossed with the swirling motion of skin on skin. Amanda began to do the same thing, watching him watching her, and soon envisioned it was Chase's powerful hands massaging her. Kelly's now felt limp and weak by comparison. She reached out her hand from beneath the sheet and blanket and extended it in his direction, longing for his touch. A moment later his hand was there, his fingers webbing with hers. His thumb gently played with each of her fingertips while her hand rested on top of his. They kept the contact while the massages continued, until Kelly sat at Amanda's head and began to massage her scalp, his fingers working up her neck and weaving deep within her hair. Chase's grip tightened on her hand, her fingers forced to drape over his now balled fist. Apparently, he considered her hair a sore spot and off limits as well. Eventually, he returned his hand back to his side, closed his eyes against it, and patiently waited for the hour to end. By the time it was over, everyone in the room had broken out into a sweat, all for different reasons.

"All done," Bobbi said, and Kelly's sigh that the ordeal was over was poorly contained.

"Is it possible for us to book another hour?" Chase politely got right to his point from his table, his eyes still closed and all the confidence that his request would be accommodated.

Following Chase's lead, Amanda remained on her table, but from half-closed eyes, caught Kelly looking desperately at Bobbi, shaking his head slightly but vigorously.

"I'm sorry, but we have other clients . . ." Bobbi began.

"That's okay," Chase continued pleasantly. "You did a great job, Bobbi, thank you. I feel completely relaxed. I was just hoping to take advantage of it, maybe take a nap, chat with my girlfriend. I'm really more interested in the room. And by all means, bill me for the extra hour, both for you and Kelly."

Kelly relaxed, thanked them, and vacated the room, telling them to have a nice day. Amanda bit back a snicker; he'd earned it.

"I guess that would be all right," Bobbi said hesitantly.

"If I don't see you back in here in thirty seconds, I'll go ahead and assume it is," Chase said smoothly, and Amanda stifled a shudder. He said it cordially, but it sounded more like he had just dismissed her, an unmistakable air of authority reflected in his tone. Bobbi was quick to respond and told them they were also welcome to wait at the fish tanks and she'd see them in an hour. If that was what he reduced a virtual stranger to, Amanda could only imagine what was in store for her.

The door quietly closed and Amanda continued to lie on her table with her eyes closed. Silence lingered and she strained to hear further movement within the room.

"Amanda," he said, finally breaking the stillness. He sounded almost amused. "It's time to face the music. Sit up."

Amanda opened one eye and looked over at him. He was already sitting on his table. She had never heard him move. He was stealthy, like all predators, silent while stalking. She sat up across from him, their knees barely touching, and tried to give him her best come-hither look in the attempt to soften his wrath.

"You are just about the naughtiest girl I ever met. What did I say about another man touching you?"

"That you didn't want me to talk about it?"

In the dim lighting of the spa room, she could see his eyes shoot out vivid green sparks along with the flash of white teeth when he couldn't keep from smiling. His shoulder and arm muscles were shiny from the oil used for his massage and they flexed while he allowed himself a single laugh before getting back down to business.

"Splitting hairs when you're in so much trouble? Do you really think that's wise?"

She didn't know if it was wise, but it certainly had been satisfying. Amanda averted her eyes to the thin door made mostly of bamboo slats. Surely he wouldn't try to discipline her here, not with a spa full of people all striving for serenity just beyond it. It was bad enough there were at least two employees with the impression that in the next hour there was likely to be some hanky-panky, which sadly was also unlikely. America's Golden Boy would never risk being called out for rutting in a suburban day spa.

"Just what were you trying to prove? Please tell me you at least had a plan?" He interrupted her thought process with the overindulgence indicative of a dominant man fully embracing his role.

"Of course I had a plan," she contended, sounding confident, which was easy as long as she was concentrating on the door.

The plan had played out in her mind that they would be forced to sit together in the secluded yet still public fish tank area, where she could sweet-talk him or further infuriate him as they lounged and rehydrated over glasses of ice water with lemon. Then after that, they would need to go get dressed, thereby giving her more time to let him cool off and she could offer to take him for lunch. Or she could get ready to hear the voice. Either way, by nightfall she'd be getting exactly what she wanted. But he had turned the tables on her. They were now alone in the same room, completely naked for the next hour. She may not have bested him at all. He had probably already formulated his course of action while watching Kelly go to work on her glutes. Now he was just going to toy with her.

"Look at me," he quietly insisted.

Her gaze drifted up his legs to his torso, stopping to quiver again at the sight of one of his huge hands, resting on the table alongside his thigh, the sheet draped casually over them. She knew all the things that one of those paws was capable of. Even his forearms were laced in muscle and bulk. His abs rippled up to the shelves that were his pecs. By the time she reached his neck, she had determined he resembled a Roman gladiator, having just finished a successful day in the colosseum. One who had slayed any opponent, man or beast, with nothing other than his bare hands; okay, maybe he'd used a stick. She briefly went back to the sheet, knowing full well it was barely covering what in her opinion was his most dangerous weapon. The thought alone was enough to set her pulse racing. She finally reached his eyes and tried not to gasp. His gaze was fixated on her, indomitable and burning.

"How long has this guy been massaging you?" Chase growled preemptively in anticipation of her answer.

"It's the first time," she said, feeling her bravado starting to go into a tailspin. "I've always used Bobbi in the past."

"Really?" Chase said blandly, in direct contrast with the vein on the side of his neck that was starting to bulge as his jaw clenched. He honestly didn't know which was worse. "So you did all of this just to wind me up and set me off?"

"You told me to give it my best shot," Amanda squeaked, all her nerve officially nose-diving.

"That I did," he conceded calmly, way too calmly. "Is it my turn now?"

Gulp. He wanted his turn now. He wasn't supposed to get his turn until later, much later, after he'd cooled down and they were alone. Not waiting for her answer, Chase removed his sheet and stood. Amanda watched his broad back and wonderful, tight buns walk over to where their robes were still hanging. He put his own on, tying the sash tightly before taking her robe off its hook and going back to her. Towering over her, he looked down at her and said quietly. "Stand up, please."

She immediately did as he bid, trying to bring the sheet with her, feeling both suddenly modest and now like she needed some sort of protection. He had to know the door didn't have a lock. He pulled the sheet away from her now-sweaty grip, placing it back on the table.

"What are you going to do?" she asked, trying desperately to keep from trembling.

"Arm, please," he requested, ignoring her question. She held out her arm and he slipped the sleeve of her robe on. He gently brought the rest of the garment around her, helping her into it, his concentration fully on the menial chore.

Then he pulled the sash from the loops on each side of the robe from one side until it was free and in his hands. He brought his eyes back up to hers.

"Hands together, in front of you," he commanded, no longer courteous or accommodating.

Amanda automatically joined her hands together. Chase took the sash and began to wrap it around her wrists. After wrapping it around them twice, he brought the ends together and held them in one hand, giving a little tug on them. He finally smiled.

"How you feeling about your plan now?" His voice was pure liquid devilry. Satisfied her wrists were secure, he released them. Then he walked back over to the door.

"I'd feel better if I knew what you were going to do," she confessed after hearing the *click*. The door had a lock after all.

"I'll bet you would." He chuckled, resuming his grasp and gently lifting the ends of the sash until her arms were suspended just over her head. He took a step closer to her, without actually making contact.

"As soon as I heard that guy's voice, I knew what you were about, although I couldn't believe it. You can take pride in getting the reaction you were looking for. Well played. I wanted to rip this entire room apart. And I think you should thank your lucky stars I don't have access to my pants, because I was seriously considering how great it would feel to take my belt off, but for now yours will have to do."

She failed at holding back the gasp this time and blinked up at him, no longer nervous but now increasingly excited. He was actually talking weapons; she had really ticked him off. A spa full of people was now the furthest thing from her mind; her thoughts were now all Chase Walker. She tried to lean in to him, her hands still over her head and he easily evaded her, maintaining full control by her wrists. He brought his mouth near her ear, again careful not to make contact, and whispered, "But then again, making me angry was your purpose for the whole exercise, wasn't it?"

She couldn't answer; she was focused on his warm gentle baritone, measured and rhythmic. She knew this voice. It was the one that made her crazy and usually ended in her rapture.

"Which leaves me with a real problem," he continued in her ear. "You've requested a very private punishment in a rather public setting. And because you control me, I have to give you what you want. And don't worry, angel, you may still get your wish." He then added, "Although I make no promises as to when."

What was that? Her pulse quickened again and she pulled her head away from his, trying to focus on him with wide eyes. Did he just say he *wasn't* going to spank her?

He laughed a little, wrapping another length of the sash around his knuckles, pulling her closer to him, still without touching her. "I forgot to mention, topping from the bottom usually backfires."

He waited for her to settle back down before whispering, "By the time I'm done with you, you're going to be begging me to violate you ten ways till Sunday."

Then he waited for the chill to pass through her before adding, "But until then, I'm not going to touch you. After all, your folks are members here."

He took a healthy lock of her hair and twirled it around his fingers, careful not to pull. "I love your hair. I'm taken by all of you, but your hair is second to only one other part of you. And although I consider even the tips of your toes mine, there are some parts that are more exclusive than others. Do you know what body part tops that list?"

Chase stepped back from her, lifted her arms a bit higher above her head, and his free hand dipped into her robe, softly grazing the underside of her breast with his fingers. He gently flicked his fingertip against an already taut nipple and he heard her breath catch deep in her throat.

"Okay," he said, low and husky, his hand moving to her other breast, lightly tracing a circle around it. "I may have lied about the touching, but you're still going to learn a little lesson about control. Come on, take a guess. What body part will you never ever share with another man again?"

Amanda had to lean back against the massage table. Between his hot breath against her ear, his hand committing a torture of the most feathery kind, and her arms still above her head, she was dizzy enough to actually faint. If it caught him by surprise, she could dislocate a shoulder when she became deadweight. That sort of embarrassment wasn't out of the question, as her history would dictate.

"I've taken the control, all of it. It's okay, baby, I've got you," he whispered before lightly biting down on her earlobe. His fingertips brushed faintly between her breasts and down over her navel. She pulled against the restraints on her wrists and spread her legs slightly apart in anticipation and he stopped.

"You may have traumatized a completely competent massage therapist out of his career. At the very least, you took ten years off his life. He looked pretty shaken up. You should feel bad about that." His fingertips danced a little bit lower.

"I do, Chase, I do. I feel like crying," she whispered, breathlessly exhaling the admission. All she had to do was tell him to stop and he would. She wasn't worried about his stopping; she was terrified he wouldn't keep going. His thick fingers made little spirals down and back up her thigh as they continued on their quest. When he passed lightly over her sex, it produced an all-consuming throb and she tried to trap his hand there by closing her legs. And he almost allowed it, but then denied her, returning to their quiz.

"That would be a logical guess and totally up there, but that one goes without saying. Try again."

He continued slowly swirling his fingertips around her thigh before coming to rest possessively on her behind. He gave it a little squeeze followed by a gentle pat.

"I think we reached the end of the riddle." She sighed softly.

"Ever heard the phrase 'You won't be able to sit for week'?" He asked offhandedly, squeezing again. "I almost want to put that one to the test."

And then he leaned into her. He was full and hard and it pressed into her stomach. He may have teased

her to the point of distraction, but there was no denying she had succeeded in arousing him as well, and he
wanted her to know it. With her arms still suspended
above her head, tight within the sash and his grip, she
blinked up at him.

"I certainly deserve it. I've been a very bad girl,"
Amanda said seductively. He let out a rush of air and
his sex pulsated against her.

"And you're so good at it," he ground out, releasing
her arms, which fell neatly over his head and around
his neck as he lifted her. His mouth covered hers just in
time to stifle her ecstasy-filled cry when he buried his
erection inside her.

Chapter 11

"Feel like taking a ride? There's something I want to show you," Chase asked Amanda rhetorically one afternoon after he picked her up at her apartment. The enjoyment in their road trips never waned. Moments alone midseason were precious and few. He didn't say anything more and they drove away from the city and headed northwest. They talked of the usual, how they'd spent the day, the chores they'd done. Amanda asked no questions and made no guesses as to their destination and Chase didn't give any clues, which had become their standard practice. Surprising each other was a contest, and not always about high stakes. Less than an hour later, they were off the highway and onto picturesque streets. At the intersection of what appeared to be a dirt road, Amanda saw a very familiar black Ford Expedition with tinted windows. Chase gave a haphazard wave in its direction and turned onto the unpaved trail, giving little thought to the damage the uneven terrain might cause to his hundred-and-fifty-thousand-dollar driving machine.

What has he found now? Amanda smiled to herself, wondering if they were going to spend a half hour marveling at some rock with a plaque near it that said George Washington rested a foot there. Chase loved history, the American Revolution in particular, and New Jersey was lousy with it. She had accompanied him to countless state parks and monuments, but he sometimes also went off the beaten path to lesser-known bridges and barns and battlefields. And it never ceased to amaze her how he could turn from a grown man to an enthusiastic juvenile whenever he encountered them. He took pictures of them with his phone; sometimes video. She recalled one of the rare times he'd pimped out his celebrity status after driving to a site that was now a private home. But the house had been meticulously preserved and was just too authentic for him to pass up. He had pulled in front of it, grabbed a signed baseball out of his trunk, and knocked on the door. And because he was Chase Walker, the proud if not surprised owners had spent nearly two hours giving them a tour. He listened and pondered aloud with the middle-aged couple over iced tea in a pristine garden what it must have been like to have been there, the trials and tribulations of the country's forefathers forging a nation. She had determined Chase really did have an old soul.

But it turned out they weren't on a road at all. They were on a driveway, a very long one. It was hard to tell exactly how long, because there were still acres of trees left to be cleared. It led to what Amanda could only describe as a castle. It was vast, complete with a round tower on one end, the kind that Rapunzel would've let her hair down from the top of. Only it didn't look dilapidated and historical. This particular structure looked brand-new. In fact, it looked like it was still under construction. The frame was sturdy and solid, the gray stonework completed, but the walkways were unfinished, much like the driveway. Landscaping had yet to be done. Chase drove up to the front of it and cut the engine.

"We're here," he announced happily while jumping out of his side of the car, practically skipping over to hers. He helped her out of the car and together they made their way to the front door. After opening it, Chase lifted Amanda up, cradling her in his arms.

"What are you doing!" she squawked, caught unaware.

"I know it's not finished and we're not married, but I'm not taking any chances," he replied with her securely against him. Then he crossed the threshold and entered the building before setting her down and closing the heavy ornate door behind them.

From the outside, the house looked imposing. From the inside it was immense. After catching her breath, Amanda looked up and around from the imported-marble-floored foyer where they stood. The ceiling was nearly fifty feet above her and there were two grand circular staircases at opposite ends of the foyer that led to the second floor. A large crystal chandelier hung from above her, patiently waiting for its final hookup to illuminate the entranceway. With the implication of his words when he lifted her up settling in, Amanda was speechless.

"Come on," he coaxed while taking her hand and enjoying her astonishment. "Take a look around while it's still daylight."

Chase began to lead her around the first floor of the expansive mansion. The walls were up and plastered, but most rooms were as yet unpainted. The windows were all installed but still needed molding. Random loose electrical wires were exposed and capped. This was obviously a project he had kept to himself for quite a while. They hadn't even been together a year yet. Either he started building this house the day they met, or he had a lot of people working around the clock.

"I'm leaving all the decorating here to you,' he announced excitedly when they reached the huge, empty kitchen, "since it's your specialty and all."

Amanda nodded mutely, still trying to fully grasp the situation.

Late-day sun streamed in from the sliding glass doors that ran the length of the back of the house. He chattered away enthusiastically about hardwoods and lighting and plumbing fixtures as they continued their tour of the first floor, which consisted of room after spacious room designed for dinning and entertaining, relaxing and living. Many of the rooms had an overhead walkway looking down from the second floor. He took her upstairs where six bedrooms awaited completion, including one in the tower, which was intended to serve as the master suite. It was private and set as far as possible from the rest of the house. It had two rooms plus a bathroom, and the closet was as big as her apartment. She counted seven full and three half bathrooms by the time she was finished with her tour, and they ended back on the ground floor in what resembled a full fairy-tale-style ballroom just beyond the foyer where they first entered.

"This is nothing short of a palace," Amanda finally said, taking note of the thirty-foot glass doors that went from floor to ceiling in the room and led out to acres of recently cleared land, waiting to be turned into gardens, pools, and tennis courts. "Fit for a king."

"And a princess," he added, grinning in the adorable way that made her heart race every time.

She stared at him blankly, once again words forsaking her.

"Mandy," he told her softly, squeezing her hand, "I'm building this house for you. For us."

"Seriously?" She laughed, embarrassed and giddy at the same time. She pulled her hand away and crossed her arms over her chest, stepping away from him, looking around again in awe. "This was a pretty big secret to keep to yourself."

"Well," he said by way of explanation, "you're always complaining about how everything in my apartment is made for a giant."

"I'm not sure this is the right direction." She laughed again, turning briefly back to him before returning her gaze out the doors at the magnificent view of the sun beginning to set. "If this is your solution to the problem, I think you may have missed the point."

"No, I didn't," Chase replied from behind her. "We're going to fill this place with Amanda-sized things."

She probably shouldn't have been surprised. The size of his apartment and everything in it had become a running joke, but she had never intended for him to take those comments to heart. She already knew he was good at keeping secrets, but figured he was done withholding anything from her. He was also thoughtful and enjoyed doing things in a big way. It was no secret he had money to burn. But this had nothing to do with money; he wasn't trying to buy her. He wanted to please her. Even if it was sentimental and completely extreme, any discord on her part was met by his immediate reaction to remedy it. It was both a blessing and a curse, the increasing responsibility to protect the image and the ego of an overgrown adolescent who also happened to be a phenom with a fetish. Chase snuck up behind her and wrapped his arms around her, leaning her against him and resting his head on top of hers.

"I thought maybe in a place like this, you could coordinate and throw some of our charity parties. You don't have to, of course; there's nothing wrong with the way they're being done now. But you ran that restaurant so well and you looked like you had fun doing it. You can involve me or not, totally up to you. I just always want you to feel like you have stuff to call your own."

Sometimes, there was just no bottom to his well of consideration. The suggestion alone brought on visions of summer barbecues and Christmas parties being thrown there. She pictured making him play dress-up and dancing with him in the ballroom, just like Cinderella. And he would do it willingly, because she was his princess. Amanda turned around within the snug confines of his arms, in a room big enough to land a plane, to tell him he really knew how to drive a point home about being a couple. But before she could comment, Chase released her and started to get down on one knee, his hand reaching into his pocket. Her glance caught something in the corner of the enormous room.

"What is that?" she asked, pointing in its direction.

Chase's gaze followed her finger for a second before turning back to her, his grin full-blown, and resumed what he was doing, kneeling down before her.

"That, my dear, is an air mattress," he answered before holding out his hands and clearing his throat. "And if you don't mind, I was sort of in the middle of something."

She noted the shiny silk sheet that covered it, the fleece blanket neatly folded up and resting on one end of the mattress and several pillows. But she also saw a brilliant sparkle catching her peripheral vision, the exquisite diamond solitaire he held firmly between his fingers. Amanda tried to sound light and casual as she held out her hand to him. All this was doing was making it official. But it still caught her by surprise, and the emotional buildup was unexpected. "We're sleeping here?"

"I don't know about sleeping," he teased, reaching out and slipping the ring on her finger. "But I'm willing to bet we'll be tired." He stood and took her back into his arms. He looked down into her face, playfulness replaced with tenderness. "From the moment I saw you, you've bewitched me. You drive me to distraction, your antics are exasperating. I can't think of anything better than spending the rest of my life jumping through hoops for you. You're everything I've ever wanted, in a woman and a friend. I love you, Amanda Cole, please tell me you'll marry me."

Amanda had barely finished nodding when his lips were on hers. She repeatedly murmured "yes" into his mouth until he silenced her by opening his wider.

"Chase," she protested weakly after being thoroughly kissed. "Probably a dozen people have access to this place . . ."

"Security is at the bottom of the driveway to tell any overambitious contactors they're getting the night off. And I'd almost pity the squatter who picked this particular time to trespass," he mused, before running his tongue lightly across her lips, then dipping inside. His hands drifted slowly down her back to settle on her hips. His thumbs hooked into the belt loops on her jeans and he gave a tug to ensure she was flush against him.

They took their time; after all, they had the rest of their lives. They slowly stripped down and rediscovered each other, this time from a standpoint of commitment and even ownership. He touched and tasted and drank from her with the only greed he'd ever be guilty of, the kind that would be satisfied only by the possession of her soul. And she gave it to him, because there was no one she wanted to have it more.

After they were spent, they rested in the corner of a drafty unfinished room, on a cold marble floor and an air mattress that had significantly less air after seeing some action. She lay across his barrel chest while he hogged the pillows and dozed. Amanda held up her hand and looked at the ring on her finger. The diamond was large, but stopped short of gaudy. Six square carats set within a diamond-lined band that glimmered in a dusk fast approaching darkness. Of course he went with the princess-cut stone. She had just agreed to marry the man who was named in *People*'s Most Beautiful edition, Bachelor of the Year in *GQ*. and one of *Forbes*'s Most Powerful Athletes, all before the ripe old age of thirty. She may belong to him, but he belonged to the whole world. She'd always have to share him, with the exception of his kink, the only dent in his Prince Charming armor.

He held her securely against him, his arm heavy across her shoulders. She listened to him breathing, deep and even. She watched him sleeping. With his eyes closed, the life force tucked away behind his eyelids, he looked so innocent and vulnerable. In the moment, he was content. But she wasn't. Something was missing. It was as obvious as the ring on her finger and the obligation she felt in committing to him.

He hadn't indulged in his kink this evening. Instead he had treated her like glass, fragile and with great care, despite his size and hunger. And because of it, her climax had been forced and unsatisfying and she couldn't quite release. She was sidetracked with waiting for it, anticipating it. Her nuances toward it were met with adoration until she had no choice except to respond. Chase Walker really did have total control over both her body and her mind. The balance was no longer even; maybe it never had been.

Because it meant she wanted it: the sting, the tears, and the dominance more than he needed to inflict it.

Translation: The flaw wasn't his, but hers. From the first moment she met him, she had unconsciously set out to provoke him, until she finally succeeded. She had tuned in to his vibe, or whatever he called it, all the while labeling it his shortcoming. She wasn't putting up with it; she was participating in it. And if that was true, that meant he had no flaws. If he had no flaws, then he really was perfect.

Perfect, a word Amanda learned didn't pertain to her. She wasn't allowed perfection. She was supposed to strive for it and then settle for everything just short of it. He was able to be all the wonderful things he was as long as she could rationalize that she was accommodating the one need in him he had a reason to be uncomfortable with. Once again, as soon as she began to view her life as a dream, it started resembling more of a nightmare. She hugged him tighter, afraid that with that realization he would disappear, or the roof would come crashing down and kill him and he'd be gone. In the stillness of the moonlit room, her mind began racing, and she began to shiver.

"You cold?" Chase murmured drowsily in response to it, reaching to pull the blanket up to better cover her.

"A little," she said, cursing that he was such a light sleeper. He could grab a fifteen-minute power nap, usually in a car or a plane, and not only be fully alert, but have the nerve to wake up looking refreshed. She prayed he would fall back asleep until she talked herself down. Hysterical drama was not how one was supposed to follow up a marriage proposal. But this would be about the time she would set herself up for the fall. In retrospect, she was surprised it hadn't happened already. Amanda squeezed her eyes shut tight, but tears slipped from between her lashes, falling onto his chest. As soon as he heard her tiny sniffle, he awoke fully.

"Baby, are you crying?" Chase asked, his voice laden with concern. "Did I hurt you?"

"No, you didn't hurt me." She sniffled again. *And that's the problem.*

He waited, readjusting the pillows before settling them back down. His hand reassuringly stroked her back and he quietly asked, "Then what? Bad dream?"

She could've lied and told him that she was overwhelmed with their engagement, but he detested lying and caught her every time she tried. "I noticed that we didn't do . . . that . . . thing we do," she choked out between fresh tears.

If she wasn't so upset, he would've started laughing. But he still couldn't keep from smiling. He began to sit back up, grabbing hold of her arm. "You want me to spank you? Come here, we'll take care of that right now."

He waited for her to play along, but she didn't. "No."

It wasn't the word itself that stopped him. Occasionally, while being particularly rambunctious and belligerent, she would say it ten times in a row. It was the way she said it. It was his job to know the difference. He let go of her.

"What's wrong?" he asked.

When she didn't answer, Chase adopted the tone. "Amanda, if you don't start talking to me, I'm going to give you something to cry about."

She couldn't tell if he was serious or just putting on the show. And then she couldn't decide which of the two choices she wanted to be the truth more.

"It's a pretty big night for us. I just sort of expected it."

"Well." The tone fell by the wayside and was replaced with a chuckle. "There's no real furniture here. I know you like those big production numbers."

She was grateful it was too dark for him to see her blush—something after all this time he still had the capacity to make her do. It was the buildup, the banter, and the threats that made for the excitement. She never confessed that to him, but he instinctively knew. And he seemed to enjoy bending her over couches, chairs, and counters almost as much as he did his knee. She had convinced herself that she was doing all of it for his benefit. His teasing served only to remind her that somewhere along the line, it had become more important to her than it was him. Even if it had crossed his mind, he decided against it, because he had the self-control she lacked. Her chin began to tremble and her voice shook. "This isn't supposed to be about me."

"You're right, it's not about you," he agreed. "It's about us."

This time he pulled gently on her arm, but it was to bring her to him and she began to cry in earnest. Amanda knew that he wasn't going to let the matter drop until he got the answer he was looking for, which was why she was suddenly so emotional. Chase held her head in his hands and brushed her tears away with his thumbs before kissing her. He lay back down, bringing her with him

"Remember our rule? You're not allowed to withdraw from me on this topic. Please tell me," he commanded into the darkness. And as she continued to weep from the safety of his arms, she spilled it all. The theory of the fatal flaw, the fact she wasn't supposed to have a happy ending but a comfortable, mediocre one and the deep-rooted desire for him to manhandle her while telling herself she was making a sacrifice.

Chase listened until she was finished, her speech ending with an all-cried-out sigh.

"Why does it have to be interpreted as a flaw in either of us?" he asked. "Why does this have to be anything more than a case of two people with the same tastes who were lucky enough to have found each other?"

"But I don't even do it right," she said, her voice still shuddering from her jag.

"There's a right way to do this?" He laughed.

Amanda pulled away from him and sat up, running her hands through her hair. Most of the time, his easygoingness was a treasure, but not now, when she was troubled and full of self-doubt. "You just don't get it," she muttered.

This time he didn't join her, but settled onto his side and propped himself up on a bent elbow. "What? That you love the action, but are bashful about the word? That instead of asking for what you want, you prefer to try to trap me into it? "

"I'm thinking about it all the time. And I'm the walking definition of topping from the bottom," she confessed.

Chase didn't need any light to tell she was truly distraught.

"Of course you are. That's what makes it all so fabulous for me," he said proudly. "You're a strong, independent woman who's fallen for a total male chauvinist who isn't above tossing you over his knee to prove the point. That's the best part. It's what makes it so much fun."

"From everything I read, it's not the way of things," she tried to argue.

"Maybe in some of these relationships it's a sticking point, but not with me. I'm bigger and stronger, that's just the fact. I'm going to protect you, even from yourself, because that's my role. And I'm going to be there to set you straight when you misbehave."

Chase didn't need to touch her for Amanda to feel his caress.

"And you let me, because you want what I have to give."

He wasn't talking about wealth or celebrity or prestige, though she'd get them by default. He was talking about stern scolding, sound spankings, and explosive orgasms. That happened to come along with hand-holding, castle construction, and countless romantic moments. And all of it combined into the most enigmatic man that ever found his way into her life.

"It makes you crazy when I withhold it. But I have to confess, it's pretty much the only weapon I have. I never expected you to enjoy it quite so much."

"You don't need to sound so smug and arrogant when you point it out," she said, and laughed weakly.

"I've got a hundred yes-men telling me I'm amazing on the daily. Sometimes I buy into the hype. Sue me." He grinned ruefully into the night and then stared at her silhouette in the moonlight. Her hair was tousled and cascaded down her naked back. He wrestled

THE SWEET SPOT · 213

between wanting her frozen in time and begging for there to be light so he wouldn't miss the smallest detail. She could feel his gaze and peered over her shoulder at him. She felt so beautiful when he looked at her that way. He was everything that had ever been said about him and so much more.

"I love it when you misbehave on purpose." There was the quick flash of white teeth from his smile.

She joined him on the mattress, leaning on an elbow of her own, and they were face-to-face.

"It just feels wrong to always go out of my way to make you mad."

"But that's what makes it all the more delightful; you only do it for me. You carry yourself so well all the time. Responsible and respectable to everyone you meet. You've taken my secret and made it your own. Everything I have belongs to you. You could be shopping. You could be vacationing or partying. Instead, you spend all your free time trying to piss me off in the most outlandish ways. You're so creative. You put so much effort into it, all because I opened up this new world for you. You're navigating your way through it."

Chase absently twirled a strand of her hair before neatly tucking it behind her ear, his fingers brushing across her jaw, then down her neck. He had so many different types of touches, and every one of them was comforting in their own special way.

He continued. "You flaunt our secret in front of the whole damn world and it's become our game. The way you work around my pet peeves is sheer brilliance. Heaven forbid you should just tell me you're in the mood. You'd rather slip your panties in my pocket right before a news conference, knowing I insist you sit in the front row when I do one. And wear a dress that's tasteful and just long enough to prevent me from completely blowing my stack. You sit there demurely with your hands folded neatly in your lap, surrounded by other people, usually men, looking remarkably proper. And the second I look at you, you cross your legs and wiggle in your chair ever so slightly, as if you're enjoying the fabric against your skin. But you and I both know it's not the touch and feel of cotton either one of us is thinking about."

Amanda suppressed a giggle. He was trying to pull off a lecture, but his voice was laden with affection and admiration. She moved closer to him, felt herself calming, and gave all the credit to his mere touch and his soothing, rhythmic timbre.

"Or when you were still full-time at the restaurant and you handed me a menu listing specials that you sure as hell better not have offered to any other customers."

She recalled his face as he sat at his table that evening, after she placed the menu in his hand and politely engaged Troy Miller and the Kings' outfielder, Sebastian Perry, whom she had seated opposite him. She stole glances in his direction and caught Chase's eyebrows raise, then quickly return to nonreaction after he opened the menu and discovered her printed inserted list of graphic sex acts, complete with an abundance of naughty words. It took him ten minutes to peruse his options before ordering his regular. Her defense that night, which she yelped from across his lap, was that she thought she wasn't allowed to *say* them. This time the giggle in her slipped out and she rested her forehead against his chest. He wrapped his arm around her.

"You've made this more about me than any woman ever has," he said with love-struck awe. "It's about you and me and no one else, even in a roomful of strangers. It tells me you're thinking of me as much as I'm thinking of you when it's inappropriate for us to show it."

"I hate having to share you," she conceded begrudgingly.

"Then maybe you only enjoy it so much because you know I do. And maybe you've embraced it because of the control it gives you over every other person who thinks they're entitled to a piece of me, as if owning my heart isn't enough for you, you brat."

He crooked a finger under her chin and brought her face up to his. She leaned her forehead onto his. In bed was one of the few places they could easily be face-to-face. Then Chase brushed his mouth lightly over hers before setting her back just far enough to let her know he still had something on his mind.

"Which leaves us with one other thing that needs discussing. What's this vendetta you have against happy endings?"

"Because it's my history," Amanda told him, trying to memorize his face in the darkness in case he began to fade away as she said it. "Because as soon as things start getting too good for me something awful happens. Every time I get too happy, I walk into a serving tray or fall down the stairs or am stricken with hives."

"We all run the risk of getting hurt," he told her.

"Yeah, but it happens to me only when I'm on the precipice of venturing out of my well-balanced comfort zone. Then look out, it's humiliation station."

"You shouldn't talk like that," he said reproachfully. "It sounds way too much like a self-fulfilling prophecy."

"It's okay," she said quickly in response. "I'm lucky and have a lot to be thankful for. But I see it for what it is. I'm used to it."

"Nobody should get used to settling," he stated firmly.

"Spoken by the man who has everything."

He paused before quietly asking, "Do you think I wanted to lose my father at twenty-four?"

Amanda was familiar with his macho posturing, his happy-go-lucky demeanor, even his anger. There was so much genuine sorrow behind the single question, a sadness that illuminated him in a different light. She'd been selfishly blinded by her own insecurities. Everything he had couldn't replace the one thing he had lost. She shook her head in response, and her hands crept around his neck. She hugged him tight. It wasn't a question that required an answer.

Chase didn't care if it showed as weakness. He didn't always need to be coming from a position of strength. Not with her. And her reaction was everything he needed to break away from their given roles and comfort him. It only reinforced what he already knew: She was the person destined to share his life. He didn't need money and he didn't need fame. Everything he needed was in his arms, showering his face with butterfly kisses.

They held each other for a time, lost in their own thoughts, before Chase said, "We can't be afraid to play the hand we're dealt, Mandy. Bad things happen. If you're happy when they happen, it's the very meaning of a well-lived life. It means you're not heaping misery on top of misery. We owe it to ourselves and our creator to make the most and sometimes the best of it. We only go around once. It's not a dress rehearsal."

Amanda knew he was, as always, speaking from the heart, and was fully aware of the advantages he'd been given. It also shed the final light on why she was so attracted to the brutelike side of him. If he was the one physically hurting her, then nothing else would have to, a fascinating paradigm.

"You're right," Amanda replied. "I'm sorry."

Chase held her face in one of his large hands and stroked her hair with the other. "You don't need to be sorry, baby. You just need to promise me you'll try to stop thinking that way. You're entitled to your happy ending. I'm here to provide it."

"I promise," she said without hesitation.

"We're a team," he said before lowering his lips back to hers.

Chapter 12

And so the King of Diamonds announced to all who were interested that he had found his queen, ending whatever speculation remained. Not a surprise. The pair had been inseparable for months. What did come as a surprise to many was his insistence that there be no prenuptial agreement. No matter who tried to talk to him about it, from his agent, Alan Shaw, to his lawyers, they were promptly shut down, with an accompanying threat that if there was any more talk of it, they were free to look elsewhere for employment. Those closest to him knew better than to voice their opinions.

Amanda was thrust into the spotlight and, viewing it a necessary evil, began to embrace her life in the fast lane, with the addition of having a wedding to plan.

And she was determined to stay true to her word and leave the negative thinking behind. It was easy to do with Chase beside her. He liked her close by, going so far as pulling her into most of his fan shots. He could manipulate any conversation and his polite requests were immediately met. They had professional pictures taken that were distributed for publicity. She gave up her anonymity and got used to strangers engaging her in conversation. He taught her that if she was nice about it, it was usually over quickly and painlessly.

But sometimes old habits are hard to break.

Amanda and her mother had an appointment with a highly recommended wedding planner. Catherine Cole was the strongest woman Amanda knew, with an innate elegance that Amanda strived to emulate, often feeling like she fell short. Catherine projected poise at all times, which always had Amanda double-checking to make sure she wasn't slouching when in her presence. It was the sort of easy refinement that Catherine could turn on a dime and use to tear down any witness without them even knowing it. She was soft-spoken and crafty, often a lethal combination when combined with a nice-fitting business suit showing just enough shapely leg. Amanda said little as she watched her mother apply the same tactics to the wedding planner.

The planner they'd met was one of the best in the business, but she just grated on Amanda's nerves. The overly made-up thirtysomething was too energetic and insanely enthusiastic, annoying traits that only intensified after she discovered who the groom was. Catherine was polite but direct, unaffected by the planner's increasing excitement, as they discussed all the best scenarios for her daughter's big day. After nearly two hours, Catherine did not confirm the woman had the job, but told her she would get back to her with a definitive answer within forty-eight hours. Then Amanda and Catherine left. They stopped for lunch before going back to Amanda's apartment to begin going over the pile of brochures about venues, food, and flowers.

"That planner lowered her fee," Amanda said, staring at the mountain of glossy paper on the table.

Catherine looked up from the catering-hall brochure she was reading. "Being able to say she handled your wedding is invaluable, from a business standpoint."

If she hadn't been raised by Catherine, Amanda would've thought she had just been reprimanded, but it was really just the tone Catherine incorporated when stating the obvious.

"Isn't it funny how that works?" Amanda said blithely. "Those who can afford to pay the most get the best deals?"

"One of the perks of being a celebrity, I imagine."

"She said Chase's name so many times she sounded like a commercial."

Catherine sat back in her chair and took off her reading glasses, a clear indicator she had already tuned into Amanda's inner turmoil. She studied Amanda, saying nothing.

"Guess I'm going to have to get used to that," Amanda said uneasily, under the weight of her mother's analytical gaze.

"Yes, you are," Catherine replied astutely. "Is that going to be a problem?"

"Of course not." Amanda lifted her chin and sat up straighter in her chair. She should've known better than to think she could put one over on Catherine Cole, not when it was one-on-one.

"That's good, because from here on out, you're going to be walking a tightrope." Catherine didn't mince words. "Your father and I were just discussing this."

"You were?"

"He seems to think you've lost interest in the restaurant."

Amanda's instinct was to deny. She had been wavering about the Cold Creek for months. But always in the back of her mind was the feeling that her parents would view selling it as the wrong choice. A foolish choice somehow equated with giving up all her rights and independence. And a slight against all they had done for her.

"We're both very proud of you." Catherine smiled slightly at Amanda from across the table.

"Maybe that's why I feel so torn," Amanda told her honestly. You didn't hide things from Catherine. She was an expert at getting to the truth.

"We were proud of you long before you started a business," Catherine said before leaning both her elbows on the table. "It's not easy being the wife of a successful man. Sometimes you feel as though you're lost in the shuffle. He gets all the accolades, but you deserve them, too. Behind every great man is usually someone who bolstered his ego when he needed it, watched him struggle in his rise to the top, often picking up the slack. When you're a wife that falls to you, often while having to multitask if you want to pursue your own ambitions."

Amanda listened quietly, folding her hands in her lap.

"But if you're partners with someone you love, you don't really mind. Both of you know you share the glory. After your father was appointed to the bench, he made sure he did everything in his power to support me in return. My success gave him the opportunity to reassess what he wanted from his own life. And now the cycle begins again. If he makes this senate run, I'll be the one standing beside him, doing my best to convince everyone I can that he's the right candidate."

"So you really can have both?" Amanda asked.

Catherine smiled. "You certainly can if that's what you want."

And in that one sentence, Catherine summed up the root of Amanda's problem. She didn't want both, but was scared if she picked one, it would look like she was throwing away the other. "What if all I want is to be with Chase?"

"I would say he's a nice something to want." Catherine laughed a little.

Amanda grinned. "I get the feeling being his wife is going to be a full-time job."

"Then make sure you do it to the best of your ability. We're very fond of Chase, Amanda. But this has to be what you want. He won't always be as prominent as he is now. And both your dad and I have the feeling his happiness is directly tied to yours."

"Sometimes the attention he gets is overwhelming," Amanda confessed.

"You can handle it. I raised you to be a strong woman," her mother told her confidently.

Amanda nodded her head and held back the giggle, wondering just what her mother would think if the strong woman she raised found some of her greatest pleasure in being spanked like a bad girl.

The coles were correct in their assessment of Chase. He wore his devotion to Amanda like a heart on his sleeve, sort of. Not quite as bizarre as his staunch refusals to even discuss a prenup, but close.

"What the hell is that?" Troy asked him in the locker room one evening in late August.

Chase quickly finished pulling down the undershirt he was in the process of putting on and muttered, "Shit."

"You got inked." A Southern boy's translation for *you fucking hypocrite.*

Chase was one of the last men standing in the locker room when it came to getting a tattoo. He steadfastly maintained he didn't personally have anything against them, except when it came to his person. He admired them on other players, but when it was suggested, Chase would laugh it off, promising that after he got his first surgery scar he'd think about it. The general consensus was he didn't get one because he thought he was so damn fly, he'd consider it a blemish. Or he was a wuss that couldn't take the pain.

"What of it?" Chase tried to sound confrontational, but it wasn't in his nature. He had gotten it in a spot that wasn't conspicuous, and with a few minor adjust-ments was able to keep it hidden for several days. He had gotten careless.

"Come on, man, you gotta let me see it," Troy pressed, determined to get a good look.

Chase rolled his eyes and lifted his right arm up, dragging his undershirt with it. It was along the top of his rib cage, hard to spot with his huge bicep cover-ing it if you weren't looking for it. It just happened to catch Troy's eye when Chase was getting dressed. Troy leaned in closer, confounded and amazed, not quite sure what he was seeing or how to react.

It was a peppermint stick, like you'd hang on a Christmas tree. At the top of it, where it curved to make the hook, were big blue Sailor Moon eyes and a full black mane that flowed to the middle of the stick part. The tip was made to look like a pert little nose and there were full, pouty lips to match. It actually sort of looked like her.

"It's really three-dimensional. I don't get it." Chase was sure Troy said it to force him into an explanation. Chase rolled his eyes again. As soon as he answered, the entire locker room would know that he was com-pletely whipped. It was something he considered before having it put there, but it didn't change his decision. He didn't care who knew how much he was in love. One way or another, he was about to take some ribbing.

"It's a Mandy-Cane," he said in the deepest voice he possessed, then blew it by blurting, "The sweetest candy on God's green earth."

Troy looked from the tattoo up to Chase's face, then back to the tat one more time, before standing and taking a few steps to create a healthy distance between them.

"Dude, I'm embarrassed for having just heard that," Troy said, like he might actually cut Chase some slack and keep his discovery to himself out of pity if nothing else. He raised an eyebrow and, keeping one eye on Chase in case he was about to get tackled, Troy announced to everyone within shouting distance, "Guys, look who finally got a tattoo!"

Most of their teammates wandered over to have a look. Opinions on its placement ranged from Chase wasn't willing to completely abandon his playboy status and didn't want to advertise by getting it on his bicep, to it looked like something a chick would get, like a Hello Kitty caricature.

All were in agreement that it was the corniest shit they had ever seen, because guys are like that.

Chase grinned, trying to keep his machismo from a full frontal assault and let them all speculate, wondering what kind of abuse he'd take if they knew it was placed there so she would always be close to his heart and secure under his arm, forever protected.

Amanda was waiting for him outside the locker room and together they went up to the clubhouse because Chase had been asked to mingle with some Japanese dignitaries and representatives from Nippon Professional Baseball, Japan's major league. It was a request specifically made to Chase in the hopes of ensuring the Kings' acquisition of Makoto Araki, currently Japan's brightest shining star. They ended up having dinner with them and the Kings' general manager, and it was several hours later before Chase felt for his car keys and remembered he'd left them in his locker after leaving in a hurry to escape the tattoo ruckus. He had dismissed his security detail since he wasn't planning to drink at dinner, so together he and Amanda strolled leisurely down the long tunnel to the locker room, hand in hand. She could never believe the difference in the sound level of the stadium after everyone was gone, the cheering done for the day, the music and vending stopped. It seemed unnatural, yet she didn't mind the quiet. He retrieved his keys and they slowly made their way back through the tunnel, out to the parking lot. The place was all but deserted, and Chase seemed pensive and thoughtful.

"Those guys from Japan seemed really serious," Chase mused, breaking the silence.

"How could you tell?" she asked teasingly. "They spent most of the time speaking to each other in Japanese. And sorry about the jeans. If you'd told me we were going out for dinner, I would've worn something dressier."

"That kid really knows how to hit," Chase thought out loud. "And he plays first base."

"Do I detect some sibling rivalry?" Amanda said, sensing a disturbance in his force. For the first time since his slump, he was voicing insecurity about his career. And he didn't use the mention of her jeans to make a smexy remark.

"Sure, they say they want to use him at third," Chase continued to grumble, not even hearing her. "But once he's on the field, there isn't a damn thing anyone can do about it."

"Why do you care where they use him? They could play you in the parking lot and you'd still be able to make the throw out at home," she said, trying to stroke his ego and thinking she'd done a good job, if she could be sure he was listening to her.

"Maybe they're going to make me the DH?" he said with a mixture of forethought and concern. It wasn't about collecting a paycheck. It was about having to sit on the sidelines.

"Babe, I think you're overtired," she responded, trying for intelligently playful. "You're twenty-eight. The designated hitter is for old guys and players who aren't effective on the field."

"Or they want to trade me?"

"Now you're just being ridiculous," she said sarcastically, hoping it might grab his attention. "No other team wants to be saddled with your contract."

"What if they trade me to Boston?" His eyes grew wide with horror at the thought.

Amanda was unable to discern whether or not he was listening and decided to make her presence known in a more bratlike fashion. Her method was to purposefully bump into him. Hard. It caught him off balance and he lurched several steps in front of her.

"What was that for?" he said dubiously, turning back to her after regaining his balance.

"So I could join the conversation. And snap you out of it. Do you hear yourself?" Amanda scoffed. "Trade you to Boston, that's just crazy talk. Even if they do trade you, what do you care as long as you get to play?"

Chase relaxed, feeling a bit foolish for having worked himself up. "You're right. Between the wedding and the house and trying to make the Wild Card, it's just a lot of balls up in the air at once."

She loved him most in his weak moments, when he left himself open and vulnerable. He let his guard down only when they were alone. Brief glimpses she knew wouldn't last. It wouldn't be long before someone wanted his attention. He couldn't be inaccessible and save the world at the same time. And she knew just how to ease him back into his comfort zone. Amanda smiled at him before taunting him further. "Of course, if they do trade you, the wedding is off. I could never marry a guy who plays for Boston. I guess I'll wait till after the playoffs to lock down a date. It would save me the trouble of divorcing you."

He recognized her brat voice when he heard it. His eyes narrowed fiendishly and he pointed a finger while stepping closer to her. "Oh, yeah? Care to venture a guess at what I'm going to do?"

Ooh. He went right into stern daddy mode, spanko foreplay. She took a step to meet him and wrapped a hand around his finger while poking him in the chest several times with one of her own, rewarding him with a pretentious eye roll. "You're going to stop acting like a baby, give someone else a chance to be a star, and get back to what's really important . . . which is me and our wedding." And then she laughed.

Her laughter was short-lived, however, when Chase took a quick look around, snaked his arm around her waist, and bent her in half, pulling her neatly to his hip. Her feet left the ground from sheer momentum and the wind rushed out of her. He released a volley of stinging swats in rapid succession to her denim-clad behind while she tried to keep from protesting too loudly. As soon as he stood her back up, she grabbed him by his jacket, hot and bothered. He gently pressed her to the wall of the long tunnel, and with his most devilish grin, brought his lips down to hers. When he finally pulled away, they were both all smiles, the thought of nearly making their antics a public display dangerously thrilling.

"That was excessive," she said, giggling at him.

"I know!" he said with boyish glee. "But did you hear it? It was echoing so loud, it was turning me on."

"You better hope no one else did," she reminded him.

"We're safe," he assured her. "There isn't anyone around for miles. But as soon as I get you home, I'm going to spank you properly."

"Then why are we standing here?"

Chase grabbed her hand and hurriedly began his race for the exit, practically dragging her behind him. But he instantly stopped when she planted her feet and gave his arm a slight tug. He turned to her and she wrapped her arms around his neck, rising up on the tips of her toes.

"Just to be clear, I'd follow you anywhere," she told him right before kissing him.

"I never doubted you, angel. Thanks for knowing just how to break a guy out of a funk."

And together they ran for the door, right past the tiny blinking red light hidden inside the innocuous small black sphere mounted on the ceiling above them.

Chapter 13

Four days later, Chase was lacing up his cleats at Kauffman Stadium, getting ready to warm up for playing the Royals. Another city, another road trip, and another three days of wishing he were home. He tried to look on the bright side. His bride had stayed behind, touring venues for their wedding, something that didn't interest him. He looked up from the bench he was sitting on inside the visitors' locker room as soon as he heard his name called.

"Walker! Coach needs to see you," the assistant coach called out from the doorway of the visiting team's management office. Chase finished what he was doing and hustled over to answer.

"You were looking for me, Coach?" Chase stuck his head in the open doorway.

Leo Bennett sat behind the desk, leaning back in his chair. He waved his hand, beckoning his star player full entry. "Come in, Chase. Shut the door and have a seat."

Chase immediately did as he was told, alert to the level of intensity that showed on the faces of Leo and the already seated assistant and batting coaches. He sat down.

The four men sat in awkward silence for several long moments.

"Am I getting benched?" Chase finally asked jokingly after looking from one unreadable face to the other.

The three remaining men exchanged knowing looks and what Chase could've sworn were sly smiles that were being held back. Leo cleared his throat and leaned both his elbows on the desk. He steepled his fingers over his mouth to hide the grin and tried to decide how best to tell the man he thought of as a son what he needed to tell him without laughing. He took a deep breath, getting ready to tackle the topic at hand.

"I just hung up with the front office. There's a situation back in New York."

Amanda was in her bedroom, finishing getting dressed for work, when the phone rang.

"If you don't get out of town, you'll ruin him," threatened the voice on the other end by way of a greeting. Amanda didn't need the caller to identify himself; the familiar skin-crawling, bile-buildup reaction was completely indicative of every conversation she had ever had with him.

"Who is this?" she asked anyway, just to antagonize him.

"It's Alan Shaw, the agent of the next disgraced athlete. Way to go." He spoke with such reproach, it instantly made her defensive.

"Alan, I don't know what the hell you're talking about, and how did you get this number?"

Another one of his slimy snorts echoed through the receiver. "Are you kidding, sweetheart? I know everything there is to know about you. While you were busy wrapping him around your finger, you forgot that he's one of those people who is constantly drawing attention. Now I'm left to do what you didn't, and that's try to protect him."

During the few times she was forced to endure him since meeting Chase, Shaw was always sanctimonious, always trying to leave her with the impression that there was some sort of inner circle that she would never know about. He had made it clear early on that he thought of her as a dalliance, and his view hadn't changed, but he was careful to conceal his opinion when forced into their company, which to Chase's credit wasn't very often. But now he had entered into her personal space, adding hostile, and Amanda was already tired of being bullied by him. She cradled the phone against her ear with her shoulder and finished putting on her pumps. "Stop speaking to me in riddles and get to the point."

"Get to the point?" Shaw shouted loud enough to make her eardrum vibrate. "I'll get to the point! At five P.M. my client and your fine ass are going to be the lead story on all the major networks. CNN and Fox may even beat them to it! You and your perverted little escapades are about to take down one of this country's most loved role models, how's that for getting to the point?"

Amanda could feel the hair on the back of her neck begin to stand on end as his venom flowed through the phone.

"What do you mean?" she rasped, all blood draining from her face, confrontational pretext gone. She closed her eyes and held her breath, praying he would say anything other than what she knew by his cryptic opening he was about to confirm.

"You know exactly what I mean." He brought his tone back down and it was now more of a hiss. "Does the tunnel under Kings Stadium ring a bell?"

The thought of Alan Shaw bearing witness to something so private was as repugnant as if he had been peeping through their window when they made love. As soon as she heard him say it, the bile in her throat became real.

"Yeah," he mocked her silence. "I thought it might. You can probably catch it on YouTube right now if you need a reminder."

She didn't need to be reminded. Her knees buckled, the bed breaking her fall. YouTube. She glanced over to her laptop on the nightstand and unsuccessfully willed it to blow up. Sweat began to bead on her upper lip and terror gripped her. "Does Chase know?" Amanda asked quietly, trying to keep her voice from shaking as badly as her hands.

She heard Alan take a deep breath, although it was far from settling. "I don't think so. Thank God he's on the field in Kansas City, and I can get a few hours head start. He still has a job to do, whether you know it or not."

"I'm going to call him—" Amanda began.

"No you're not," he cut her off abruptly. "I just told you, he's on the field. He can't answer. You're going to shut up, stop wasting time, and do exactly what I tell you."

"I'm not doing anything till I speak to him. He'll know what to do," she said aloud, mostly to calm herself.

"Know what to do?" Alan's voice started rising again. "He hasn't done anything right since he got mixed up with you. Making a damn fool of himself, following you around like some lost puppy. I don't know what kind of spell you've put on him, but don't you think you've fucked him up enough?"

The tears were in her eyes in a blink. No matter how much she despised Alan Shaw, there was truth to his words, and he was using them to his full advantage, throwing them in her face.

"How did you find out about this?' Amanda tried to sound focused and rational and not like she was about to start bawling.

"It's my job to stay one step ahead, something you obviously didn't think of," he scoffed, refusing to divulge his sources and opting instead to continue the verbal beat-down. "You would think with a family on the political fringe, you would be better at it."

Her careless actions would now also cost her parents. Amanda laid her head in her shaky hand to try to steady them both.

"It's not that bad." But her words didn't even convince herself.

"Oh yeah? How do you think Nike is going to feel when 'Just do it' becomes the catchphrase of wife beaters worldwide?"

"It's not even like that," she replied, filled with humiliation, a compilation of every kind imaginable.

"And I'm pretty sure it's not what AmEx has in mind when they boast about membership having its privileges," he spat out sarcastically.

"Alan, enough," she snapped, pushing against the wave of dread that was swelling with every biting word he spoke. At least having him to fight against brought out the last of her chutzpah and made her feel tougher. "You're not helping by berating me."

There was silence on the other end as Alan regrouped and tried a different tactic.

"And you're not going to help him by being here when this story breaks," he told her, still unsympathetic but marginally civil.

"But we're a team," she weakly parroted the line Chase faithfully told her, while glancing at the ring on her finger and feeling the dread wave cresting over her head.

"No, the Kings are a team, a team that's invested the next five years in him at great expense. And they're going to want to know exactly when their golden boy became a domestic abuse offender. You really want to be the one to explain it to them?"

Amanda shook her head to both clear it and answer the man she detested without having to confirm it with words. Words would've revealed that she was on the verge of a total meltdown.

He took her silence as the affirmation he needed. His voice became calculated and conspiratorial. "Here's what you're going to do. You're going to go on a little vacation, two weeks, maybe three. By then this thing will have run its course. You may want to lay off the television; speculation about your character will be flying fast and furiously. Stay off the phone and Internet, too. The fewer people who talk to you, the better."

For a moment, Alan sounded rational and like he really wanted to help, but she should've known better than to believe he had any of her interests at heart. If she wasn't so stupefied and worried about vomiting, she would have noticed just how premeditated his plan was.

"And you're to have no contact with Chase whatsoever." He said it as if he took perverse pleasure in knowing it crushed her.

"But why?"

"Because he's going to be pissed as hell, that's why." Alan's voice began to rise again, in response to her having the nerve to question him. "And he already can't think straight when it comes to you, as his lapse in good sense has already proven. He needs to focus on controlling the damage here."

Something in the logic didn't make sense, but Amanda's mind was racing with too many scenarios to break it down. And she was ashamed to admit it, but he was offering her a way out. He was not only giving her permission to run away, he was recommending it.

"You ready to stand next to him in front of fifty cameras and microphones and listen to him explain away your sex life?"

The thought alone was enough to make her gag. She flashed to a few particularly hateful comments she saw on social media since their engagement was announced. Faceless trolls who labeled her everything from fat and unworthy of their hero to a gold-digging slut. It was nearly as repugnant as the comments from men who freely speculated on exactly what Chase saw in her.

Shaw went in for the kill. "Or maybe withstand a sneak attack of paparazzi? Not only are they not known for their couth, but you know he's going to defend your honor. He can add an assault charge to the list of bullshit."

The dread wave crashed down upon her.

"He'll find me," she gasped on the last gulp of air before she started to drown in panic and degradation and sadness.

"He won't have time to look," Alan quickly replied, trying to downplay the victory and get her in motion. "I'll text you when the coast is clear."

"He's going to be furious," Amanda whispered brokenly.

Alan Shaw finally laughed. It was as cold and harsh as he was. "When this is all over, he can give you a good spanking." And then he was gone.

Oh my God, she thought, *he actually said it*. She swallowed another round of shame and revulsion. When Chase said it, it was passionate and erotic and tantalizing. To hear it coming from Alan Shaw, it was tainted and depraved and warped.

In Amanda's mind, it was already all over, her fairy tale, the love of her Prince Charming, and even her previous life as she knew it, back before she met him. If it was only going to be half as bad as he made it sound, it was going to be unbearable. She stared at the phone in her hand as it went from silence to dial tone and ultimately the high-pitched scream designed to alert that it wasn't hung up. She pushed the Off button and threw the phone on the bed as if it were covered in poison.

You'll ruin him.

She hugged herself and began to rock slowly, her eyes darting wildly around the room. She spied the television and her stomach cramped. It was no longer just about ruining it for herself.

She wanted to go on automatic pilot and finish getting ready for work, but her legs refused to lift her.

How was she supposed to go about the mundane business of applying mascara when she couldn't even bear to look at herself in the mirror? How in heaven's name was she going to walk into the Cold Creek and face her customers, or worse yet, her employees?

And worst of all, she knew there was no way for Chase to protect her. He was states away and maybe it wasn't far enough. She had tempted and teased him knowing full well he couldn't resist her. The result was that she had single-handedly revealed America's Golden Boy as some sort of sadist. The one thing he specifically said he wanted to keep to himself. What had started as a romantic interlude was now a travesty. She would call his reputation into question all because she was too immature to control her jaded tastes in public.

Her phones began to ring. And ring, independently and then simultaneously. She remained on the bed, unable to rise, unable to move, just staring at the dark screen of the turned-off television. Her imagination ran amok with what would be happening if she were foolish enough to turn it on. Minutes turned to hours and day to night before she pulled herself off the bed. Halfheartedly hoping her manager showed up to work, but not really caring if the place burned down, she picked up the phone. The tone that indicated she had messages sounded. It wasn't until she dialed her code and heard that she had sixteen messages that she hung it up, unable to cope with any of it. Her cell phone was beeping like crazy, and she weakly lifted it off the table and returned to the bedroom, lying down and curling into a fetal position. She saw that Chase had called ten times. There were multiple text messages. With shaking fingers, she dialed into her voice mail.

"Honey, call me when you get this message." The inevitable change was already taking place. He sounded apprehensive. And he always called her "angel" or "baby." Calling her "honey" sounded grown-up and forced. It only proved Shaw's point that Chase was operating from outside his element.

Followed by: "Amanda, where are you? I really need to speak to you. The Cold Creek says you haven't shown up. For God's sake, call me."

Next was: "It's me. I sent someone by your place; they say they got no answer. You're starting to frighten me. Please, if you won't call me, call someone. Let them know you're all right."

Then there was a message from her mother, her attorney, the Cold Creek twice, Nicki and her father, all asking her to call them right away, but saying nothing more. They were all embarrassed for her, refusing to even touch on the real reason they were calling. Tears streamed down her face. How could she ever face any of these people again?

And finally: "Listen, honey, I know you're freaking out, I just know it. This is going to blow over, trust me on this. I know it seems awful right now. I'm mad as hell, too, but this is nothing more than the product of a slow news day, you'll see. I love you, Amanda, we'll get through this. Together."

If there were any other messages, she didn't bother listening to them. Her tears had turned to choking sobs and she hugged herself until she fell asleep, praying for two things: that Chase was right and an ax-wielding psychopath would go on a rampage to grab the headlines.

But it wasn't forgotten. It only got worse. When Amanda struggled to open her eyes the next day, still swollen from crying, she lay there for a few seconds, confused, until the memory came rushing back. Still in her clothes from the day before and her mouth dry, she dragged herself up and padded to the kitchen to get a drink of water. She felt detached, scattered, and desperate for the normalcy of the day before. Before she picked up the phone and once again Alan Shaw made her life turmoil. Too afraid to turn on the television, she opened the front door, mostly out of habit, and retrieved the daily newspapers she received for the nights when Chase slept over and to check for ads that she ran, keep up with her stock holdings, and any pictures of him. What greeted her was the front page of the *New York Post*. In bold letters, complete with still photo, was the headline:

WALKER HAS LAST WORD . . . ALWAYS

If she hadn't been so mortified about her backside looking like the cover shot of some tawdry porno, she would've patted herself on the back. Her current workout program with Logan had really paid off. And the jeans were a good choice, after all. A dress hiking up would've been the only way it could've been worse.

And not to be outdone, the *Daily News*, while not having a front-page photo, had the headline:

WHY COLD CREEK SHOULD CHANGE ITS NAME
TO HOT CHEEK

As new tremors began to rack through her body, Amanda reached for the phone. Before the new tears completely blurred her vision, she did the only thing she could think of.

She dialed her father.

When Rupert Cole walked into his daughter's small eat-in kitchen, he did a double take. Amanda was barely recognizable. Her eyes puffy and her face pale, she sat at the table, the newspapers spread out in front of her, all opened to either stories or pictures or both. Even the *New York Times* had a blurb about it in the sports section. He was almost afraid to touch her. She looked so fragile. He opted for scooping up the papers and making his way to the trash. He waited for Amanda to turn red eyes to him before dumping them in the garbage.

"It is these people's jobs to sell papers. Celebrity sex scandals do that job nicely." He dropped the papers in. Going to the fridge, he poured two glasses of orange juice and came back to the table, setting one down in front of her and taking a seat. He waited patiently for her to take a small sip before quietly saying.

"A lot of people lost sleep last night because of you. Thanks for texting your mother that you were just ignoring everyone." Catherine Cole was the only person who sent a message that Amanda answered. It was perfunctory, asking only if she was in physical danger, and she didn't text again after Amanda's two-word response: *rotten night*. Amanda wouldn't lie to keep up appearances for Catherine, who would be the first to agree. Her daughter had found herself in a rather unpleasant situation. She would rationally tell anyone who inquired that her daughter wasn't taking calls, and give them all the space needed to digest the information. Alerting the police would only garner more unwanted attention. Amanda sent the text right before falling into a sleep that was like a body shutting down, unable to process one thing more.

"I'm sorry. I should've sent it earlier."

"Amanda, does he abuse you?"

"No, Dad," she denied quickly. "It's nothing like that. We were just fooling around." Here it comes, the next in her series of awkward conversations. How do you talk about sex with a father who still maintained babies were brought by storks? Not that it mattered one way or the other. Her secret was out.

Rupert believed his daughter and didn't want to make it any harder on her. "Look, pumpkin, I know that you never bargained for anything like this when you and Chase got serious, but I really think that you might be making more out of this than there really is." Rupert finished the contents of his glass and leaned back in his chair. "For Christ sake, they spend all day slapping each other's asses, so this is really no surprise to me or anyone else."

Amanda let out a laugh in spite of herself. It was a moment of normalcy. Then her chin began to tremble, and she looked at her father with the saddest eyes he had ever seen.

"I probably ruined your chance for a career in politics," she murmured, tears brimming in her eyes again.

"I was only considering that anyway." Rupert chuckled reassuringly. "But now I'm probably going to get real pressure to be on the ticket. People are so funny about the bandwagons they jump on. And I think I need to remind you, you weren't alone in this."

"What am I going to do here?"

"Well, if it were me, I would have been at the restaurant last night buying rounds for the house every time they aired it." When he got another little smile, he went on soberly, "But I can't tell you what to do here, kiddo. What I can tell you is that I support whatever you decide to do. Do nothing, spank him back, write a book, kill him, it makes no difference to me. But I do know one thing, the longer you let this eat at you, the longer it will stay an issue in your life. What's done is done. There is only so long you can keep your head in the sand."

"I know, Dad, I know." He was right and she knew it, but it was little comfort this morning.

"You don't live in Nebraska. You're not getting ready to marry a dairy farmer. You live near New York City and your fiancé is a famous pro athlete. These things come with the territory." He went on, wanting to see her reaction. "You know, he called the house last night, frantic. Your mother spoke to him, but I'm not sure it helped. You really should have called him."

"I can't face him, I just can't." She exhaled pure misery, crossed her arms on the table, and laid her head on them. She held back from telling her father about the conversation with Alan Shaw, mostly out of disgrace. When all was said and done, this was her fault, and it was breaking her heart in two. "I don't think I can face anybody right now."

While he was hoping Amanda would do the right thing, dig her heels in, he knew it was a lot to ask. Her fighting spirit was on hiatus, somewhere gathering strength. Rupert already knew more than he wanted to about his future son-in-law, and his main concern was the happiness and well-being of his only child. He waited only a moment.

"Senator Warren just remodeled his summer home in North Carolina and was hinting around about looking for a fall or winter rental. He hates that the place is empty. Maybe it would do you some good to take a break from all of this, go someplace quiet and get your head together."

Amanda picked her head up. "What about the Cold Creek?"

"Don't worry about the restaurant, pumpkin. When you hired Liam, you made a good call. I'll do what I can to help things along." He stood, walking to the door. "You go pack. I'm going to make a few calls. You can be there by nightfall."

She stood and practically ran to her room. "Thanks, Dad, I love you."

"I love you, too. But, Amanda." She stopped short and turned to meet her father's compassionate yet firm gaze. "Remember what I said. The longer you hide, the longer it takes."

Chase got out of his car, shut the door, and took a deep breath. Squaring his shoulders, he strode purposefully right to the Cold Creek's front door. The restaurant would not be open for several hours, but most of the staff would already be there, getting the place prepped. He had been calling Amanda every hour for days, unable to stop himself from dialing. As soon as he returned home, he started going by her darkened condo all hours of the day and night, with no sign of her. The presses hounding him had finally begun to die down, and he was beginning to feel like enough was enough. He was leaving for an eight-day road trip and determined to see her before he left. Someone in there knew where Amanda was, and he wasn't leaving until he found out who.

What he found was Rupert Cole. He was sitting at the bar, going through the mail, when he looked up and saw Chase standing in the doorway. He waited for his approach before giving him a gruff nod. He knew it was only a matter of time before the boy came here looking for her.

"Chase," Rupert said curtly.

They sized each other up. Rupert was smooth, polished, always prudent, never raised his voice. Chase wondered just what the man knew, what Amanda had told him, and how he felt about it.

"I need to find Amanda."

Rupert's expression remained impassive as he studied his would-be future son-in-law. "I have to give you credit. For someone who's caused so much havoc for my daughter, you certainly aren't afraid to step up to the plate."

"I love her beyond reason. I can't begin to tell you how sorry I am about this," Chase told him, shaking his head before looking uncomfortably away and down at his shoes, shuffling his feet. It was a gesture so genuinely humble and full of remorse, Rupert had to take a second to remember that who he was dealing with was not only a grown man, but an influential one.

"Let me just start out by saying, if I thought for one minute you hurt my daughter, there is no one on this planet who would be able to save you. But Amanda assures me that's not the case, and I believe her. That having been said, I'd still like to know how the hell this mess happened."

"Some scumbag from the stadium's security department caught it on a hidden camera, looped it, and peddled it to some gossip rag. He's been fired, the Kings are pressing charges, as am I, but I'm afraid the damage has been done."

Rupert got up, went behind the bar, and poured himself a scotch, offering one to Chase, which he politely refused. "Ah yes, the damage. You know, Chase, when it became apparent that you and Amanda were becoming serious, the hardest thing for her to cope with was the constant attention. While I'm sure you have been used to it for quite a while, it was all new to her. Her privacy was something she didn't want to give up. But she always maintained that you were worth it, and the more we got to know you, the more inclined we were to agree." His eyes took on a wistful look, as if he were recalling a time long ago, and he went on. "You know, in all of her life, there was only one time I spanked Amanda. Funny, I can't even remember what it was for. But I will never forget the look on her face when it was over, those big sad eyes so bewildered. I could tell that she wasn't able to reconcile the love with the pain. I knew I would never be able to spank her again. But she was a good girl, and lucky for us both, she spared me ever having to agonize over that choice again." He came back to the present and the corners of his mouth turned up ever so slightly. "Her mother, however, is an entirely different matter. There has been more than one occasion when I thought a good old-fashioned spanking would have benefited her immensely." He gave Chase a little wink, and the tension eased between them.

"I have seen the footage," Rupert concluded diplomatically. "And it didn't look like she was having too much trouble with reconciliation."

"You know where she is, Rupert. Please tell me."

The man took on a look of true compassion, laid both his hands on the bar, and waged the battle of the decision.

"Look, Chase. I like you. You're a good kid. Do I think Amanda is making too much of this? Yes, I do. Do I think the longer she stays away, the bigger she makes the problem? You bet. But only she can decide how and when she can make peace with this. She was always so concerned about doing the right thing, making a good impression. I love her with all my heart, and her happiness is my only concern. I can tell you that she's been in touch and that she's safe, but I'm sorry, son, I can't tell you where she is."

Chase's shoulders slumped, dejected. He understood Rupert's hidden message. He knew exactly where his daughter was. The last road to Amanda had effectively been blocked. He stood up and made his way out the door. He still had a game to play. The one constant, where he still felt in control and at the same time could take a break from the calamity his life had become. He needed to leave it all behind and get back on the field. Before he got to the door, he heard Rupert's voice, in a tone that reminded him of his own father.

"Hang in there, Chase, she's worth it, too."

He went back to his car, pounded the steering wheel until the horn went off, and let out a broken sigh.

Chapter 14

Amanda sat alone on the nearly deserted beach. September in the Outer Banks of North Carolina brought with it a certain measure of seclusion, especially midweek. Families were sending children back to school but would return for the weekends to grab the last remnants of summer. Other seasonal houses were boarded up and battened down in the hopes of withstanding any potential storms. The remaining full-time residents randomly roamed the beaches. They all politely greeted Amanda in passing when they encountered her and returned to going about their business. At least she stopped thinking in terms of every interaction as an aspersion cast upon her. It was a relief. She had been wearing her guilt as a mask that she couldn't take off. Every person who crossed her path became her judge, jury, and executioner. Even the feeding gulls and egrets sounded like they were laughing at her. Every trip to the supermarket was an exercise in how to handle a panic attack. Amanda felt she had made great strides by refusing to give in to the voice in her head telling her to wear a wig, but she did don a hat and sunglasses. It took her at least five days to get over the feeling that she was constantly being watched or followed. But she never walked with her head down because that just wasn't in her nature. She may have been beaten, but she wasn't broken. Or was it the other way around?

Now, two weeks later, Amanda occupied her same spot in the sand, her knees up and arms wrapped around them. She watched the changing of the tide, wave after wave washing onto shore, cleansing the beach. If only the waves of her varying emotions could be so dependable. She tried to assume a pose conducive to meditation, as she had every day she claimed her spot, but it was still a waste of time. She started with the best intentions; was sick and tired of being sick and tired. It was time to think on the matter logically and rationally. It didn't take long before she was daydreaming, reliving, and rehashing.

The first week had been the worst. Like a rubbernecker unable to keep from looking at the crash despite the severed head rolling across the road, when she got to the spacious, airy house, she immediately turned on the television. With a false sense of security created by the distance between her and New York, she surfed the channels, tearing her eyes away only when the actual tape was being shown. But then she found herself searching it out, not to watch a careless moment forever memorialized, but to see him. And see him before her reckless disregard for his reputation ruined it all for both of them. But there were way too many brief glimpses of him coming in or out of his apartment surrounded by security, unsmiling and dogged. She was grateful she didn't have access to his games. Either he would appear cheerful and not tortured like she was, which would cut her to the core, even if he was acting. Or he would be disturbed and his numbers would show it, and then she would know she had managed to destroy the only other thing he'd ever loved.

It all happened in real time and at lightning speed. There were the jokes and the debates. Late-night shows always made some sort of reference, and while a few of the suggestive and subjective one-liners actually made her laugh out loud, the humiliation far outweighed the moments of humor. Talk shows all weighed in on whether Amanda has single-handedly set the feminist movement back decades or if Chase was really the devil in disguise. The one thing she and Chase had wanted to keep to themselves was being slowly dissected like some sexual science project. After hating to admit she should've listened to Alan Shaw, she finally turned the television off for good after a day. She had stopped calling into her home voice mail, as the calls from the bizarre left her equally violated. It was amazing just how many people were able to get her number. Kinky crackpots, S&M magazines asking for interviews, the list went on and on. Her number would be changed by the time she got back. She kept her cell phone off, but turned it on intermittently to read and ignore every text and listen to, then delete each voice mail. The message from Alan Shaw never came.

Chase only called once, about a week into her self-imposed exile. His message had been heartbreaking. Even though he sounded as bad as she felt, she read the single attempt to reach her as proof he was more concerned with repairing his image. In contradiction, he sounded like a forlorn child trying in vain to win back the approval of a disappointed parent, which only made her more depressed and confused.

"Mandy, this has been so hard to do without you. Alan told me about your little vacation. But I just wanted to let you know, everyone else has moved on, it's yesterday's news. I know you're mad at me, I get it. And I hope this isn't about me punishing you. You can f-bomb me till the cows come home, but you have to do it in person. You're killing me here. I won't bother you again."

She saved that message, played it over and over again, until the tears were blinding. Now she listened to it for the last time, and when it finished, the only sound she heard was of the methodic, pounding breakers as she sat alone on the beach, all cried out, with nothing but the memories of what she had had and what she had lost.

She leaned back in the sand, looking at the gray sky with its accumulating clouds and recalled their last time together, when she was foolish enough to think she was allowed to believe in fairy tales . . .

As soon the door was closed to his apartment, Chase grabbed her around the knees and upended her over his shoulder, bearing her down the long hall to his room. After placing her back on the floor, he sat on the bed, pulling her between his legs. His eyes glued to hers, he expertly undid the button of her jeans and pulled them down. She stepped out of them, gave him a slow, lingering kiss, and with his help, laid herself over his lap. With his index finger, he hooked her panties in the middle and ever so slowly pulled them down, his finger trailing a line down the cavern that separated her round cheeks, tickling her.

The sensation still so vivid that even as she lay in the sand, she couldn't help but wiggle. He adjusted her panties to right below her backside, framing it. And then she held her breath and waited. The first slap was always the hardest, and it took her a while to figure what he was about. He wanted to admire his handiwork.

He would look at her bottom, trying to find the right spot, and bring his hand down hard, enough to take her breath away. His objective was to leave a perfect print against her skin. Sometimes it worked, sometimes it didn't. He would never do it twice, and if it wasn't what he wanted he would give an exasperated "humph," but if he got his desired effect, she could swear she heard him purr, and he would take a few moments to appreciate the sight, at times even tracing the outline his hand created on her soft skin. He found his sweet spot that night, and she relaxed, readying herself as he marveled. She knew when he was going to get down to business by the slight pressure he created at her waist as he held her in place.

He knew how much she could take and always gave only slightly more. There had never been a safe word between them; it never occurred to her to ask for one. She turned herself over completely to him, guided by faith and love that he would never go beyond what she could endure. His hand rained down over and over, precise and effective, until the heat began to rise, her wriggling turned to kicking, and finally the release of all her control. But she'd better not start crying, because her crying was something he couldn't take for long even if it was brought on by euphoria.

"Do you promise to be a good girl?" he asked authoritatively, but with the distinct undercurrent he knew she was as good as it gets.

"I promise, I promise," was her sob-filled response. The first one said in response to his question, the second for all the things he would ask of her in the future.

He stopped spanking her, waiting only a moment before lifting her back up, and while she tried in vain to rub out the burn, he kissed away her tears, murmuring words of love, telling her over and over again there could never be another, his own eyes becoming glassy with emotion.

They tore at each other's clothes, buttons flying and material ripping in the effort to feel the other's skin against their own. He lifted her again and impaled her in haste with this throbbing sex, his hands on her hips. She rode him slowly, savoring each and every thrust. He hugged her so tight, she was afraid he might break her ribs. And as he climaxed deep inside her, her name became his song. She followed right after, her spasms his reward as they both collapsed on the bed, over-whelmed by the intensity of it all.

There were no words to say. They took each other in, the unspoken declaration of love shining brightly in the room lit only by the light from the hallway. She couldn't remember who finally gave the stare up to sleep, but it was almost as if fate was giving them this last time to hold on to.

Now all that was left was the memory.

Amanda continued to lie in the sand with her eyes closed even after the first drop of rain landed on her face. The day had started out overcast, the wind had started to kick up, and a storm was likely to hit the coast by nightfall. But she wasn't ready to leave the daydream yet. As soon as she opened her eyes, it would disappear, and instead of being in Chase's arms, she'd be alone again, on a beach with only infamy to keep her company. She'd have to return to the quagmire of regret and self-loathing she'd been stuck in for weeks without an end in sight.

Dear God, please help me.

Another drop hit her forehead, followed by a gust of something, but it didn't smell like salty sea air. Amanda opened her eyes and two big brown eyes were staring back at her. She was nose to nose with a golden retriever with an apparent slobbering problem. One that she never heard approach to investigate her as she lay in the sand reliving the last time Chase took her and she dared to believe in storybook endings.

She yelped in surprise as she struggled to sit up and the dog jumped back several feet into the sand, as startled as she was. It began to wag its tail from its spot several feet away, its hind end up in the air and leaning on its front paws. The two regarded each other closely and the dog barked.

I'm going to be mauled by a wild dog, that'll be a new one, Amanda said to herself, thinking that it was about time she somehow got hurt physically. Her penance would be that for all eternity, she would get hurt just thinking about him. It was actually a comforting thought, being put out of her misery.

"Bingo! Bad dog!" Amanda heard the reprimand from above her, and Bingo took off toward it.

The voice belonged to a woman. A woman Amanda had seen before who was now heading in her direction. She looked to be in her seventies and slender, wearing denim capris, a tank top with an opened button-down shirt as a cover-up, and white Keds canvas slip-ons. A big floppy straw hat covered her pulled-back gray hair.

"Sorry about that," the woman said jovially as she joined Amanda.

"That's okay," Amanda said. "He just surprised me."

"He's harmless, but thinks he's a cadaver hound," the woman continued, and Bingo ran around her twice before bounding toward the water. "I know he should be on a leash, but by now it's usually locals. Mind if I join you while he takes a swim? He can't resist the sea foam that comes with the storms."

"Not at all," Amanda eagerly replied, thinking the timing couldn't be better. Her own voice had begun to sound foreign.

"I'm Gertie," the woman introduced herself as she gingerly sat down in the sand next to Amanda. "I think we're neighbors. You're in the Warren place, no?"

"Mandy," Amanda said guardedly and with a stab of melancholy. There was only one person who ever called her Mandy, the final time he did was still fresh in her mind and saved on her phone. But she was supposed to be incognito. Small talk itself now presented a challenge. "I'm visiting."

If Gertie sensed Amanda's hesitancy, she didn't let on. "You picked a good time if you're looking for peace and quiet."

"Hmmm," Amanda agreed absently, trying to figure out if Gertie mentioned peace and quiet because she recognized her. She had been sitting in the same spot every day, even before the crowds thinned out. Having to second-guess every conversation for the rest of her life was going to be arduous.

They both continued to look out at the horizon, watching Bingo running along the shoreline, occasionally playing in the surf.

"This one's coming in from the east," Gertie said matter-of-factly.

"Should I be nervous?" Amanda asked.

"I don't think so," Gertie said reassuringly. "I haven't floated away yet, and I've been here for fifteen years. They did have to drag me out during Hurricane Ophelia back in 2005 when I missed the evacuation warnings. I don't watch much television."

Amanda felt as if she'd been touched by an angel. Another random comment sent at a most opportune time. They wouldn't be talking television. Her tension started to ease.

"That must have been harrowing," Amanda said.

Gertie snorted with good humor. "Not really. I enjoy riding out a good hurricane. I think in my next life I'd like to be a storm chaser. I did feel bad about putting all those first responders at risk, though. Now they just call to make sure I'm okay and tell me if it looks like leaving is the smart choice. The locals are pretty tight-knit here."

The sky got darker, and Bingo ran from the ocean and back to intermittently check on them. He was wet and full of sand and Gertie didn't seem to care.

The more she talked and Amanda listened, it appeared there wasn't a whole lot that Gertrude

Millicent Bach got worked up about, ever. She had moved to the Outer Banks after retiring from her job as a labor room nurse and coming into a healthy inheritance from her mother.

"My mother was years ahead of her time," Gertie said. "She up and left my father back when those things were seriously frowned upon. She was a real trailblazer. Moved me and my two brothers to a new town, started her own seamstress business, and taught us all to think for ourselves. It's probably why I never married. I was having so much fun blazing my own trail, I didn't want anyone getting in the way."

"Any regrets?" a fascinated Amanda asked.

"Hell no, regrets are a waste of time." Gertie laughed, then looked pensive. "But I will admit to this, watching a mother and father hold their newborn for the first time sometimes got to me. Not enough to make me go that route, mind you. I was a little too set in my ways to want to give up the freedom. Dogs seemed to feed my mothering urge well enough."

As if on cue, Bingo ran back up to them. After giving Amanda another investigative sniff, he plopped down in the sand next to his owner.

"You all tuckered out, Bing?" Gertie said to the golden retriever, petting his wet head and asking, "How long you here for?"

It should've been a simple question, but nothing was simple anymore. Gertie certainly wasn't prying. Amanda knew she couldn't engage in a conversation and withhold information at the same time. She ached to take a step forward. If she really believed in divine intervention, then maybe this independent, spirited woman was sent to her in the effort to help Amanda reclaim her life. And while still hesitant, Amanda knew she had to start somewhere.

"I'm not really sure," Amanda answered honestly, but before she could elaborate, the wind picked up and was accompanied by a clap of thunder.

"I'm thinking it's time to get off this beach," Gertie said while beginning to slowly rise. "Can I interest you in waiting out this storm over some coffee?"

Amanda jumped up and reached out to offer the older woman a hand.

"These old bones just aren't what they used to be," Gertie said into the now-howling wind and accepting the help. "Come on, I'm close by."

Together Amanda, Gertie, and Bingo the dog walked the short distance to Gertie's house, four houses away from where Amanda was staying. The rain began to fall but none of them rushed. Gertie even turned her face up to it, enjoying the feel of it. Amanda found herself doing the same, and for the first time in as long as she could remember, she felt herself breaking away from the grip of self-loathing. She needed one more round of tears and the rain provided them.

Gertie's house was cute and eclectically cheery, a small boxlike ranch. The closer they got, wind chimes hanging from the back porch clamored in the now-gusting wind and teeming rain. Gertie opened the unlocked door and invited Amanda in while she stayed behind to quickly towel off Bingo.

Once inside, Amanda was greeted by the scent of patchouli. The kitchen windowsill supported a planter of herbs—basil, dill, cilantro, and thyme. Seeing them reminded her of just how long it'd been since she thought about cooking. Plaques hung on the walls with sayings that read HAPPINESS IS AN INSIDE JOB and OF ALL THE THINGS I'VE LOST, I MISS MY MIND THE MOST.

The living room managed to look cozy despite the house's open floor plan. There was an abundance of candles in all shapes and sizes in jars and holders. There were figurines of angels and Buddhas. Books were neatly stacked near a wing chair. Planters sat near or were hung from windows, beads dangling from them. Incense burners rested on the coffee table. Amanda smiled. She had been sent an intrinsic hippie.

And then Amanda began to frown. In the corner of the living room was a television. The all-too-familiar feeling of anxiety began to nudge her again. She wondered if there was any possible way to casually go and feel if it was still warm from recently being used.

Stop it, Amanda reprimanded herself, *the woman has a television. Big deal, she says she doesn't watch it.*

"Coffee's on," Gertie said from behind her and Amanda jerked. She had removed her hat. Her face was weathered from years of sun and had lots of laugh lines. Her forehead furrowed when she exclaimed, "Where are my manners? You look soaked to the skin. Let me get you a towel."

Amanda sat down at the kitchen table, comfortable with the distance between herself and the television. She took a deep breath, and whether it was because of the environment or sheer mental exhaustion, it worked. By the time Gertie returned and she dried off, Amanda felt a serenity that had been inaccessible since that fateful day when she picked up the phone and it had all come crashing down around her.

"You know," Gertie said as she moved about the kitchen, "I've seen you for days sitting and staring off at the ocean. If you don't mind my saying so, people who spend that much time alone on a beach usually have a lot on their mind. I just thought maybe you'd enjoy a little break in your routine."

Amanda could almost feel another cosmic wheel turning. There wasn't any point in lying, especially if this lady was the answer to the prayer.

"I just broke up with my boyfriend," Amanda said, satisfied with the white lie.

"Sorry to hear that. Slacker?"

"No!" Amanda was quick to defend Chase, then caught herself. "It's complicated."

"Men usually are." Gertie laughed. "How do you take your coffee?"

They sat at the kitchen table for most of the afternoon as the storm raged outside. Over coffee and then lunch, Amanda was introduced to exercises that involved tranquility and little else. Gertie pulled out two miniature Zen "gardens," which essentially were small boxes of wood with a rim about an inch high. Inside the box was finely grained white sand, a few highly polished stones. Each garden also had a tiny rake made out of thin, tightly woven bamboo. They puttered around with the rakes in the sand intermittently while making chitchat about nothing in particular. It was pacifying to delicately drag the bamboo claws through the sand, make designs around the stones. The stones were polished so smooth that no grains would stick to them. She'd stop for a while but it was impossible to not take it up again. Amanda soon felt comfortable enough to talk about the restaurant, and it segued quickly to cooking. Gertie didn't probe and focused instead on broader topics. She admitted to not owning a computer, but she did have an iPad she rarely used and an old-style flip cell phone.

"Gotta keep up with the times," Gertie said.

She was laid-back and nonjudgmental on most subjects, something she credited to her tenure as a nurse and to seeing firsthand just what a miracle life was. As the afternoon wore on and they tended their little gardens, Amanda felt all her angst dissipating. Enough to consider opening up a bit more, maybe even confide in this total stranger with kind eyes and a peaceful soul.

"I miss the boyfriend a lot," Amanda said sadly, testing the parameter of the subject, "It's mostly my fault."

"I'm not so sure about that," Gertie replied easily. "It usually takes two to tango. And if you miss him, why don't you just call him, extend the olive branch?"

"It's not that easy," Amanda said. "There's a story behind it."

"We all have a story," Gertie pointed out. "What we don't have is limitless time. Seems a bit pointless to make a decision and then spend the rest of your life second-guessing it. It sounds like this relationship has really put a damper on your chi."

Amanda knew what chi is. According to Taoism and the other Chinese thought, chi is the vital force is believed to be inherent in all things. It is the balance of positive and negative energies in the body. It was that knowledge that lent itself to Amanda's conclusion that every time she tried to venture away from hers, catastrophes were likely to follow. To hear Gertie say it made perfect sense.

"I think mine could use a little feng shui," Amanda admitted.

Gertie studied Amanda for a moment before announcing, "You know what you need?"

Amanda grimaced uncomfortably. That particular question was one Chase had asked her playfully a hundred times. The answer to it was exactly what had landed her where she currently found herself.

"What?"

Gertie was already reaching for the nearby phone, mounted old-school to the wall. "Drum circle."

Chapter 15

Gertie took Amanda inland to the house of friends. There Amanda was introduced to three women and one man. Their ages varied, but Amanda guessed the youngest to be about fifty. Like Gertie, they were all mellow and easygoing, dressed casually and comfortably. The hostess led them to a windowed sunporch in the back of her house. Fold-out chairs were arranged in a circle in the center of the room. Along the wall were a dozen drums of various shapes and sizes. There were big freestanding drums and smaller handheld bongos. Everyone picked out a drum and moved to a chair. Amanda chose a medium one.

"What do I do now?" she whispered to Gertie after taking the seat next to her.

"You play your drum." Gertie smiled at her, saying nothing more.

Amanda hesitated, lightly running her fingers over the skin on the top of the bongo that was wedged between her legs. The other members of the circle began to play their drums while she watched for a minute. Some held their drums differently, like under their arm. One drum was big enough to sit on the floor independently. Some members closed their eyes while others seemed to enter into a trance, staring off into space. All were unconcerned about the others in the room. Amanda tentatively tapped her drum.

The sound was barely heard within the sounds of the other drums. Then she tapped it harder. The vibration reverberated from the drum between her legs, and she patted it several times in a row. It felt good to hit something. It was as if all her anger and frustrations about her current situation were being called up to the surface. She banged her drum harder. Chase popped into her mind. Suddenly she could see the allure that spanking held for him and what it was like to be on the other end of it. She thought about his secret, which he dragged her into without warning or permission. How he seduced and charmed her before introducing her to his fetish and then converted it into hers. How he made it the touch she sometimes wanted most. It didn't take long before she was beating her drum over and over, picturing his ass and then his face as she let out all her unexpressed feelings of having no control and things she couldn't change. All the insecurity and responsibility he had bombarded her with since he first walked into her life and insisted she share his. By the time she was done a half hour later, she had broken out into an exhaustive sweat. And she was the only one left drumming.

She looked at the other members of the circle. In her frenzy, she had forgotten they were there. They were all waiting for her to finish up, all with small, knowing smiles. Drum-circle newbie.

"Good job," Gertie said as she and the rest of the members got up and returned their drums to the wall. Amanda did the same, but awkwardly and with the general sense that she had done something wrong. They were all placid while she had to catch her breath. She remained quiet as they enjoyed water flavored with mint and the others spoke of local goings-on.

"We'll see you tomorrow?" the hostess asked politely as she walked them to the door.

For the next five days, Amanda and Gertie went back to the drum circle. With the exception of the hostess, it wasn't always those she had met the first day. But everyone she met was gracious and accepting of her. No one was the least bit interested in her backstory, or even if she had one. They weren't interested in forcing their histories on her. They were all very meditative and introspective, always talking and acting positively and in the moment. She stopped worrying about who might or might not recognize her.

And for five days, Amanda continued to beat the living hell out of her drum. During that time, she focused mostly on Chase. She used the opportunity to view him in a different light. As the entitled and spoiled cocreator of the mess her life had become with shades of he was a total package complete with pluses and minuses. She left each drum circle mentally and physically exhausted, all anger depleted. Gertie would drop her off at her house and she would immediately fall into a deep and dreamless sleep. Amanda would wake up the following morning refreshed and calm. She started acknowledging his part in their fiasco instead of blaming only herself.

On the sixth day, something changed. Amanda wasn't angry anymore, with herself or anyone else. Beating the Chase drum no longer held the same savage appeal. She had finally realized that Chase Walker wasn't some superhero or demigod, but a flesh-and-blood human being, complete with imperfections and subject to making mistakes. Just like her. And when she finally allowed him to be a mere mortal, she began to hear the sounds of the other drums. She started to find beats and rhythms, something that seemed to have escaped her previously. When the circle was done, she wasn't sweating and heaving, but as placid as the other drum-circle participants. It was a significant change and it felt great.

"There's something I need to tell you," Amanda said to Gertie as they drove home.

"I know." Gertie smiled.

"How do you know?" Amanda asked, surprised by the older woman's response.

Gertie paused before explaining. "When you are in a drum circle, the objective is to find balance, to share the rhythm and get in tune with yourself and each drummer. To form a group consciousness by feeding off the energy generated by the other members. It becomes a collective voice that emerges from the individual members as they drum together. Today you became part of a beautiful voice. Before then it was all about working out whatever issues you were dealing with on that poor drum."

Amanda laughed. "Yeah, that thing didn't stand a chance."

"I knew you would get there. We all did. We have faith in you. What did you want to tell me?"

"I didn't really break up with my boyfriend. In fact, he's not even my boyfriend, but my fiancé. I ran away from him when he needed me most. He doesn't have a clue where I am and in all probability is terribly worried." Amanda felt an intangible weight lifting off her shoulders with finally coming clean.

"I see," Gertie replied.

"I know it sounds awful. You probably don't think very much of me now."

"It's not my job to judge. I'm sure you had your reasons for what you did," Gertie told her.

"He's rich," Amanda blurted; it was time to lay it all out there. "And he's famous. We sort of got caught up in a scandal."

"That's one way to put it," Gertie mused.

It didn't take Amanda more than a few seconds for her newfound friend's words to sink in.

"You know who I am?" Amanda asked, torn between betrayal and the all-encompassing relief that she had just been saved from telling the story out loud.

"I said I didn't watch much television; I didn't say I lived under a rock." Gertie gave a half laugh.

"How long have you known?"

"A while," Gertie said noncommittally as she pulled into her stone driveway. "I found out quite by accident. Want to come in and talk a bit? Have some chamomile tea? If I drink coffee now, I'll be up all night."

Amanda wanted to be cross with the woman, but it was impossible. Gertie had spent the better part of a week helping Amanda sort through her feelings from the sidelines. She had helped her see her way through the dark and back into the light without trying to sway her in any direction. Gertie had been an answer to a prayer. And prayers are not always answered in the way you expect or even want.

Amanda followed Gertie into the house and took her regular seat at the kitchen table while Gertie put on the teakettle and let Bingo out into her small fenced-in yard.

"Do you think I'm sick?" Amanda finally asked.

It was the first time since they had met that Gertie conveyed a sentiment that was other than completely tranquil. "That's the problem with young people. You all think that every time you stumble across something, it's a new discovery. People have been tying and beating each other up for centuries. Haven't you ever heard of the Marquis de Sade?"

"Didn't they stick him in prison?"

"You do have a point there." Gertie's cheerful disposition returned as quickly as it had departed. "And sometimes I think a jail cell is a better alternative than having to answer to the court of public opinion. Thanks to modern technology, folks who aren't qualified to make a decision about what's for dinner now have the ability to make snap judgments at a moment's notice, and what's worse, the ability to voice them without having to stand behind what they say. It gives whole new meaning to the words *witch hunt*."

The teakettle began to whistle and Gertie got up to pour their tea as Amanda silently watched. Gertie was not only wise, she was savvy.

"You know what else I find interesting? Your generation really seems to enjoy their pain. They seek it out. Back in the day, you got one tattoo of something that was really meaningful, telling everyone how excruciating it was to have it put there. Now kids cover every square inch of their bodies with intricate designs and elaborate detail. They get all these piercings, some with holes in their ears big enough to drive a car through. They don't try to escape pain; they move toward it. The marquis would've been proud. At the very least, he was onto something."

Gertie wasn't only sharp, she was thought-provoking. It was clear that Gertie had given a lot of thought to Amanda while still keeping her own counsel.

"I never really looked at it like that," Amanda said.

Gertie brought the mugs over, and after placing one in front of Amanda, sat back down across from her. Both of them began the unconscious ritual of lifting their tea bags in and out of the hot water while Gertie finished up what Amanda surmised was as close to a tangent as she got. "And I always take television with a grain of salt. I watch a lot of BBC. I don't know what the fascination is with all these programs on regular TV. Game shows I get, but the reality-show nonsense? What's so dang interesting about watching someone else living their life?"

They sipped their tea while Gertie regained her center after ranting.

"How did you find out?" Amanda asked, trying out her first real post-scandal conversation.

"You want to see?" Gertie broke into a grin that could only be defined as girlish. She didn't wait for Amanda to respond before standing up. "Come on, follow me."

They went into the living room and sat down. Gertie picked up the remote and turned on her television, going to her DVR lineup. She chose an episode of Derrick Baxter. Baxter was a popular political commentator with an hour-long show on one of the news cable networks.

"You record Derrick Baxter?" Amanda asked, puzzled.

"Never miss him," Gertie replied with a big grin. "He's so distinguished, very sexy."

It was funny to think of Gertie getting all giddy while watching the bow-tie-wearing, salt-and-pepper-haired conservative. But as Gertie rewound to the spot she wanted Amanda to see, the video began showing a blurry image that was instantly recognizable and Amanda felt the blood start to heat up right in her veins. Gertie stopped at the beginning of a segment and Amanda started squirming in her seat.

The piece started about a country that put too much emphasis on its perceived heroes, and although she would've liked nothing more than to turn away, she couldn't. She was busy looking at the picture of Chase that was in the upper right-hand corner of the screen as Baxter spoke, his words barely registering. There was a scene of him that she had seen before when the story first broke, surrounded by security as they quickly escorted him to or from his apartment. All the warmth she felt when she saw him immediately started simmering. Then the shot cut to video footage, a clip of Chase standing at his locker in the Kings locker room, surrounded by bright lights and a sea of reporters. Amanda's breath hitched. He was live, and this was the first time she had seen him in weeks. She wanted to rush to Gertie's twenty-inch television and touch the screen to try to get closer to him, but didn't want to miss a second of what she was seeing. Him.

He looked relaxed, lucid, and unruffled, despite the microphones and tape recorders that were above and all around him. Baxter's show didn't air the question that was asked, only Chase's small smile and his careless shrug before he spoke:

"I realize you guys have a story to work, but I would ask that you try to be mindful of one thing. This isn't someone I picked up off the streets to engage in what is being labeled by some as twisted behavior. This is the woman I love and was hoping to marry. Depending on how well you do your jobs, that may or may not now be possible. I'm starting to call a doghouse home."

There was a general rise of laughter and Chase joined in with a small laugh of his own before he continued. Amanda was hanging on every word, trying to memorize every expression he made. "We are two consenting adults who were having a silly private moment that someone unfortunately chose to take advantage of in the hopes of making a quick buck. If there's nothing earth-shattering going on in the world right now that this needs to be a front-page story, I guess we're grateful. I wish our charities got this much attention. That's my official statement, and from here on out, I'm going to get back to baseball."

The television cut back to Baxter, and he started spouting off his opinion. To Amanda's surprise, Derrick

Baxter was taking the *there's no longer any honor among thieves* side, and accused the mainstream media of purposefully neglecting to show the rest of the tape and the make-out session that followed, which, in his humble opinion, effectively blew any abuse allegations out of the water. And two kids who might play a little rougher than some made bad poster children for domestic violence, a topic that deserved serious attention.

Chase had spoken in terms of "we" and "our" as if she were still with him and not cowering behind Ray-Bans in Nags Head. He had covered for her even though she was states away and he was clueless as to her whereabouts, had even alluded to the fact she had every right to be angry with him. He was still being a team player, a team she had forsaken when the going got tough.

And as Derrick continued to air his views, the screen cut to a stock photo taken of them at a fund-raiser, and Amanda felt all the breath leave her. She tried to inhale, but the grip of missing him combined with the scope of what she had done to him wouldn't let go of her airway.

Gertie pushed the Stop button on her remote and the image was gone. Amanda finally reached oxygen.

"You two look beautiful together. You both radiate. Good aura all around that," Gertie said, before adding, "And he's hot."

Hearing a seventy-year-old woman use the word *hot* with such vigor set Amanda to laughing out loud. "Yes, Gertie, he is. But he's also incredibly sweet. I don't think since I met him, he's ever said an unkind word to me."

"That says a lot about a man."

"Do you think I made too much of this?"

"I think you made as much of it as you had to."

"Do you get ESPN?"

"I have basic cable." Gertie pretended to be insulted.

"Do you mind if we put it on? He's got a game."

"And just how would you know that, missy?" Gertie smiled knowingly.

"Because I started watching some television and checked the cable guide. If I hadn't had my catharsis, I was going to swipe a drum and beat it every time they showed him. Now I'd just like to see him while I figure out if I should call him as soon as the game's over or wait to see him in person."

They turned on the game at the bottom of the fourth inning. There were sweeping shots of him that made Amanda's heart flutter. But it wasn't until the sixth when he got up to bat.

She wasn't ready for the alteration.

His smile had been replaced with a scowl. His eyes were dull. Not vacant—there was still plenty of fire—but there was no joy. All the boyish sparkle was gone. What was left was scary to see. Amanda hoped she was the only one who saw it. That it was only guilt brought on by having to watch her consequences in action. She prayed that, to the rest of the world, he just looked like the King of Diamonds getting his A-game playoff face on. He fouled off the first three pitches in a row. She could feel his fury every time he took a swing, and when the fourth pitch was thrown, he hit it with such force the bat splintered. He stood there watching it till it made its way out of the stadium. He ran the bases, his expression never changing, and jogged his way back to the dugout. Before ducking in, he stared right into a camera, the coldest, iciest stare Amanda didn't believe him capable of, and her gasp was audible.

It was like he knew she was there.

"That's the man you've been telling me about?" Gertie asked, trying not to sound alarmed.

"Yeah," she replied, feeling the most awful twist in the pit of her stomach.

"Honey, I think it's about time you start hightailing it back to where you came from. You don't want that boy coming to find you."

Chapter 16

Chase kicked the treadmill's speed up a few more notches, the incline as well, and ran at full speed for another three minutes. Sweat poured off him, but the same focused expression he had been carrying around for weeks never changed. There was an untouchable coldness to him, and while he was never rude to anyone, he was definitely not the same man. After he finished, he took only a minute to catch his breath, pacing the whole time. When he set the bench press's weight up another ten pounds for the third time and went to lie down, Logan felt it was finally time to step in.

"Hey, man, is it working?"

Chase gave him what could only be construed as a growl. "Is what working?"

"The unhealthy risk-taking?"

"What the hell are you talking about? The playoffs are coming up."

Logan gave him an indulgent grin, not fooled. "You've been training with me for, what, seven years now? I've seen you through how many postseasons? In all that time, I can't remember a single instance where my program wasn't enough for you."

"Why don't you just fuckin' say what's on your mind?" Chase spat out, adrenaline surging, aggression surfacing. But they had known each other a long time, and Logan was unconcerned about any potential backlash.

"If you don't mind me cutting to the chase, pardon the pun, all of this won't bring her back."

Chase shifted his weight from one foot to the other and back again. He had been itching for an altercation that with a second look, he wasn't ready to have.

Don't say her name, don't say her name, don't say her name drummed in his head. He broke out into a smile that never made it to his eyes and tried to sound nonchalant.

"Oh, that." He gave an overexaggerated wave of his hand. "That's old news, buddy. We were pretty much done before she took off. You know me better than that. What have I always said? So many women, so little time." Chase picked up the front of his shirt and wiped his face, thereby hiding it. It gave him the time he needed to settle in, continue the farce.

"If that's true, then how do you even know who I'm talking about?" Logan continued to provoke.

Chase settled both hands on his hips, let out a rush of air. "Who else could you mean?" *Don't say her name, don't say her name.* "The spoiled brat who bailed as soon as the heat turned on."

Logan merely smiled "Spoiled brat? Heat turned on? Interesting choice of words, given the circumstances." He was the first one of Chase's friends who had even broached the topic since it happened. Everyone had been either too scared or just plain not interested. In Chase's circle, almost everyone had a least one skeleton in his closet. When it happened to one of their own, it only sent the message that next time it could be them.

"You know what I don't get? What the big fucking deal was." It was all Chase needed to finally let out the steam he had carried around for weeks, anger that had kept him solitary and withdrawn. "I go to the ballparks and chicks are screaming, 'Spank me. Spank ME!,' They carry signs, they have shirts made. They send naked pictures of their asses to the Kings' website. It's not like I set up a video camera in our . . . MY room and did a Kim Kardashian. She was always so annoyingly pious." His rant done, his spleen vented, he seemed to relax. Then he acquiesced. "Sorry if I stepped on your toes, you're the boss." He checked the clock on the wall. "At least for another fifteen minutes. Can we get back to work?" As Logan took the extra weight off the bench press Chase gave one last puffed-up sneer. "What made her think she was so damn special anyway?"

Logan bit back a smirk of his own. You did, my friend, you did, he thought.

Chase entered his apartment, threw his wallet on the table, and took off his shirt, wiping down his chest with it. He skipped showering at the gym, deciding to jog home, figuring the fresh air could only do him good, as fresh as the air got in New York City during September at any rate. He wandered into the kitchen, pulled out a bottle of water, and downed it. After spending a few seconds flexing his pecs, he walked over to the phone to check for messages. Relieved at hearing nothing but a dial tone, he returned it to its cradle, yelled out to Lena that security was on its way to pick him up and he'd be ready in twenty minutes. Then he headed to his room to shower.

"Hello, Chase," she said just as he was walking into his closet.

As soon as he heard her voice, she saw him visibly stiffen. His back to her, he took a minute to place his control firmly in check before he turned around to face her.

There she was, every bit as pretty as he remembered. Only tan. Damn her. He was spending night after sleepless night with haunted visions and she was soaking up the sun somewhere. She looked downright healthy. The little bitch. He waited till he was sure his voice wouldn't give him away before he spoke.

"Came to return my keys, did you? You could have left them with the doorman."

Amanda, seated in a chair in his bedroom, looked at a man she didn't know. The Chase standing before her now, though still the sexiest man she had ever seen, was the same man with the icy stare that she'd felt through the television only a day ago. This was the man she created, and the time for her running was over. It was her turn to step up to the plate.

"I missed you." *There, good job, Amanda. That oughta do it. You can sweep me up in your arms now.*

"Really? How very kind of you to say. I've been right here, all along. Good old Chase Walker, spanker of wayward women." His voice was drenched with sarcasm, his hulking, shirtless body still dripping with sweat. Both gave her strength, for entirely different reasons. And if she was smart she'd be scared, but she was finished with her head leading, and there was only one place her heart wanted to run.

"This is all your fault, you know," she said, confrontational in response, crossing her legs.

"My fault?" He was incredulous, his self-control starting to give way, and they had barely even begun. "My fault? What was my fault, Amanda, why don't you tell me? Oh, that's right, I saw a hidden camera and decided to spank you in front of it. Then I called security and told them to alert the media." Afraid if he continued, he might actually strangle her, he made his way toward the door. "Look, I have a game in six hours, so if you don't mind, I'm going to have to cut this short."

She was up in a flash, refusing to let him duck out of the fight. She marched right up to him, poking him in the chest. "Don't make like you're the victim here! You're the one who couldn't wait twenty minutes. Twenty stinkin' minutes."

He backed away from her and she thought he might exit stage right. She followed closely behind him and jumped in response to how loud the door was when he slammed it. It sent the clear message to anyone within the apartment: Stay away from this room. He rounded back on her. "You sure didn't seem to mind when I was doing it. And I think there's a tape somewhere to prove it!" he shot back at her, starting to ball his hands into fists.

"How dare you! Of course you would have no problem joking about it. It only made you more of a national hero, you pompous oaf!"

He grabbed her by the shoulders, violently shaking her, stopped only when her eyes grew wide and frightened. "And do you know why that is? Do you? Because I stayed here and looked everyone in the eye as they judged. I took the phone calls, I made the statements, laughed at the jokes. I tried to protect the person I loved. I didn't go running to my daddy, begging him to hide me like I committed some sort of criminal offense." He released her abruptly, as if touching her disgusted him. He stomped over to the other side of the room, hoping it was enough distance between them. "You think this happened only to you, Amanda? It happened to me, too. It happened to *us*. For all the words of togetherness we ever shared, I was the only one who seemed to mean them." Then, with remarkable ease, he punched a hole in the wall, the plaster crumbling in response to the unleashed fury. He looked at the destruction and lowered his head, his hands on his hips, and she could tell by his heaving, he was trying to hold back the rest of the rage.

She should have been terrified. She should have run. But every word he spoke was the truth, and though the reasons were different, they both were to blame. Determined not to cry, she cautiously joined him and laid her small hand on his granite bicep, gently urging him to turn to her.

"You're right, Chase. But where do we go from here?"

He didn't want her so close, didn't want her to touch him, but she kept ever so slightly pulling, until he dropped his arms and she slid into him, her arms curling around his waist and up his back. Placing her ear on his slick chest, she waited to hear his heart regulate itself. As if his arms had a will of their own, they wrapped around her. He rested his cheek on the top of her head and breathed in the scent of her, the mixture of perfume and shampoo he knew so well. He closed his eyes.

"I don't want to love you," he said despondently, almost to himself. "It hurts too much."

"I can make it up to you. Please let me try," she pleaded, her pride no longer relevant inside his strong embrace, the safety she had been looking for all along.

He exhaled and his tension eased a bit. His arms had been without her for too long. "What am I going to do with you?" he asked wistfully.

"You're going to make me pay, in all the best ways," she teased, sensing the worst of it was over.

"I don't even know where to start, little girl," he said, making the shaky attempt to pick up where they'd left off, although they both knew it wasn't going to be that easy.

"Start right from the beginning, when Alan Shaw told me to get out of town."

His arms noticeably began to stiffen around her.

"Wait. What?"

Chase felt like he'd just been plunked in the rib cage by Justin Verlander's fastball. Right on the tattoo of her he could no longer bear to see. He set her apart from him.

"What did you just say about Alan Shaw?"

Amanda could tell in one look that whatever her answer was, it was going to be the wrong one.

He repeated a disbelieving "Alan Shaw told you to get out of town?"

He asked it the same way he would if he were accusing her of having an affair, all gut reaction. The tone of his voice alone was enough to cause panic. She nodded.

"He told me you'd need to concentrate on damage control," she said quickly.

Still struggling to wrap his head around it, he repeated louder. "You ran away from me on the advice of *Alan Shaw*?"

Chase stepped away from her into the middle of the room before turning to face her again. He was composed to the point of indifference.

"Alan told me you called him at his office after you left and said you were so mad that you didn't want to speak to me. That if you ever stopped being pissed off, I'd be the first to know."

"That's completely not true," Amanda corrected him, hoping the truth would make things better. "He was the first call I got. He pretty much insisted."

But he only got more glazed over. "So let me get this straight. You took off because Alan Shaw told you it was a good idea? The greasiest, sleaziest, greediest . . ."

His sputtering reminded her of Yosemite Sam describing an altercation with Bugs Bunny. She waited to see if he was going to finish it up by calling Shaw the "pole-cattin-est, flim-flamming-est varmint he ever did see." But if he was blustering, surely they had to be on the road to recovery. Of all the things she expected to happen, he did the one thing she never thought he would. He started making his way to the door.

"Amanda, you have to go." He said it so calmly, her blood ran cold. He held his bedroom door open, his hand pointing to the way out and down the hall. She could see Jack hovering in the doorway of the neighboring room, in response to the housekeeper's concern about the way Chase slammed the door. When Jack wasn't discharged, Amanda began to realize how bad it was going to get. He had just allowed another person access to the conversation.

She'd expected that they would start making love or have a knock-down-drag-out fight, or that he would give her the paddling of a lifetime. In a perfect world, she'd have gotten all three. But he was always going to forgive her.

"But . . . why?" she asked through the tears that were already glistening on her eyelashes.

"Because it's the rule," he stated coolly. "You left me. I told you, only once."

"But a minute ago . . . " Amanda looked back to where they were standing. Hugging and reconciling.

"A minute ago, you were at least brave enough to have run away on your own accord. I need someone I can trust, not someone who would take orders from the most immoral character I can think of instead of her future husband. Leave my keys. I don't want you to contact me again."

She heard it in his voice. It was the worst voice she'd ever heard, devoid of any passion or emotion. She couldn't see it in his eyes, because he refused to glance in her direction. His jaw was set and his lips tightly drawn together. He looked from the ceiling to the window to the door he still held open.

There were two things Amanda could do. She could grovel or she could leave. By the all-encompassing change that had taken place in him, the sheer magnitude of his apathy, she didn't think groveling would make any difference. With the few remaining shreds of dignity she had left, Amanda walked past him, then Jack, down the hall, stopping only long enough to take his keys off her keychain and placing them on the table next to his wallet.

"Make sure she finds her way out of the building, Jack," Chase said flatly from his bedroom, like she was a fan who had become a nuisance and needed to be removed.

She held it together while in the elevator. The shock was still fresh and she'd gotten good at feeling like the sky was falling and still remain mobile. Jack said nothing, as rigid and unresponsive as his employer instructed. She made no attempt at conversation. The man had just been given the order to kick her out. She got in her car, the useless convertible Chrysler Sebring she wouldn't let Chase replace. Thank heaven for small favors. The only way it could have been more melodramatic would have been to be banished and then have to board the crosstown bus. She began driving out of the city, starting to feel the full effect of him sending her away. He was bone-chillingly cold. It wasn't open for discussion and he wasn't making an idle threat. He simply dismissed her. She'd seen him do it with others, always from his circle of luminosity she had once basked in. But not anymore, he had just seen to it that she'd never be in his presence again. She didn't have a game plan for the rest of her life without him. It was already getting darker without him shining down on her. With that thought, her tears began to flow freely and she let them, brushing at them just enough to keep them from blinding her while driving. She drove past her own exit and kept heading west. She picked up the parkway and drove mindlessly, heading north, trying once again to escape.

It was no surprise when she ended up in Mendham. She was drawn there as part of her cosmic wheels directing her where she'd be able to sort it all out. It felt as natural as it did finding Gertie on the beach. She would start at the place where she was first told she deserved to have it all. It would feel like he was near until she figured out what to do. She would drive right up that long driveway, and if anyone was working, she'd just turn around. And if no one was there, she'd stare at it and wait to see if it gave her a sign.

Her heart cracked in half as soon as she saw the real estate sign posted at the beginning of the driveway.

Chase had put their house up for sale. It wasn't the kind of sign she was hoping for.

Amanda pulled her car over into the driveway and finished crying. He was acting rashly. She refused to believe he'd stopped loving her. He was too loyal to give up on anyone for one mistake. Whenever he made this decision, it was when he thought she left because she was furious and not mortified. She dialed the number on the real estate sign. She sniffled her way through analyzing in a way that would make her mother proud. She wasn't sure what she was going to do, but it was going to have to be something drastic. She needed to stop being a damsel in distress and get her act together.

Amanda Cole was getting her man back.

Chapter 17

C hase came off the elevator at his lawyers' office, security in tow, and was promptly taken into a conference room. His real estate agent was already there.

"Thanks for coming down, Chase," his real estate lawyer said, extending his hand. "It was nice that you agreed to do this. I know it's unorthodox."

"Meeting a grandmother who wants to see her children enjoy their inheritance is hardly a sacrifice. Thanks for making me sound like a hero, but I have to be honest, I would do almost anything to unload this property." Chase hated to sound so callous, but it had been getting more and more difficult to keep it from slipping out occasionally when it came to her. Once the house was gone, he'd be one step closer in his exorcism.

He needed to make a decision about his lawyer's recommendation that he send a demand letter for the return of the engagement ring. That would be the final tie severed. But he was torn. What was he supposed to do with a six-carat diamond? He could use it to cut glass or try to carve the tattoo of her off his body. As soon as it was in his hand, it would make one more clean incision into his heart.

"We'll try to make it quick," his lawyer said. "They called a short time ago. They're just a few minutes out."

"We really tried to keep it private," the real estate agent apologized, "but these are the kinds of rumors that easily spread."

"It's all good. If it means that much to a fan, it means a lot to me."

Chase waited with a cup of coffee. He made business small talk, mostly about the playoffs, free-agent trades, and the baseball-crazy eccentric who was throwing her capital away before going to her grave to buy an extravagant gift for her child, and giving the asking price in exchange for a photo op. Who insisted the deal be done quickly and quietly because time was of the essence.

The intercom buzzed that the buyers had arrived.

As soon as she walked in, the room lit up, as did he. But it was short-lived as the realization he may have been duped hit home. She was flanked by two lawyers and a real estate agent of her own.

"Amanda, what are you doing here?" Chase said quickly before turning to his lawyers and real estate agent. "Is this some kind of joke?"

"Don't bother blaming them, Chase. They're probably as confused as you are," Amanda told him smoothly, though her insides were quivering, a mixture of the usual rush when she saw him and adrenaline-fueled excitement.

"We're supposed to be meeting with a large family and a generous . . . " Chase continued to his handlers, ignoring her completely in an effort to keep from looking at her again. As the pieces of the ruse came together, he pursed his lips tightly, started shaking his head, and exhaled, "Baseball-loving matriarch."

Chase took a moment to get fully in check, and to the casual observer he probably succeeded. But his jaw had started to clench ever so slightly, and the fingers on his right hand started curling around his thumb. He looked curiously at the individual faces of the uncomfortable members from Amanda's team, who had the courtesy to look apologetic, then away. He finally rested his gaze on her and broke into his Hollywood smile, the one that never quite makes it to his eyes.

"You actually got all these people to lie for you in an effort to bring us to this point?"

"Not your people, only mine," Amanda replied breezily. "You want to sell a house, I want to buy one. I don't really see what the big deal is."

"You played the frail grandma card," he commented drolly.

"Oh. Did I say elderly woman's dying wish? I meant bitter ex-girlfriend."

If she wanted to play this sort of game, he had no choice but to go along or risk embarrassing himself in a roomful of strangers. Embarrassing her, however, wasn't out of the question. He continued to smile at her, but his tone became one of condescension.

"You can't afford this purchase, Amanda. Even your parents don't have the kind of money to buy my house, not if they want to try to run a campaign."

"Nice of you to worry about my folks, but I think they know what they're doing. I guess you haven't heard about my new venture," she replied in kind, feeling another rush but also grateful for the safety in the number of people in the room.

"What?" he said as if he were speaking to a child. "You think opening the Cold Creek for lunch is going to make a difference?"

"Of course not, silly." She laughed. "But the interview and the book deal sure do."

As soon as the words were out of her mouth, his smile was gone. His face momentarily registered with shock, then passed quickly into barely contained fury, and in the next second well-polished aloofness as her threat and everything it implied sank in. He took one more moment to fully absorb it and began lightly drumming the fingers of one hand on the table. He rested his other elbow on the table, casually stroking his chin, while he considered his options. Amanda knew he wouldn't take long, and seized the opportunity.

"Would you all be so kind as to give us a minute alone?" she asked pointedly, her eyes never coming off Chase. She met his stare of carefully contained emotion head-on and displayed neither relief nor apprehension when he briefly shifted his attention to the other occupants in the room and slightly nodded his approval, his expression never changing. Chase and Amanda continued to stare at each other from opposite sides of the table, while everyone else stood up and filed out of the conference room. As soon as the last person closed the door behind them, the pretenses were dropped.

"You're going to talk about *us*?" His jaw went slack and his face molten with disbelief.

"Of course I'm going to talk about us. Well, mostly you. You're the one everyone wants to know about. The sweetest, most wholesome deviant America ever produced. You would be surprised by just how many of your past partners are willing to come out of the wood-work. There's even interest in a reality series, all of us living in one place in a big city, trying to find a suitable replacement. A re-Chase-ment, if you will."

She had to be kidding him, it was so preposterous. He could feel a headache starting above his left eye. "Very funny, Amanda, enough with the jokes. You and I both know you aren't going to do any of those things. You melted down with a minute of exposure, now you're suddenly willing to live under a microscope? I don't think so."

"You underestimate your own ability. It was you that convinced me I was allowed to have it all. Not to be afraid to play the hand I was dealt and make the most of it. And I don't know, something about being part of a sisterhood makes me feel bolder. It won't be so bad, after all, it's not like any of us are actually mad at you. Some of those actresses tell a pretty compelling tale. There may be a few who are flat-out lying, but I'll be damned if I can tell the difference. I'll let you figure it out with them in court."

Chase's temple throbbed again. "You're bluffing."

Amanda shrugged dismissively. "Maybe. But now you need to figure out just how far I'm willing to go to stay in. The interview went to the highest bidder and the check for it is already in my possession. They gave me the mortgage based on the letter of intent from the publishing company and my father's signature. He thinks you're acting like an ass, too, by the way. Your willingness to sell for such a reasonable price only made it easier all the way around. I should probably be thanking you."

"You know who you should be thanking? The fifteen lawyers standing on the other side of the door; they're the only thing preventing me from dragging you across this table."

He was already making threats, a wonderful sign. He wasn't aloof and patronizing anymore, but he was far from losing his cool. Amanda stood and leaned both elbows on the table, essentially bending over it, and said seductively, "Want me to meet you halfway? I promise to keep it quiet."

It was so over-the-top, designed to goad him. She knew exactly what she was doing. It was absolutely working. Chase remained in his chair, his elbow on the armrest, propping the side of his head up with one finger. He was glaring intensely, his eyes practically glowing. "Trust me, the way I'm feeling right now, if I got my hands on you, they'd hear. I'll tie you up in court for all eternity to keep any of it from happening; you do know that, right? "

Amanda looked at him with such feigned innocence, still fully bent over the table, he had to keep himself from leaping out of his chair and pouncing on her. "Tie me up? If we were still together, I'd be giving that some thought. But instead I'll think about how a long-drawn-out court battle would keep it in the headlines for a good long time. I can see where that sort of publicity might be helpful to me, but I'm not really seeing the benefit in it for you."

She had him. This little girl had fucked him up good. He could almost hear the sound of his endorsement deals drying up, something he could live with, but eventually his game would suffer. If she was going to expose them anyway, better to take the hit quickly. One more round of damage control. The house meant nothing to him. He certainly didn't want it, why didn't he just let her have it? Because it'd be bought with proceeds earned at his expense. *Oh, I'd like to let her have it*, he thought. His heart pounded painfully in his ears. He had her all wrong. He had dreamt about her, agonizing dreams full of want and longing. Because deep down Chase still thought she was made for him, the only woman he'd ever love. Someone he could trust, even if she hadn't exactly stood by him. Not someone who would go out of her way to try to destroy him. He studied her from across the table where she had retaken her seat, politely waiting for him to respond. He had hoped by now she'd be nothing more than a faceless distraction, the one dull, aching scar in his otherwise charmed life. Seeing her brought back all the memories, even the ones he'd tried to forget. And worse than that, he knew that in the end he would give her what she wanted, for no other reason than she wanted it. That even as it killed him, now that he saw her, he knew he wouldn't be able to deny her. The one time he sent her away was all he had in him. After the initial feeling of betrayal had worn off, he had waited for weeks in hopeful anticipation that she would contact him again. But not like this, not to drive the final nails in his coffin. Damn, she still had the ability to take his breath away, her round blue eyes and bow-shaped mouth as captivating as the ones tucked away within his memory. Her fitted Donna Karan dress created perfect recall of her every curve. There was just one difference; she was safe in his memory. He could protect her there, better than he did before. Not feed her to the media machine, to be spit out into the kind of woman who was now sitting across from him.

"Why do you even want the house, Amanda?" he finally asked, teetering off furious and closer to resolved defeat.

"Because it's mine. You were building it for me. It's mine and I want it."

The words were bratty enough on their own merit, before she added the tone. She didn't stamp her foot, but she did sit straight up and cross her legs. Was she still deliberately trying to tweak him? There was something far more natural about it. Chase quirked an eyebrow. "So you get it. You honor your commitments and make us both look like a couple of idiots, then what?"

Amanda's mouth formed a tight line, a look she perfected for him. "I'm going to burn it to the ground."

Chase blinked, startled by her response. "That's the most ridiculous thing I've ever heard."

She leaned back in her chair, crossed her arms, and dared to smirk. "Would you rather I keep it? Settle down? Raise a family?"

The thought of her carrying another man's child slammed into the side of his head like a sledgehammer. His look hardened again. A look so hard that came on so fast, Amanda was afraid that she may have pushed him too far. She couldn't help from reacting and she jolted when he suddenly stood up. He walked away from the conference table and over to the wide picture window on the other side of the room. It was getting too difficult to maintain a semblance of control with her so close. His hands clasped tightly behind his back, he stared out the window, a panoramic view of a parking lot. His one hand clenched and unclenched into a fist, his other hand holding it in place behind his broad back. Several long moments passed.

"Why are you doing this to me?" Chase asked, so befuddled and sad, Amanda thought he might begin to cry and wondered how she was going to get through the next few minutes without starting to as well. But it was her turn to be strong for both of them, and it was now or never.

"Because you're stubborn as a mule," she replied. "And I had to be sure."

Even through his suit jacket she could see his shoulder blades begin to come together as his back stiffened and his fist clenched again.

"Sure of what?" he asked wearily, in direct contrast with the tight fist being restrained by his other hand.

"That you weren't really over me," she told him.

"I'll never be over you," Chase said quietly, still staring out the window. "Happy now?"

"Almost."

"Get everyone back in here. Let's close this deal. You can have the house."

"I don't want the house, Chase. I think you know that."

"I don't know anything anymore," he blurted despondently to the window, dropping both hands to his sides and his head in surrender. Shaggy blond hair,

314 · STEPHANIE EVANOVICH

much in need of a trim, fell partially onto his forehead. He ran his hand absently through it and heaved a heavy sigh. "What more do you want from me?"

Amanda got out of her chair and walked to the corner of the conference table near where he was standing, his back still to her. She pulled herself up and sat on it. Her legs swayed slightly as they dangled.

"There is a way out of this for both of us, you know," she stated simply.

"Is there?" he asked, snorting in disgust, hating that he already sensed she had gotten closer even before she spoke. "Obviously, I've missed something."

Amanda shook her head slowly. The solution was right in front of him and he honestly couldn't see it. Had she set him so far off-kilter his instincts no longer kicked in?

"Why do you insist on torturing yourself?" she asked randomly.

"It's better than torturing you, isn't it?" he bit back.

Silence hung thick in the air. She could almost see the aura of pain that surrounded him. It dulled all his charismatic light. He wasn't talking about torturing her physically. He really believed she'd orchestrated what was happening in retaliation and the attempt to further tarnish his reputation. It was heartbreaking to see him so lost, knowing she was party to it. She was never so grateful to have him presenting his back to her. To see that despair reflected in his eyes at that moment would've killed her. She just needed a few minutes more. If she could stay strong and resolute, not crumble and force him to save her, she'd conquer the last of the barriers that stood in her way and finally enter nirvana. Getting there would mean nothing if he wasn't with her.

"When I first took off, I wasn't sure if you would try to find me. Afraid I wouldn't have the time to think things through," she said quietly.

"I could've found you," he mused to the window. "I have the resources."

"Don't you think I know that, Chase? I've known all along you didn't come after me because you knew it was what I wanted. I never expected it to take as long as it did to figure it all out."

"But you don't understand, and I keep telling you, Amanda, as soon as you left you were gone. I told you, only once. I didn't come find you because that was the rule."

"Come on, Chase, you know this doesn't have anything to do with any rule. But for the sake of argument, your rule was based on something that didn't fall within the confines of our agreement. The rule was I couldn't leave when *you* made me uncomfortable.

You never set down the rules for when *Entertainment Tonight*, ESPN, and Fox News took a stab at it."

"A technicality." He sighed sadly. "You knew all those things came with the package."

"Not when it came to our secret," she said emphatically. "And you're right; it wasn't fair for me to leave you worrying about where I was while you were in the middle of trying to handle the crisis. But you knew I was safe, because my father told you I was. It was convenient to blame Alan Shaw, but I really did what I thought was best for both of us. I wasn't going to be any help to you, Chase. I was freaking out. I needed to go someplace to just be mad at you for a while. The kind of mad that didn't want to concern itself with repercussions of *any* kind. Not only did I not want to worry about setting you off when I went on obscenity-laced diatribes, I didn't want to worry about feeling guilty watching you punish yourself as you scrambled around trying to make me not be mad anymore. And I had to take the time to really forgive myself. I knew what I was doing that night; I was just as thrilled by the thought of getting caught as you were, until it actually happened. I failed you, too; I didn't take very good care of your secret. I had no idea you would consider my listening to Alan a total breach of trust. I should've. But I assure you, the choice to leave was all mine. My father tried to tell me to stay, too. And I knew running away would never be a decision you would make or let me make. I made my own decision. I probably made the wrong one, but I'm new to the people-knowing-my-name thing. I made a mistake and I'm sorry. Don't you think we've punished each other, and ourselves, long enough?"

Chase turned back around to face her, but instead of the pain she heard in his voice, something a tad different had settled in as well. The tiny yet distinct flicker of the man she knew. Amanda didn't miss it. It drew her in and began warming her, a kind of warmth that only he knew how to create, one of the many things she wanted and needed. It was the spark of everything she ever wanted, every dream she ever could have. It was a beacon just calling to be blown on. It would burst into flame and incinerate the entire room. She knew she had the wind power.

"I've always said you were clever, Amanda," he said, not the least bit sorry she saw it, "but you're wrong."

She leaned both her hands back on the table behind her. The movement hiked her dress up above her knees. She began to gently kick her left leg.

"You may have gotten me to believe that twenty minutes ago. But now?" she practically sang. "Not a chance."

He wasn't sure if she did it on purpose or subconsciously, but it hardly mattered. He was caught up watching her transform right before his eyes. From the elegantly dressed, refined, efficient businesswoman to the sexy, mischievous naughty girl who starred in all of his favorite fantasies. Her leg continued its gentle swaying, and she was literally spread out on the table before him. She peered up at him from beneath long lashes and blinked as if she'd just been chastised for some made-up offense. He already knew what he was going to do about her, but he didn't see the harm in taking a few minutes to admire the view. Chase leaned back onto the windowsill, crossed his arms over his chest, and took on a hint of a smile.

"You sound pretty sure of yourself."

She nodded before saying softly, "I am. You really don't know your other option?"

"Once again you have me at a disadvantage," he responded dryly.

"I'll back out of all the deals if you keep the house and we live in it together, like you planned."

A slow, genuine smile spread across his face, the first one in weeks. She was brilliant and beautiful, and Chase was sure he would never tire of her attempts to top him from the bottom.

"Amanda Cole, did you really do all this because you're trying to blackmail me into reconciliation?" He laughed. She thought it was a most glorious sound.

She pouted, a personal favorite, because she only ever did it for him. "I guess, technically, yes. But blackmail makes it sound diabolical. I prefer to think of it more as an intervention."

He laughed again, this time at the irony. "What if the only thing I need saving from is you?"

He tilted his head and she tilted hers, too. They scrutinized each other. If there was anyone else in the room, they might have thought Chase and Amanda were sizing each other up, getting ready to go for the jugular. But what they were really doing was deciding how much longer they would continue to play the delicious game when there was so much time to make up for. Amanda pushed her lower lip out a bit farther.

"I love you so much, Chase. What do you say? Please take me back. Let's finish building the castle and living our fairy tale. You can teach me a lesson I'll never forget in every single room. We'll live slappily ever after."

The game was over. Chase bolted off the windowsill, and she quickly sat back up in an effort to close the distance between them. He slid her by her stocking-clad thighs to the edge of the table in one motion, and his hand reached behind her neck into her hair in the next. His mouth crashed down onto hers. She cupped the sides of his face to make sure he wasn't going anywhere. Weeks of pent-up passion exploded in one breathless kiss. When they finally came up for air, Chase set her back down on the table, his irreplaceable boyish grin having fully returned.

"You drive a hard bargain, lady. I hate to break it to you, but you just went through a lot of trouble for nothing. If you really wanted to apologize, all you had to do was call me. I'd already made peace with the fact I'd never be able to fend you off a second time."

"I would've never called you again." She smirked, using her thumb to remove her gloss off his lower lip, deliriously happy to be back in his arms. "I do have my pride, you know. I had to get in the same room with you, someplace public where I could have a few minutes to really get under your skin."

"You've been under my skin from the moment I saw you. I'm not that hard to find. And Security has a standing order if they see you. That's bringing you right to me."

Her features flashed with mischief and no small amount of jealousy. There was only one place where sighting him with security would be guaranteed. "I was not about to go to that stadium and compete for you with a bunch of *fucking kinky bitches*."

His eyes widened briefly, then narrowed meaningfully as he shook a stern finger at her. "Okay, now that one was blatant."

She giggled and wrapped her hand around his finger, then brought him back in for another chance to smear her gloss. This time he removed it completely.

"Come on, angel," Chase said after reluctantly pulling away. He reached out, taking her hands to help her down from the table. "Let's bring everyone back in here and ruin their day."

"Not everyone's," Amanda replied, standing up and smoothing her dress back to its proper length, "just the producer, the publisher, and the real estate agents. The lawyers will just bill us anyway. Your agent will probably consider it a happy ending, too."

Chase chuckled while watching her shimmy her dress down. "You really were keeping a low profile. I fired Shaw the minute you left my apartment after telling me. He's been crying breach of contract to anyone who will listen ever since. I'm going to let him whine a little longer and then pay him off."

"Oh, I knew that. It's what convinced me you were as miserable over our breakup as I was. He called me soon after. You should've heard that phone call. I told him he got off easy; I wanted to hit him with a bat. I meant your new one."

"So sassy. God, I love you."

He made several strides in the direction of the door, pulling her behind him before stopping short and giving a little tug on her arm. She halted and regarded him curiously. He looked deep into her eyes, and his fingers tightened around hers. He said earnestly, "Mandy, I don't think I could live through you taking off on me again."

She stared at him with all the love her heart could hold, awestruck once again by how readily he conveyed his vulnerability. Without hesitation, he gave her complete control over him and balanced out the power between them. Did he really believe she could survive without him for one single minute for the rest of her life? She slowly shook her head, then smiled, hoping it translated into even a fraction of what she felt for him.

"Chase, unless you're about to tell me there's a full-on sex tape of us out there, I vow never to leave you. I watched you be a perfect gentleman and protect me through this whole thing. I'm confident there's nothing you can't handle." She took a step and then halted again. "And if there is a video of us about to go viral, it's not my leaving you'll have to worry about living through, it's my staying."

He couldn't resist giving her one more kiss and the well-deserved swat he'd been holding back since she'd first come into the office.

Chase opened the door, expecting to find a galley of faces staring back at them. But the waiting area around the conference room was deserted. So was the hall. Amanda wasn't really surprised. She had told her own lawyers that if there was no sound of an altercation coming from behind the closed door after three minutes, it was safe to assume it was going to end positively. She had never felt so confident in her new role as a risk-taker, and she knew exactly who to thank. They found the nearest secretary, who got all the attorneys and real estate agents out of a nearby office. They all went back into the conference room, only this time with Chase and Amanda taking seats next to each other as far from the rest of them as possible. They were the only two members on a very exclusive team. The attorneys added Amanda's name to the house, and the real estate agents were dismissed. Then they began to go over the strategies for any and all repercussions that would follow the change in the previous game plan. When it turned into all legalese on subject matters he couldn't care less about, Chase reached over and took a piece of paper from the pad of the lawyer across from him. He pulled a pen out of his own suit jacket pocket and began scribbling, not the least bit concerned with looking interested. When he was finished, he put the pen back in his pocket, folded up the piece of paper, and slid it in front of her.

At first she had no intention of reading it; he had seemed so impolite while he was writing it. But maybe it was something important that he wanted her to tell her own lawyers. She brought the folded paper below the table into her lap and opened it up before looking briefly down at what he wrote:

> As soon as I get you alone, I don't know what I'm going to do first, but at some point, I'll be saying "This is going to hurt me more than it does you."
>
> I am so not going to mean it.

Amanda's face remained completely impassive. She looked back up, and her attention resumed to focusing on what the attorneys were saying around her. Chase did the same, calm and composed as he ever was. Then, when both were confident they could pull it off and perfectly timed, they looked directly at each other. Her eyes widened playfully and his pupils dilated predatorily. They looked away from each other in the nick of time, preventing one from directly blowing the other's cover. She shifted in her chair and recrossed her legs. Discreetly folding the note, she stuck it in the inside zippered compartment of her handbag.

She considered it a binding contract to her personal happy ending.

Chapter 18

C hase walked briskly in the underground parking garage with security keeping up, preoccupied
and too impatient to wait for them to bring his car. The
gradual buildup of tension surrounding his wedding
had taken a turn toward drama, and they still had three
weeks to go. It was to be a lavish winter affair, taking
place in the small window of time falling between New
Year's and before they left for spring training. One for
which the Coles spared no expense. Amanda insisted
she not burden his only relative downtime and did her
best to leave him out of the planning as much as she
could. He trusted her judgment regarding cake tast-
ings, menu planning, invitations, and flowers. He knew
she could handle their wedding party getting to the size
of a philharmonic orchestra with aplomb. Both Rupert

and Catherine came from large families, and his mother's invitation list was long as well. But he saw trouble on the horizon when Amanda moved back into her own place, citing some old folklore about how it would add to the proper nuptial buildup. What rubbish. It wasn't a prizefight he had to reserve his stamina for; it was a marriage. And a month before the most important day of his life was no time for her to go all virginal on him. When she called earlier that morning to make the final decision on their honeymoon he could tell she was stressed out and scattered. But instead of being supportive, he spat back.

"I don't really care where we go, just make sure the room is nice because by the time this shindig is over, we're not going to leave it."

Amanda hung up abruptly after grouching that he sounded more like a drill sergeant giving her marching orders, and she was going to go "man up." The whole episode left him with a rotten taste in his mouth. As he picked up his pace in the cold garage, Chase considered blowing off his lunch meeting and tracking her down. But what good would that do when his only solution would be to try convincing her to sex him up until they both felt better?

Chase didn't notice the black sedan accelerating and coming toward him until Jack and his partner started taking affirmative action and rushing in front of him. The car's brakes squealed, a sound made louder by the echo created in the garage, and the car fishtailed, then spun halfway around before stopping a few yards away from the trio. Even with the half-empty garage, it was still a tight maneuver.

The men stared in stunned silence as Amanda jumped out of the backseat and rushed up to them, her hand secure in the pocket of her beige trench coat. She reached out with her hand firmly ensconced within the coat, the outline of her pointer finger and thumb protruding from the top and side of the coat's pocket as if brandishing a revolver.

"Stay back and no one gets hurt," she ordered, jerking the hand in her pocket toward the running car. "He's coming with me."

Upon recognizing her, the two security guards marginally stood down. Still with their hands on their own holstered weapons, they looked briefly at each other and then at their boss, who was smiling broadly.

"Better do what she says, boys. That finger looks pretty serious," Chase said, already moving in the direction of Amanda's getaway car.

"That was easy," Amanda remarked, taking her hand out of her pocket and heading back to the car. She briefly turned back to the silent guards, who had broken into small grins, even Jack, who wasn't known for smiling. She added, "I'll have him back in three days, make sure they clear his schedule?"

Both men gave a single nod. Amanda and Chase got into the backseat of the car.

"Hey, Ricky Bobby," Chase said good-naturedly in reprimand to the driver as he slid into his side behind the man. "That's my fiancé you almost smashed into another car."

"Sorry, sir," said the driver, a man of about thirty, who grinned sheepishly after making eye contact from the rearview mirror. "She told me to make it dramatic."

"No surprise there," Chase drawled as Amanda closed her car door after taking her seat beside him. He took her hand. "Okay, I've come along quietly. What's this all about?"

Amanda leaned over and kissed him quickly before settling back in her seat and saying victoriously, "You'll see."

The car sped out of the parking garage and into city traffic. With a third person in the car, Chase and Amanda refrained from further conversation. He continued his grasp of her hand, absently playing with his ring on her finger. He leaned his head back against his headrest and closed his eyes, but couldn't stop smiling. He had given up control without having a clue where they were going, yet he couldn't remember ever being happier. In a matter of minutes he was sleeping.

When she woke him, the car was on a tarmac at what he assumed was Teterboro Airport. A short distance away, a Learjet was awaiting their arrival. The driver popped the trunk of the car and handed over an overstuffed backpack to Amanda before leaving.

"I do have my own plane, you know," he told her, intercepting and taking the heavy backpack from the driver as they made their way to the stairs of the open hatchway to board.

"What kind of kidnapper would I be if I used your own stuff to kidnap you?" she asked.

They took their seats and were given glasses of champagne while the flight crew began preparing for takeoff.

"At least tell me what's in the backpack?" he requested.

"My wedding dress," she replied.

Chase's eyebrows rose in response. He stared at the bulging bag that was full of satin and crinoline that the flight attendant was storing in a nearby compartment across from them. "Your Vera Wang original is in that thing?" he asked with a chuckle.

"Don't laugh. I've got one your tuxes crammed in there, too. Lena handed it over to me while you were in the shower. Don't be mad at her, I held her at finger-point, too," Amanda fibbed. Chase's loyal housekeeper was the only other person she'd told of her intentions. Because Lena possessed a romantic heart and had noticed the gradual buildup of agitation taking place in her boss's demeanor, she was more than willing to help.

A picture came together in his mind of Amanda's plan, and he wasn't sure how to feel about it. He didn't care about their destination, he certainly didn't give a tinker's damn about his wedding, and at least this time she wasn't running away without him, but concern started overshadowing his face.

"Baby," he said quietly, "you're not losing it on me, are you?"

"Of course not," Amanda reassured him. "I can't remember ever feeling saner."

"I think maybe it's time you explain to me what's going on," he said with all the benevolent authority she had come to love.

Amanda took a deep breath, could feel herself relax in response to it. They were minutes away from being in the air. The most difficult phase of her mission was already accomplished. She had him all to herself, at least for the next three days.

"I don't know," she began on a sigh. "Suddenly it just all seemed so ludicrous. I think it may have started around the time World War Three broke out over the bridesmaids' dresses. Just because Nicki thinks she looks good in everything doesn't mean the rest of the girls do. Off-the-shoulder, sleeves or no sleeves, gowns versus short dresses—do you know how hard it is to get six women to agree on a dress? Just thinking about picking out shoes gave me a headache."

Chase grinned, more in amusement than actual sympathy. "I can imagine."

"Then the photographer, who I know doubled his price because it's you, called to pitch a hissy fit because there may be other photographers there."

"Who knew a guy could be such a diva?" he asked in commiseration, his smile widening.

"I'm opening responses to our wedding invitation from people I've never even heard of!" she exclaimed.

"I hear you there," he readily agreed.

"I hate my condo now," she continued miserably. "I only went back there because my mother sort of pressured me into it. Every night she's calling me with some sort of lame excuse, like I don't know she's really doing a bed check. I think marrying off her only child is secretly making her crazy."

Chase could see her eyes begin to well up and her voice shake. "And while I'm glad I'm making it easier on her, I don't quite know how to tell her that waking up without you is starting every day off gloomy and depressing, no matter how wonderful the end result is supposed to be."

Chase could feel his insides turning to mush. He was so focused on his own stranded libido, he'd never taken into account that his bride might be feeling the same way. He squeezed her hand in unspoken apology.

"Our cranky conversation this morning was the capper. I went for what felt like the umpteenth fitting of my dress. I thought it looked fine. But when the seamstress began clucking about how I'm going to need at least one more fitting because 'most brides want to shed those extra fifteen pounds,' something in me snapped. I couldn't take any more."

Chase said nothing, just slightly nodded his head and listened, waiting for her to succumb to a full crying jag. Yet he wasn't surprised when Amanda instead straightened in her seat and shrugged. "I just thought, if I have to deny myself a decent meal for the next three weeks to fit into a dress my husband can't wait to tear off, I'm going to blow a gasket. I told her to give me my dress right now, walked out, and, well, you know the rest."

His laughter filled the plane's cabin. In less than four hours, she had managed to raid his closet, charter a jet, kidnap him, and who knew what else. He pulled her in for a sound kiss, the only thing he could remedy on the spot. "That's my girl."

"You still haven't told me where we're headed," he said after their lips finally unlocked.

"Vegas, baby," she proclaimed.

Amanda had thought of everything. A stretch limousine was waiting their arrival when they landed and would be at their disposal for the duration of their stay. She secured the penthouse suite at the Bellagio, with a magnificent view of the legendary fountain below. She'd instructed the hotel's concierge to obtain all the toiletries they would need, including his favorite cologne, her perfume, and lingerie. She saw to it that their clothes were made wrinkle-free after being intricately and strategically folded into the backpack, a feat he considered amazing in and of itself.

If anyone else had told him he was about to be married by Elvis, Chase might have been skeptical.

Instead Chase found himself standing in front of the gold-lamé-suited, pompadour-sporting, hip-swinging impersonator. Next to him was James Dean, his impersonating and impromptu best man, wearing jeans, a white T-shirt, and worn leather jacket with its collar up. Apparently, his appointed groomsman had no interest in baseball or seemed to fully embrace his rebel role. He was only slightly more enthusiastic than the real James Dean, which meant he basically acted as lively as a corpse.

The same could not be said for the maid of honor, Marilyn Monroe. She couldn't stop giggling and sashaying in her form-fitting black dress or batting her false eyelashes. In his mind, it wouldn't have mattered if she was the real Marilyn; there was only one woman on the planet that would ever captivate him again. And while Chase indulged her in one of his rakish smiles, as soon as he caught that first glimpse of white strapless gown at the back of the small chapel waiting for "Love Me Tender" to start playing, the blond bombshell became invisible.

He wasn't interested in making small talk, even though both Elvis and Marilyn had tried to engage him in their shtick. All he saw was his bride. Her makeup was minimal, her ebony hair cascading in its natural state of unblown waves, just like that fateful night when he'd met her, only now it rested on her bare shoulders. After all this time, she still took his breath away.

Amanda couldn't recall a time Chase ever looked more handsome, although she'd seen him in a tux a hundred times before. His eyes were iridescent, his smile so dazzling, it was like a magnetic force field pulling at her from where she stood. The recorded music started playing, the Elvis started singing, and she began the short walk to join the man who was minutes away from becoming her husband.

And per her explicit instruction, there wasn't a photographer in sight. However, there was a single unmanned stationary video camera set up in the back. Thanks to a written and signed confidentiality agreement, it would have its content turned over to Amanda in exchange for a hefty sum. The next fifteen minutes she intended to selfishly keep for them alone.

Amanda stepped down the small aisle, past the several rows of empty chairs, forcing herself to keep from racing, her gaze locked on Chase. When she reached, then joined him, they still were made to wait. Elvis had a chorus to go, despite the fact there were only two anxious people the performance was for. Apparently, they were going to get the full treatment. Marilyn swayed and James Dean jammed his hands into the back pockets of his jeans and slightly bobbed his head to the music.

"When does he stop?" Chase whispered in her ear as Elvis continued gyrating all around his stagelike platform.

"I guess when he's good and ready," Amanda whispered back and they both tried not to laugh.

The song finally ended and Amanda handed her small bouquet over to Marilyn. At Elvis's request, Chase took Amanda's hands in his.

"Uh, we are gathered here, before God and," Elvis began, addressing all the empty chairs, "and these two witnesses to celebrate the love this man and this very handsome woman have for each other."

Amanda could feel her palms getting sweaty. This was it, she was about to marry the man of her dreams, breaking millions of girls' hearts in the process. She blinked up into Chase's loving gaze. He winked and gave her hands a reassuring squeeze before leaning over to Elvis and politely interrupting him. Elvis stopped his speech and drew his head closer to Chase. They shared a brief, private exchange in which both pulled away smiling after Elvis gave an affirmative "Uh-huh-huh."

"Amanda, your hunka hunka burnin' groom thinks it might be best if you went first, so you won't feel so nervous," Elvis continued in full act. "So I . . . I . . . I want you to repeat after me. I, Amanda, take you, Chase, to be my wedded husband."

"I, Amanda, take you, Chase, to be my wedded husband," she repeated through the tears of joy starting to brim in her eyes. It was happy-ending time. Her fairy tale was about to come true.

"I promise never to leave you at the Heartbreak Hotel or step on your blue suede shoes," Elvis preached loudly.

Way to lighten up the moment, Amanda thought as she repeated it, giggling.

"I promise to love, cherish, honor, and obey. . . ."

"I promise to love, cherish, honor, and . . . " Amanda halted before saying waspishly, "Beg your pardon?"

"You heard him." Chase grinned and pointedly said, "Obey."

Amanda took a quick look around at the other three people in the room and pursed her lips together. "They don't say that anymore."

"But you will," Chase stated boldly, his grin getting wider.

Amanda pulled her hands out of his and took a step back, landing them on her hips. "I'm not saying that," she said sharply. She heard Marilyn's small gasp of either shock or hopefulness followed by a carnal breathy "Oh" and Amanda jerked her chin at the maid of honor in warning. James Dean began to look interested.

"Come on now, little sister, don't be cruel" could be heard coming from the platform.

Amanda snapped her head in its direction. "Pipe down, Elvis, this doesn't concern you!"

Elvis took a big step back with another "uh-huh-huh" and started pulling at his collar in a way that was more similar to Rodney Dangerfield getting ready to plead for some respect.

All the while, Chase remained in his spot and watched, unconcerned and thoroughly amused, waiting to see what his bride would do next.

Amanda rounded back on Chase, itching to slap the smile off his face, one that only moments ago she adored and which now infuriated her.

"Why on earth would you choose to act like a wise guy on our wedding day?" she hissed at him.

"I can't let you have all the surprises, can I?" he calmly asked, his eyes bright and laughing.

She swallowed her anger and took a step closer to him, lowering her voice. "I realize our life is an open book on this sort of thing, but you're embarrassing me."

"Not my intention," Chase continued mildly. "Frankly, you looked so nervous, I wasn't even sure you would notice."

"Well, I did," she huffed. "Now, can we stop this madness and get back to our wedding?"

"Certainly, just as soon as you say it."

"I'm not saying it," she repeated through teeth clenched in frustration.

"Then I guess we're at an impasse," Chase said seriously. "I'm not going to be the only one to do it."

Amanda could feel herself blushing even before hearing Marilyn's sensual sigh and Elvis's relieved one. Chase had successfully gotten her to set herself up. She didn't know whether to laugh or cry or kick him in his shin. She already knew life with this man was never going to be dull.

"You're saying it, too?"

He smiled tenderly, offering his hands to her. "Of course, even though it's really just a formality. I'd never expect you to abide by it. Old-fashioned, remember?"

She placed her hands back into his and leaned closer into him. "Please tell me you would never have done this at a church full of our friends and family?"

"Are you kidding?" He bent down to murmur into her ear, remembering he wasn't supposed to kiss her until he got the final go-ahead. "I wouldn't have done it here if it wasn't for that confidentiality agreement they all signed. I have to snag these opportunities when I can get them." Chase snuck in a quick kiss to her temple before adding impishly, "Wait till you see how angry you got."

Amanda could feel his fingers, webbed within hers, tightening ever so slightly, probably as a precaution in case she tried to slug him.

"I really like this better when I'm the one making *you* mad," she pouted.

"Then let's wrap this thing up so you can get back to it," he told her before straightening to his full height and ordering, "Hit it, Elvis."

The original "King" resumed his official duties, and both Amanda and Chase promised to love, honor, cherish, and obey, forsaking all others until their dying day. James Dean produced the two plain gold bands from his pocket, purchased spur-of-the-moment to replace the carefully designed rings that were still waiting for them back home, and they slipped them on each other's finger. And as soon as he heard the word *pronounce*, Chase pulled Amanda in close. With one powerful hand securely on the small of her back, he wove his other hand deep into her hair. Then he sealed it all with a kiss.

But instead of vacating the building, which would have been their plan, Chase and Amanda were obliged into celebrating with their first dance to a very long-winded rendition of "Can't Help Falling in Love." So long, in fact, that James Dean proffered his hand to Marilyn and they joined the bride and groom while Elvis worked himself up into a sweat of passionate crooning.

"Next time, let's get married by Earth, Wind and Fire," Amanda sighed into his chest.

"Anything you say, Mrs. Walker," Chase replied, right before lifting her off the ground to bring her face-to-face and kissing her again. He set her back on the ground and resumed their dance, singing into her ear. "Got to get cha into my life."

Eventually they were allowed to leave. The DVD and a flash drive, the only tangible pieces of evidence that a wedding had occurred, were secure within their possession. Chase and Amanda got back into their waiting limousine to head back to their hotel, while Marilyn and Elvis threw confetti at them from the entrance to the chapel and James Dean smoked a cigarette. They accepted the driver's congratulations and engaged in few minutes of well-mannered conversation. Sitting on opposite ends of the big backseat, each took a moment to privately appreciate the enormity of what had just taken place. Amanda stared out her darkened window at the passing scenery, where desert met debauchery, overwhelmed with bliss. Her life would never be the same. With Chase by her side, there was nothing she couldn't accomplish. When she gave herself over to him, he only made her stronger. She knew she would never be loved so completely again. And slouched from his side, as she watched the bustling activity on the Las

Vegas strip whizzing by, Chase watched her. The most beautiful, maddening angel come to earth was his in every sense of the word. He really was a man who had it all.

"You know, there are a whole bunch of people back home who still think there's going to be a wedding," he mentioned casually as his finger depressed a button near where he was sitting. "People who went to a lot of trouble."

"They'll get over it," she said vapidly, her gaze still out the window, but catching the partition separating driver from passengers start to rise from the corner of her eye.

"That's not very nice," he continued sternly once the divider was fully in place, ensuring their privacy. "And your behavior in that chapel was deplorable. Borderline to a tantrum, I dare say."

She turned her gaze from the window to fleetingly double-check the partition before settling it on her husband. Chase did his best to appear as the strict disciplinarian. Amanda gave a halfhearted attempt at looking contrite. Both were completely bogus.

"I'm not sure what came over me," she said, more pleased than sorry.

"You know what has to happen here," he said with all the disapproval he could muster, which still made

344 • STEPHANIE EVANOVICH

for a good show. He sat up and shifted to the middle of the long bench seat, extending his hand in her direction.

Boy, do I! Amanda thought with glee as she took his hand and he pulled her gently across his knees. He began to lift her dress as he said unconvincingly, "I hate to have to do this."

"I'll bet," she sassed from beneath yards of material now over her head. She felt strong fingers hooking into both sides of her panties followed by the familiar cool rush of air on her skin while he peeled them down. She held her breath in anticipation as his hand began the sensual tracing and dancing before coming to rest on his favorite place, right where her bottom ended and her thighs began. Her sweet spot.

"Do you have anything to say for yourself, young lady?" A rhetorical question answered only by Amanda wriggling against his muscled thighs in erotic delight.

Chase righted her seconds before the Bellagio's valet opened the door on his side of the car, scooping her panties off the limousine floor and stuffing them in his pocket. He helped his flushed new wife out of the limo, taking her hand and walking with purposeful strides directly to the hotel elevator. He deliberately and uncharacteristically ignored anyone who recognized them.

Nobody saw them for two days. When they returned to New York they still had the party, but they left their fancy duds in the closet, and everyone was encouraged to wear what made them comfortable. A light snow began to fall on their way home, and it gave Amanda the idea of a fairy-tale whim. They put their wedding clothes on, her white flowing gown and his black tie. Chase drew her into his steely arms and she delicately placed her hand in his before he rested them both over his heart. And they danced alone together in the ball-room of their recently completed castle.

Acknowledgments

When I first found out *Big Girl Panties* was going to be published, I was so naïve, on the level of Forrest Gump. I knew very little about publishing. Almost nothing. I hung up the phone after getting the word and thought, *Well, that's good . . . one less thing.* I've learned so much since that phone call, mostly about all the really hard work that caring, dedicated people would undertake on my behalf. Enthusiastic folks who took me and my book into their hearts and helped guide me through my new learning curve. Saying thank you doesn't begin to scratch the surface of the appreciation I'd like to express. It is with that thought and deepest gratitude that I'd like to thank the following:

Rachel Kahan—for believing in me when I doubt myself and feeling my characters almost as much as I do. She is an editor extraordinaire.

Liate Stehlik—for trusting me and the editor extraordinaire to tell this story. Having Liate in your corner is like being touched by an angel.

Heidi Richter—for being so smart and savvy and keeping me organized. She always knows just what day it is. Woot!

Kathy Gordon—for having more energy than a can of Red Bull—the kind of energy that's contagious.

The team at William Morrow/HarperCollins—Trish Daly, Angela Dong, Dianna Garcia, Kaitlin Harri, Jen Hart, Virginia Stanley, Shelby Meizlik, Doug Jones, Lynn Grady, Tavia Kowalchuk, Rachel Levenberg, Erin Gorham, Lorie Young, Julia Meltzer, Lisa Stokes, Mary Schuck, and Andrea Rosen. For making hard work look like fun.

Andrea Cirillo and Meg Ruley—for making me feel sane, even when I know I sound completely off my rocker.

Rhonda Ritter Witkowski—for being the first friend I ever made, back when we were five, and hanging around for the duration. She is likely the only person on this earth who can truly blackmail me.

Ava Johnson—for always being ready to bust out a little "I'm Sally O'Malley"!

Amy Caswell—for helping me see the humor in everything and her uncanny ability to relate it to a Seinfeld episode.

And finally, from the bottom of my heart, I want to thank every wonderful reader who took time out of their day to make mine. Whether you reached out via the World Wide Web to lend your support, or recommended me to a friend, or shared a few minutes with me while I was passing through, you've enriched my life in a way I'll cherish forever. Thank you.